CAROLINA JEWEL

A Novel By

Mary Dodgen Few

Published By

HALLUX, INC.

Anderson, S. C.

End Paper Art By Elizabeth Belser Fuller

Standard Book Number: 87667-058-3.
Library of Congress Catalog Card Number: 73-117160

MANUFACTURED IN THE UNITED STATES OF AMERICA
Book Design By Hallux

To
Joe

FOREWORD

Two hundred years and a generation ago, a strange and flamboyant figure cut a wide swath through the wilderness of South Carolina. By a stroke of luck, or pure genius, that is recorded with awe in the existing journals of the Indian traders who accompanied him on his colorful journey, Sir Alexander Cuming, Bart. was the instrument of an uneasy peace between the white pioneer and his red antagonist, the Cherokee Indian, which existed with periodic aberrations for thirty years. Sir Alexander got no credit for his genius. Unfortunately his ability as a diplomat was not complemented by an equal ability in the field of finance. In his brief but effective stay in the Province of South Carolina in the year of our Lord 1730, he managed to make way with an enormous fortune without benefit of collateral. To his red brothers he remained in eternity the Great White Warrior; to his white brothers, a crackpot and charlatan who died in poverty.

Most of these facts are known to any casual student of the history of South Carolina. There is no official record that his daughter Elizabeth ever came to this country; but some of the more poignant pages of history are not found in the Public Records.

PROLOGUE

The great house was quiet and only the howling of the wind could be heard above the scratching of the quill. A huge man sat writing in intense concentration at a polished desk. Sir Alexander Cuming had removed his gaudy coat, waist coat, and gorgeous red wig and wrote with characteristic haste. Occasionally he scratched his head with an ivory wig scratcher in his left hand without however disturbing the rhythm of the pen in his right. His pen flew across the paper.

And so, my dear Elizabeth, I have been fortunate to purchase for you the splendid plantation of Mr. Roderick Cameron who has lately moved to Barbadoes from whence he came to Carolina some years ago. In the great plague of 1728 he lost his dear wife and has had no stomach for Charles Town since. For you I have renamed it Whitehall.

All is well with me and my affairs prosper. The state of the currency here is appalling and the planters are in great need of immediate funds which I have been pleased to supply on promissory note at ten per cent, a rate somewhat less taxing than the prevailing twelve to fifteen per cent. Tomorrow by packet I am sending five hundred barrels of rice which I charge Mr. Fant to dispose of at twenty-three shillings which is under the English market. The proceeds he will properly invest in your name.

Until this week the weather has been very mild and tropical blooms are in profusion. You will find that this is no frontier post but rather a glittering society with a finery and gaiety of dress hardly surpassed by the Court of London. The plantation houses are of a proportion and excellence of construction which denote masters of taste and discernment. They follow the lines of the most elegant of the European countries their owners represent. The gentlemen seated in the country are very courteous, live very nobly in their houses and give genteel entertainment to strangers and others who come to visit.

Tonight we drank a toast in a good sound Beer made from the native corn plant. It is strong and heady. By maceration when duly fermented, a strong spirit like Brandy may be drawn off from it by help of an alembick.

Both the ladies and gentlemen dress and appear as gay in common as courtiers in England on a coronation or birthday. There are tokens everywhere of style, luxury, and even magnificence. Before leaving Charles Town I sent to you and your mother a pair of humming birds stuffed with sand and perfumed. They are pretty delicacies for the ladies who hang them at their breasts or girdles.

Six gentlemen of the Council will accompany me tomorrow on my trip to the Cherokee country for the Royal Society. Along with them will be Colonel George Chicken, the Indian Agent, the account of whose trip some years ago inspired my desire to visit these natives and unearth some of the treasure their soil must hide. Mr. Eleazar Wigan, one of the ablest traders, I'm told, who knows the Indian tongue and whom the Indians regard with respect; Mr. Joseph Cooper, interpreter and guide; and Mr. Jon Fenwick, a Charles Town gentleman representing Mr. Eveleigh, the merchant who is engineering this journey. A very interesting young man. We will be accompanied by a train of twenty horses with three pack-horsemen to tend and cook.

I return with Captain Arnold on the Fox April 20 and he promises me a swift crossing. Three months at sea even in the commodious modern vessels of today is at best a cramped existence. There is scarce deck space for a limited constitutional.

Have Mr. Fant also prepare our house in Spring Garden for you and your mother. I know that London is not pleasant in summer but I shall wish to find you there when I arrive. I shall not tarry long. Make ready to travel to Carolina as soon as I can set my affairs in order.

I salute you, dear daughter. Embrace your mother for me.

Your obedient servant,

Alexander Cuming

Newgilmerton
Charles Town
March 12, 1730

Tossing his quill aside impatiently, Sir Alexander sanded the sheet and rising went to the window. Throwing it open he drew in great draughts of damp air. While he was writing the wind had shifted and the rain ceased. A soft breeze was blowing from the gulf stream redolent of the fragrant exotic growth of the West Indies. Fleecy wisps of scudding clouds were chasing each other across the smiling, silvery face of a full Carolina moon.

Tomorrow would be a fine day.

"Carolina is a rich jewel which it has pleased God to add to the crown of our King."

Thomas Ashe to the British Board of Trade

BOOK ONE

THE DREAM

1730—1732

Chapter One

Elizabeth felt a sense of elation as her eyes swept the harbor of Charles Town with its beautiful bay sparkling bluely in the cold December sun. The memory of the long and bitter voyage, the angry parting with her father dimmed, replaced by a thrill of excitement as the deep throated guns of Fort Johnson boomed a five signal salute to the new Governor of South Carolina.

"There's Mama!" squealed Margaret Johnson at her side. "Hannah! See! See! Mama! Mama!"

"Miss Peggy," the old Negro woman remonstrated sternly, "when you gonna stop bein' a chile? You is a young lady already presented at cote and de guvnah's dawtah tuh boot."

Margaret whirled saucily and giggled good naturedly.

"If I must be a lady, Hannah, stop calling me Peggy. Margaret is a lady's name."

"How ahm gonna tell you frum yo ma? One Miss Magrit is enuf fuh one fambly.

"Deah's Mistah Henry," Hannah smiled broadly toward the approaching dock. "Why don you squeal at him?"

Margaret sniffed and tucked her hand through the arm of the tall, blond young man who leaned on the rail at her side.

"Henry's just a child." She laughed gaily at Gavin McBride as he smiled fondly down into her eager face. "I prefer doctors anyway."

"What's wrong with lawyers," a slender young man with a very straight back and an infectious smile leaned across Gavin McBride to smile at Margaret.

Margaret grinned back at the dark young man.

"Oh, Andrew! You too! Isn't it wonderful to have so many suitors?"

The Governor's fifteen year old daughter hastily jerked her bodice and straightened her furred cap with its captivating lappets.

"You might be a better choice, Mr. Rutledge," she pretended to consider gravely. "I can see by the look in your eyes, Sir, that you shall amass a great fortune with your cleverness and your book learning." She cut her eyes up at Gavin. "And Uncle James says no doctor worth his salt has tuppence to burn a hole in his pocket."

"Uncle James?" Gavin inquired absently as his eyes swept the approaching wharf, the tall palmettos whose deeply cut fan-shaped fronds waved lazily above their eighty feet of erect trunk, the five or six hundred fine homes guarded gracefully by the towering spire of Saint Philip's church, the great live oaks of White Point.

"Your partner, goose! Dr. James Kilpatrick. He isn't my uncle. I'd just like for him to be."

Hannah scolded her charge crossly.

"Tain't fitten fuh you to take on so . . ."

"You hush, Hannah," Margaret stormed but immediately relented. She retrieved her hand from Gavin's arm and patted her nurse fondly on the shoulder. "Don't fret, Hannah. I'll marry Henry some day when he grows up. I've picked Dr. McBride for Betsy anyway."

"Lawd! Lawd!" Hannah threw up her hands helplessly as Elizabeth's blush added rich color to her already vivid face. "Ah sho is glad tuh git you home tuh yo ma."

"You are a wicked minx and I shall call you Peggy to punish you." Elizabeth laughed to cover her confusion, but her eyes did not fall before Gavin's searching blue ones as they met over the heads of mistress and maid who squabbled on comfortably while the guns of Granville, Craven, and Broughton Batteries spoke out as the ship glided to a stop against the wharf.

In the joyous scramble of reunion on the dock, Elizabeth stood aside with her Aunt Vadie as Gavin McBride and Andrew Rutledge helped her Uncle Roy gather their modest mountain of boxes and parcels. As she watched Margaret's happy reunion with her mother after the long months spent in far away London with her father, Elizabeth's heart contracted with sharp pain at the thought of her

16

own father. Now that the long weeks of the uncomfortable voyage lay between her and her quarrel and bitterness, she could scarce remember the hurt and anger with her father when news of his high financing in Carolina the preceding spring had hit the London journals.

> *We have lately had a most successful cheat put upon the whole country, by one Sir Alexander Cuming, a stranger. . . .*

Only sorrow stirred in Elizabeth as she recalled the words of the letter from South Carolina which the *Eccho* had shouted from Edinborough, published in its degrading entirety. Those words had destroyed with immediate finality the vogue that Sir Alexander was enjoying in England at the moment. His signal success with the Cherokee Indians in getting them to agree to a treaty at the Indian Capital of Keowee had immediately evaporated in the chill climate of royal disfavor. Her father was ruined, bankrupt, and disgraced. Only what he had shrewdly placed in the name of his daughter had survived the debacle.

Tis computed, the letter ran on inexorably, *he has carried off no less than* 15,000 *pounds sterling and we have only this comfort left for the loss of our money — that no man can laugh at his neighbor, or rather, that every man may laugh at all his neighbors. . . .*

"Miss Elizabeth!" A hoarse voice broke in on her gloomy reveries.

Elizabeth was taller than the seamy-faced man whose crisp white curls were bared to the brilliant sun. His soft buckskins hid the wiry crookedness of his spare frame. Elizabeth's eyes were glad as she clasped Eleazar Wigan's gnarled rough hand in farewell. She sought and could not find words to express her gratitude to this strange man who had been her almost constant companion during the hectic voyage.

Gavin McBride had been kept busy tending the many sick in the four vessels of the convoy. During a terrifying storm Elizabeth had volunteered her services, along with a huge indentured man O'Gilvie, to Gavin as he ministered to the injured and ailing in the stinking holds of the ships. But after her run-in with a slatternly wench named Nellie over Elizabeth's efforts to clean up the filth of the steerage, Gavin had forbidden her, although, to O'Gilvie's grim delight, Elizabeth had emerged the victor in the encounter.

Andrew Rutledge had buried his nose in his numerous and ponderous law books, thereby avoiding the high stakes of the games of loo in Captain Anson's quarters. Uncle Roy tended Aunt Vadie, seasick and helpless for the first time in her busy and orderly life. Hannah and Margaret Johnson suffered together in freezing but stuffy misery in their cabin while the endless games of loo occupied the few who could keep from retching on the turbulent fury of the wintry Atlantic.

Elizabeth had ridden out the storm on the comparative comfort of a coil of rope, sheltered from the bitter spray by the cabin wall. There Eleazar, the Indian trader returning from his unwanted assignment as interpreter to the Cherokee delegation Elizabeth's father had taken to London to attest the astounding treaty, had found her and whiled away the uncomfortable hours with his vivid tales of life and people in the Province. At a safe distance huddled Onconecaw, youngest of the Cherokee travelers, listening avidly to the bewildering formation of sounds that made up the white man's language. A peculiar friendship had grown up as a result of these three cornered lessons.

Onconecaw and his red brothers failed to fathom the subleties of the white man's mind. They understood only that they had promised Sir Alexander — not the great King George who pretended to be father to them all — that *he* might . . .

. . . make haste to plant corn and to build houses from Charles Town towards the town of the Cherokee behind the great mountains . . . to brighten the chain of friendship. . .

In Elizabeth, Onconecaw saw the image of her father, known to his Nation as the Great White Warrior, the only white man they had seen fit to tolerate, nay welcome even, with any semblance of affection — if such an emotion could be said to exist in the red man.

Perhaps during these conversations Eleazar had come to guess a bit of what had happened in the stormy session between father and daughter held behind the massive doors of Sir Alexander Cuming's London library that had culminated in his daughter's hasty departure for the Carolina plantations. Through the heavy oaken doors Sir Alexander's voice had roared in anger.

"You shall not!"

During a short ensuing silence, Aunt Vadie, scurrying by on one of her numerous domestic errands, had presumed that Elizabeth was expressing herself with equal if less audible determination. Aunt Vadie jumped and scurried on as her brother-in-law's huge fist pounded his desk as he bellowed with just a shade of uncertainty.

"You shall not, I say!"

Only then was Elizabeth's voice to be heard in an equally angry and determined tone.

"I shall!"

Now here they were. Elizabeth had had her way. She tried to fight down a feeling of dismay that vied with her excitement at her arrival in the fabulous new land of adventure and romance – and perhaps fortune? She had defied her father, cajoled her aunt and uncle, and set for herself the monstrous task of resolving her father's debts and effacing his shame in the eyes of the Carolinians.

Amid the hasty good-byes and the equally hasty introductions Elizabeth remained thoughtful, trying to conquer an unwonted feeling of fright. The Governor was drawn away to be fittingly welcomed in the pomp and circumstance of a great parade and the reading of his commission from His Majesty King George II. This formality was greeted with restrained *huzzahs* as the ladies were ensconced in their carriage which clopped sedately over the cobbles to New Keblesworth, the Governor's property from his former tenure as governor for the Lords Proprietors ten years agone.

As the carriage disappeared, the gentlemen relaxed from rigid formality and protocol and turned to the more congenial task of greeting their friend Robert Johnson. There was much hearty laughter and many strong handclasps as they turned to Shepheard's Tavern where a handsome entertainment was provided. Toasts were drunk to King and Country, Governor and Council, and many other matters that gentlemen find worthy of toasting. The winter sun was low when the Governor finally tore himself away to go to his waiting wife. The gentlemen left the tavern with an expansive feeling of well being. To one and all, the future looked rosy as they sought their respective homes to bedeck themselves for the great ball in honor of the Governor. There they might resume the toasting where it had been left off.

At Crowfield, magnificent manor house just completed as a

19

wedding present by President of His Majesty' Council Arthur Middleton to his son William, the Governor's party arrived early. Robert Johnson and his wife must be in line to receive the distinguished guests who would be on hand for the gala occasion. The atmosphere was light hearted and gay. In the hands of such a man as Johnson, the future of the province looked secure and bright.

The liquid light of hundreds of candles shone on the polished black walnut panelling of the great marble paved entry hall. The young ladies, ushered by a satin clad Negro butler, passed under the carved arms of George II Rex over the arched doorway of the twelve foot wide hand carved stairway into a tremendous bedroom where they were to remove their cloaks. Elizabeth paused in awe at such magnificence. Even Sir Alexander's vivid descriptions and Eleazar's accounts had not prepared her for the ease and wealth in which the great estate holders of South Carolina lived. Two mammoth four poster beds hung in red damask faced each other from opposite walls. Between the two, a large round table hung with fringed canary yellow velvet held a carved silver bowl containing a riot of scarlet camellias. The high ceiling walls were hung with yellow damask and a Fereghan rug in dark blues and reds covered the waxed parquet floor with a carpet of closely woven flowers that seemed to glow in the candle light. Identical Queen Anne highboys with polished brass pulls stood by each bed. The carved marble mantle of the fireplace at one end of the long room was flanked by a pair of high backed Chippendale chairs which had petit point foot stools. With its heroically proportioned furniture removed, the room would easily furnish a commodious ball room for the Governor's guests this evening.

Mrs. Johnson and Aunt Vadie hastily repaired the damages of the jolting carriage ride from town and left the girls to a more leisurely toilette. Giving her scarlet lined cloak to Hannah, Elizabeth turned her back to the pleasant warmth of the crackling fire. Dressed completely in white, she made a regal picture in the beautiful room. Her dress was of heavy clinging China silk folded cleverly at the bosom and devoid of any ornamentation. Around her neck was a simple collar of mussel pearls from the streams of Carolina, a gift from her father. At Aunt Vadie's coaxing and with her help, Elizabeth had dressed her hair in the new French fashion that her mother affected. Drawn up from her face it formed a coronet of small curls on the crown while a large fan of hair covered the back of her head. Tiny clipped white ostrich feathers were secured in the curls. Her wide mouth was dark red, and the ripe-peach color of her cheeks was heightened by excitement and anticipation.

Margaret Johnson was watching her with obvious admiration as she turned over her cloak to Hannah.

"You are just like a duchess. Do you suppose I'll ever grow to be as statuesque and beautiful as you are?"

She pirouetted for Elizabeth to see and came to a stop laughing. "I'm the runt of the litter, Hannah says."

Elizabeth joined her infectious laughter. "I'm too tall for a girl and my mouth is too big. You're as pretty as a picture and nobody could resist your happiness. What more do you need?"

"Poof! I look like everybody else. You're different and your mouth is the best part of you."

Sounds of approaching voices put an end to their conversation. A high trilling laugh and the heavy odor of perfume preceded a tiny blond girl into the room. Voluminous hoops had to be turned at an angle to admit the rustling taffeta and lace of her elaborate gown. A small face of pink and white perfection was crowned by piles of silky, golden curls. Jewels flashed at her throat and ears. The apparition paused for effect on the threshold.

"Margaret, dahling, how sweet you look, my child. Do tell me about the simply marvelous trip to London." She swept across the floor and embraced the Governor's daughter, enveloping her with her heady perfume.

Margaret stepped back with a hardly perceptible snort and tried not to wrinkle her nose against the overpowering scent.

"How do you do, Charlotte? May I present my friend Miss Elizabeth Cuming? Betsy, this is Miss Stanyarne."

Charlotte Stanyarne turned swiftly to face the girl before the fire. Without greeting, she flung her cape to Hannah who deliberately let it fall to the floor before she lifted it and holding it as far away from herself as possible laid it on a chair in a far corner of the room.

"How d'you do?" the high sweet voice was syrupy. She looked the tall girl up and down from head to toe insolently. Turning from her scrutiny to the dressing table she meticulously arranged her fluffy curls.

"Is the very plain garment you are wearing some new style?" She asked cuttingly without turning from the mirror. "My mantua maker's new fashion dolls show no such simplicity. Or perhaps for rural affairs —"

Margaret Johnson cut off the insulting voice.

"With such ridiculously exaggerated hoops as yours, Charlotte

Stanyarne, Mr. Middleton would have to limit the number of guests he could invite to meet the Governor. Come on, Betsy. It's nicer downstairs."

Taking Elizabeth's cold hand in hers, she dragged her from the room. "Don't mind her, Betsy," she pled as they went down the stairs. "Charlotte Stanyarne may be the belle of Charles Town but to me she's just a cat. Oh — there's Uncle James." She dropped Elizabeth's hand and ran the rest of the way into the open arms of a stooped, grey haired man. His smile was glad, his eyes sparkled with humor.

"Little Miss Peggy is a lady fresh from court. I suppose now you'll stop sitting on my knee and listening to my senile babblings!" He held her at arms length and looked into her vivacious face.

"I shall sit on your knee and eat all your licorice until you call me Margaret. I never listen to your 'babblings' anyway!" She giggled. "Uncle James, look what I've brought."

Old man and young girl turned to Elizabeth who stood waiting at the foot of the stairs.

"This is Elizabeth Cuming. You'll love her. Isn't she beautiful? She's going to live here." Margaret's excited voice ran on.

"Well, Miss Elizabeth," Dr. Killpatrick looked at her with appreciation. "You are a sight to warm an old man's heart. Goodness knows what you'd do to a young man."

His smile and warm handclasp restored Elizabeth's feeling of ease and as the orchestra struck up they entered the ball room. Double doors were thrown open on a long high ceilinged room with paned windows from floor to ceiling. Three matching, heavy, silver and crystal chandeliers sparkled with many candles. The walls were covered with an imported wall paper alive with exotic birds and plants. In a far corner twin Italian pianos tinkled a rhythmical minuet with an orchestra composed of oboe and strings. Elizabeth passed down the impressive receiving line with Margaret, Gavin, Andrew, and Dr. Killpatrick. Each guest looked at Elizabeth with an admiring smile until he heard her name. The smile then changed to one of stiffness and acidity. Some would have been openly rude had they not been informed that she was a guest of the Governor. A cold lump of misery and shame formed in the pit of Elizabeth's stomach. Her charming smile faded, her lips became stiff, her greetings automatic. Gavin, Andrew, and Margaret grew more and more uncomfortable and Dr. Killpatrick's blood pressure hit a new high. Finally he directed them from the line and asked Elizabeth for the first dance. As they swung out on the floor, heads turned in their direction and ladies whispered behind their handkerchiefs. Gavin stayed constantly at her side and endeavored with all his charm to protect her from the coolness of her reception. Elizabeth looked around for her aunt and uncle, but they were nowhere to be seen.

Uncle Roy was in his glory. In the study a lively game of loo was in progress. The pleasant room, lined from floor to ceiling on two walls with books and on the other two with gold tooled leather, was aromatic with smoke from the gentlemen's pipes. The long voyage on the *Garland* had been made bearable by such smoky hours in the captain's cabin. Uncle Roy had played loo in a desultory manner before but never with such exciting tenseness and high stakes. Fortunately, he had kept comfortably ahead and had developed into a surprisingly astute and cautious player. Now he sat again with Captain Anson, but the other faces were new. On his left sat Thomas Gadsden, one of the wealthiest men and largest land owners of Charles Town. Uncle Roy had been told that he owned a large part of the city. Next to Gadsden, Augustine Perreneau, gross father of spindly Phillip, sweated profusely, not because of the heat but because of the high stakes and his diminishing pile of ivory counters. On Roy's right, Jon Fenwick's dashing figure slouched elegantly in his chair. Jon, an indifferent gambler, enjoyed the game not as an opportunity to make a fortune which he did not need, but as a vehicle for the study of the frailties of his fellow men. Apt in character study and quick to ridicule others, he rarely saw the weaknesses in his own reflected image. Now he sat cooly contemptuous of the bourgeois sweating of Perreneau and the overwrought aristocratic tenseness of Gadsden who were putty in the cold, calculated hands of Captain Anson. The captain played for blood, not for pastime, but emotion never clouded his cool judgment whether he was winning or losing. Consequently, he rarely lost. Perreneau was dealer. His sweaty fingers stuck to the cards, making the process a slow one to Gadsden's obvious annoyance.

"Stakes, please," called the dealer as he started his third and final round.

Captain Anson poured six tiny ivory fish into the center of the table and turned to Jon who tossed in one. Roy did the same. Thomas Gadsden licked his lips and gathered up nine counters from his meager pile. Anson watching him keenly, spoke out coldly.

"The limit was set at six, Mr. Gadsden."

Gadsden paused and looked venomously at Anson's pile of

counters. An angry purplish color crept into his face.

"Dammit to hell, how can anyone recoup his losses at such a limit?" he roared angrily. "You are scarcely the one to set a limit, Sir, with your winnings."

Captain Anson's hand sought his missing sword unconsciously. He withdrew it as quickly and replied with dangerous softness.

"I did not set the limit, Mr. Gadsden. It was decided amongst us." He shrugged and turned inquiringly to the other players. "For my part, it can be easily removed."

Uncle Roy moved uneasily. The stakes were already dangerously high. Reluctantly he pushed back his chair.

"My position does not permit that I play with unlimited stakes. Perhaps someone will take my chair. If you will excuse me, Gentlemen." Someone quickly took his place. Jon had pushed back his chair to follow suit when some daredevil urge made him reconsider. A few minutes were consumed in honoring Uncle Roy's counters, and Perreneau, whose asthmatic breathing had increased, resumed the deal. Gadsden cast in his nine counters. Augustine turned up the trump card of the remaining deck — the seven of spades. Jon looked down at his hand — three small hearts.

"I play," said Captain Anson.

"Pass," Jon laid his cards face down on the table.

"Pass," the newcomer echoed on his left.

Thomas Gadsden hesitated. Uncle Roy, who had remained to watch, saw that he held the ace, deuce and trey of diamonds. A fine bead of perspiration broke out on Gadsden's forehead.

"Miss," he spoke from a dry throat. Putting down his hand, he took up the "Miss" in the center of the table.

"Faugh!" Augustine threw his cards down in disgust.

Captain Anson raised his eyebrows. "Are we to understand that you pass, Mr. Perreneau?"

"Just that, Captain Anson."

"Very well, Sir, I play."

"Your lead," snapped Gadsden.

"I am well aware, Mr. Gadsden," Captain Anson replied coldly, leading the ace of spades.

Tensely the crowd which had gathered behind the players watched the play. The captain took three successive tricks and drew the pile of counters toward him.

"Do you wish to be excused, Mr. Gadsden?" the captain's rapier-like voice cut through the silence.

Thomas Gadsden half rose. When his hot eyes met the sneering ones of the captain of the *Garland* his face mottled with rage.

"Indeed not, Sir," Gadsden returned to his chair.

"Your counters are gone?" There was a question in the captain's voice.

"But not my credit, Captain. I place my property on Elizabeth Street as my next stake."

Jon's chair scraped over the polished floor.

"We are after all in a private home," his voice was heavy with disgust, "and not in a public gaming house. I beg to be excused. My chips just balance."

As he strode from the smoky room, the crowd closed in nearer to the table and behind him he heard the shuffle of cards and the captain's even voice,

"I play!"

"Jon, oh, Jon," Charlotte Stanyarne's high voice called across the refreshment room where a crowd of young people had gathered around a laden table.

Jon left his scrutiny of the dancers and turned in their direction. Charlotte caught his arm, batted her eye lashes charmingly, and looked up into his handsome face. He laughed down at her pink-and-whiteness.

"Well, my Cherub. Do you seek to crack a shell as hard as mine with your coquetry?"

Charlotte stamped her foot prettily and pettishly jerked her arm away from spindly Phillip Perreneau who sought her attention. Jon was drawn into the crowd and acknowledged his introduction to the newcomers. Gavin and Andrew he liked at once. His eyes widened as they fell on Elizabeth. He checked an appreciative whistle hardly in time.

"Miss Cuming? Then you must be – –", Jon began.

"So, Miss Cuming, is it?" Charlotte trilled as if she heard the name for the first time. "Could you by *any* chance be a relation of a certain –," she paused as if searching for a word – "*gentleman* of the same name who recently paid us a rather *expensive* visit."

Elizabeth's warm smile faded and the rich color left her cheeks.

"If you mean Sir Alexander Cuming, Miss Stanyarne, he is my father."

"Then I shall *warn* my father to have his steward *nail down* our portable goods."

The feeling of abject misery that her first encounter with Charlotte Stanyarne had caused, changed to one of furious anger. Rich color flamed back into her cheeks and the stormy Atlantic was again reflected in her eyes.

"Perhaps Mr. Stanyarne could also have his steward give his

daughter a lesson in good manners!"

Few had heard the encounter. A stunned silence accompanied admiring glances that followed Elizabeth's straight figure as she turned and swept out of the ball room in the direction of the stairway. Jon Fenwick's appreciative laughter broke the spell. He looked wickedly into Charlotte's furious face. Pinching her cheek, he spoke into her ear but not too softly.

"There's one filly even you can't bridle."

Charlotte slapped his hand from her face and turned to Phillip Perreneau who alone remained at her side.

"Go get me some punch, you ninny," she snapped.

Jon was waiting at the foot of the massive stairway when Elizabeth hurried down, her heavy cloak on her shoulders. When he sought to detain her, she stepped aside.

"I am going home," she said without looking at him.

"Home?" Jon asked.

"To Governor Johnson's," she answered.

"That's quite some walk," Jon bowed with mock gravity. "May I offer my carriage?"

Elizabeth hesitated. In her haste she had not thought of transportation. She looked at Jon's dark handsomeness for the first time.

"Mr. Fenwick? Mr. Jon Fenwick? My father spoke often of you." She drew her cape around her and turned as if to leave. "But I do not wish to be further embarrassed, Sir. Pray, let me pass."

He made no move to do so.

"Don't tell me that anyone who looks like you can be frightened off by that venemous tongued chit in there. Besides," he looked pointedly at her high-heeled satin slippers, "You are not shod for such a distance as I have already pointed out. However, if you must leave, my carriage is at your disposal."

Elizabeth hesitated again, but only momentarily, before she smiled slightly and took his proffered arm.

"You are very kind, Sir. I have no choice."

Jon spoke to the doorman as they left and ordered his carriage as they stepped out into the crisp air. They waited in silence in the brilliant December moonlight. The carriage clattered to a stop and Jon handed Elizabeth in. She turned to bid him goodnight and found him settling himself opposite her.

"Mr. Fenwick, you offered me your carriage."

"And myself along with it, Miss Cuming."

Before she could make further protest they were whisked away into the night.

Jon endeavored with all his charm to break the shell of Elizabeth's preoccupation and to turn her thoughts away from the fiasco of the evening. It was uphill work, and he was about to give it up when she suddenly exclaimed.

"I can not keep the Governor in such an equivocal position. As his guest I can only embarrass him and cause him to be looked at in askance by the very people whose confidence he needs to gain." She turned to Jon. The certainty had returned to her eyes with sudden decision. "Please drive me to Whitehall. It cannot be far."

"Whitehall?" queried Jon.

"Yes, the plantation my father bought —," she stumbled over the word, "from Mr. Cameron."

"That I know, but you cannot go there alone," he protested. "The place has been closed for months."

"But my father left an overseer and servants in readiness for his own return."

"O'Dwyer? He's a filthy rascal. Only the fear of the local militia has kept the slaves from open rebellion. Whitehall is not for you."

"Mr. Fenwick," Elizabeth spoke with spirit, "it is not for you to tell me what I may or may not do. You can only refuse to drive me there. If you do, I shall find another way."

Jon's eyes gleamed in the fragrant moonlit darkness while his gay smile broadened.

"To anyone with such spirit I can refuse nothing." He struck his silver headed cane on the roof of the carriage which drew to a halt. "Whitehall on Goose Creek, Abel," he called to the coachman.

The old Negro on the box neither moved nor answered while his eyes rolled in terror. Whitehall, left to the mercy of its evil overseer since Mr. Cameron's departure for Barbadoes, was a byword among the Negroes. They only spoke of it in whispers.

"Abel," Jon thrust his head out the window and called sharply. "Did you not hear me?"

"Nah Suh, Mistah Jon, ah didn."

"Yes, you did. Drive on!"

Abel reluctantly clucked up the horses and hitched his coat collar higher around his ears.

While they rode on through the night, Elizabeth spoke to Jon of O'Gilvie. When the ships had docked that day in the harbor of Charles Town, Elizabeth told him, she had seen the files of indentured men pass a small desk on the dock to be sold as workmen or overseers to the highest bidders. Because the better

27

grade of purchasers were busy welcoming the Governor the bidders were a sorry looking lot. From the carriage Elizabeth, who knew of the system from Eleazar, saw O'Gilvie's great, silent figure step up to the desk to be examined and poked like an animal. When his big fist had balled up in automatic protest, Elizabeth had stepped down from the carriage before she thought and had placed a bid in her clear voice. The amazement aroused by a bid from a woman had caused the time to pass, the auctioneer's gavel to fall, and O'Gilvie was Elizabeth's as much to her surprise as to the Charles Town representatives of Jeb Leister, merchant of London.

O'Gilvie's muffled voice had merely said, "Thank you, Miss," but his eyes had spoken his gratitude.

"Now what will I do with him," thought Elizabeth. "Heaven knows we can't spare the money." Then she thought of Whitehall. She had directed Uncle Roy to pay her bid and to have someone direct O'Gilvie to Whitehall. She had given him instructions for O'Dwyer, the present overseer at Whitehall, to have the servants prepare the house for occupancy and had told him she would see him in a few days.

Jon listened to this lovely, tall girl talk as matter of factly as if such situations were daily fare. With every sentence his admiration grew. The miles flew by quickly. Suddenly the dark gates of Whitehall loomed in front of them. The carriage rolled to a stop.

"Well?" Jon called impatiently.

"Mistah Jon is yuh sure yuh wants to go in heah?" the Negro's voice pleaded with his master.

"If you don't drive on, I'll leave you here," his master threatened.

The horses jerked into a run down the dark tree tunnel of the avenue. Not a light was to be seen. The house loomed up in front of them as the carriage crunched on the crushed shells of the courtyard circle. For a moment when they came to a standstill neither Abel nor his passengers moved. Finally Jon sprang out and the brass knocker echoed hollowly. They waited. Jon struck the knocker again impatiently. Finally a tiny light flicked in the far reaches of the house and moved forward hesitantly. The door swung open a crack.

"Light Miss Cuming's way with your lantern, Abel," Jon ordered over his shoulder. "Open up for Miss Cuming," he called to the silent figures behind the door.

"Don know no Miss Cuming," a frightened voice answered as Jon forcibly swung the door wide.

The carriage lantern cast its thin light on a tousled haired Negro man with a slatternly looking woman hiding behind his back.

"This is your new mistress. Clothe yourselves properly, fetch candles, and direct my man to some firewood." He turned to Elizabeth who stood big eyed on the threshold. "Be quick," he warned as they stood dumbfounded. "Where is Mr. O'Dwyer?"

The two Negroes looked at each other fearfully.

"He sick," the man answered.

"Has your master been so long gone that you've forgotten your manners?" He advanced ominously.

"Naw, Suh! Naw, Suh!" They backed away.

"Fetch O'Dwyer."

Elizabeth saw the terror in their eyes.

"Not tonight, Mr. Fenwick. Just have them call O'Gilvie. Let's leave Mr. O'Dwyer until tomorrow. He doesn't sound very pleasant, I'm afraid. He'd best be dealt with in the light of day."

While they had talked in the wide hallway, the slovenly looking woman had lighted several half burned candles in the wall sconces of a pleasantly large drawing room. Dust lay thick everywhere. A mouse scurried by as Elizabeth lifted the rich whiteness of her skirts to avoid the dirty floor. A glance into the drawing room revealed gray wallpaper alive with white rice birds, heavy gold silk draperies and a mud tracked oriental carpet. Elizabeth shivered. Jon guided her to a smaller book lined room where Abel was cleaning out the remains of an old fire and laying a new one. He soon had a blaze crackling and Elizabeth rubbed her chilled fingers in front of its welcome warmth. There was a fluttering in her stomach and her mouth felt dry.

Jon looked at her pityingly. "Do you still wish to stay?"

Elizabeth tried twice before she forced her voice to answer him with a husky tremor.

"I'll stay." She cleared her throat nervously.

Firm footsteps echoed in the empty house and O'Gilvie looked shocked when he saw Elizabeth. She strove to control her voice as she greeted him and explained her presence at this hour.

O'Gilvie shook his head. "This is no place for you, Miss. You'd best go back to the Governor. May be you could come back later — maybe." He looked around at the dirty room helplessly. "This is no woman's job, m'am."

With warmth, Elizabeth's courage was returning. "I can't return to the Governor, O'Gilvie. I am afraid I've made a hasty mistake — a mistake I cannot make the Governor pay for." She spoke as if to herself.

Resolutely she squared her shoulders.

"I'll stay. Mr. Fenwick, thank you for your kindness. If you would direct my aunt and uncle to please join me here, I shall be again in your debt. I shall make my apologies to the Governor tomorrow."

"Do you expect me to leave you alone."

"I am not alone, Mr. Fenwick. O'Gilvie is in my employ and I trust him implicitly."

"Nevertheless, I shall stay until your aunt arrives. Abel can take O'Gilvie to fetch your aunt and uncle and what you need for the night."

Reluctantly Elizabeth agreed.

When O'Gilvie and Abel had left, Elizabeth began to shiver again with nervousness. Jon spoke to the Negro man.

"Fetch a bottle of wine for your mistress."

"Ain no wine — suh," he added as an afterthought.

"Why not?" snapped Jon.

"Mistah O'Dwyah don tuk hit all," he looked fearfully over his shoulder.

Elizabeth saw the Negro woman slip unobtrusively into the room. A vivid bandana hid her frowzy hair, a shapeless garment hung from her shoulders to her bare feet.

"What is your name?" Elizabeth asked pleasantly in her direction when she could control her trembling.

"Blossum," her eyes rolled toward the man, "M'am," she added when she saw his face.

Elizabeth suppressed a smile. How could such an ill fitting name fall the lot of this wretched looking woman?

"Blossom, could you fix us something to drink, please? Tea, perhaps, coffee? Anything, just so it's hot."

Blossom stood stock still. Months had passed since she had been addressed by a pleasant voice, heard the word, "please."

Elizabeth smiled encouragingly.

"Yas'm." Blossom fled on silent feet.

"And your name?"

"Clem."

Elizabeth ignored the omission of a title of respect.

"After Blossom has prepared our drink, I'd like for you to help her prepare three of the cleanest beds. I suppose there are sheets?"

"I s'pose dey is — M'am," he added truculently as he caught sight, out of the corner of his eye, of Jon's tall figure.

"And, Clem," Elizabeth waited.

"M'am?"

"See that you both wash your hands."

"Yas'm," he replied and disappeared.

Elizabeth looked up into Jon's admiring eyes.

"Bravo," he spoke without sarcasm. "You'll get along."

30

Chapter Two

All Charles Town was agog the next day over the happenings at the Governor's ball. Tea cooled unnoticed in Dresden cups while the ladies' elaborate powdered wigs drew together in excitement. The Cuming affair took decided precedence over the fact that Thomas Gadsden had lost practically half the village of Charles Town to Captain Anson. Charlotte Stanyarne was not to be reached for comment. The town beaux who had witnessed the encounter between Charlotte and Elizabeth found their ardor for the blond siren somewhat dampened. Their thoughts turned pleasantly to the stunning girl in her strikingly simple white gown who had come off the decided victor in the duel of words. The vitriolic tongues of their indignant mamas and envious sisters soon brought their thoughts back into line, albeit reluctantly.

"The very idea! How dare she show her face in Charles Town," mamas berated shrilly. "Such boldfaced impertinence. Thomas," (or Charles! Pierre! or William!, as the case might be), "stop your mooning and tell Hugo (or Caesar, or Pompey, or Inigo) to bring the carriage around. I have a few calls to make."

And as Thomas left the room, wigs converged again.

"And they say she rode alone, mind you, with that Jon Fenwick."

Shocked faces drew back in delighted horror.

"— alone in that ruined house with a drunken overseer who ought to be taken into the custody of the marshal." Uncle Roy's and Aunt Vadie's presence there was either unknown or deliberately ignored.

"Oh, but, my dear, did you hear about the incident on the dock? She herself bought an indentured man —. So brazen that she doesn't know a lady never transacts business personally, only through her factor."

In the stunned silence that followed, the owner of this choice morsel proudly surveyed the indignant faces of her listeners. Thus, inner conflicts were forgotten as the dowagers of Charles Town sharpened their claws and united forces against the common enemy. The husbands felt a bit sheepish this morning at having been led by their ladies, like ring-nosed bulls, into such a heartless snub. Had the pressing affairs of a muddled government not demanded their instant attention and complete absorption, the outcome might have been different.

Governor Johnson was very angry and concerned for Elizabeth. She has written him an apologetic note on a sheet of musty paper which she had dispatched by Jon's coachman when he returned with a flustered Aunt Vadie and a protesting Uncle Roy. She explained the stand she had taken and pointed out that she had no alternative. Her presence as his guest could only hinder his effectiveness and she begged him to withdraw his sponsorship. She pointed out that she wished a few days to think out her future plans and that she would discuss them with him at his convenience. While Governor Johnson bowed to the wisdom of her thoughts, he deplored the hastiness of her actions, and steadfastly refused to withdraw his sponsorship. He sent Madame Johnson to her with provisions and her own overseer while he attended a called meeting of the Council.

When the Johnson coach arrived, the Governor's wife found Dr. Killpatrick, Gavin, and Andrew Rutledge already in the dusty drawing room. Dr. Killpatrick was in a towering rage, and Gavin was pleading unsuccessfully with Elizabeth to abandon her foolish plan and return to Charles Town.

Perilously near tears after a sleepless night on an unaired mattress, Elizabeth stood backed against the mantel.

"Please," she implored, her eyes huge with fatigue, "can't you see you are only making it more difficult for me? You are the kindest friends, but you must see that my position in Charles Town is untenable. Your friendship with me at the moment will only harm you," she looked directly at Gavin with misery in the depths of her dark eyes. Her words were for him. "You have a reputation as a doctor to build up. You can't afford to incur the enmity and suspicions of your prospective patients."

"Bah!" Dr. Killpatrick interrupted Gavin's instant protest. "These lily livered bas —," he cleared his throat and hitched the shoulder of his coat, "pardon me, Madame," he bowed to Mrs. Johnson, "— I seek in vain for a more appropriate word — had better not snub my new associate. If so they might find themselves under the treatment of that fool Dale. I know no worse fate! Miss Betsy," he had taken Margaret's name for her, "you are as sound as bed rock and as rare as a diamond. What we need here is more like you. Come, Dr. McBride, there is much sickness to attend. They need no doctor here — at least not professionally." He chuckled as he took Elizabeth's strong, young hand in his heavily veined, old one. "I only wish I were as young as these blades here." He looked with admiration into her grateful eyes. "You'll get along." Elizabeth's thoughts flashed to Jon Fenwick's parting words last evening.

Gavin left reluctantly. Getting Elizabeth's pledge to take care of herself he promised to return soon. At Elizabeth's request, Andrew remained to advise her in her encounter with the dreaded overseer, O'Dwyer. O'Gilvie had sat up the remainder of last night in front of the flickering library fire and had prepared the breakfast himself from meager rations collected by Blossom from various slave cabins. Elizabeth had already walked around a limited area of the grounds but had wisely stayed away from the quarters, on O'Gilvie's advice. The place was a shambles. Weeds and lush growth were taking the pretty informal gardens. The house itself was a gem. Though not large and by no means to be compared with the great mansions at Crowfield, Newgilmerton, Silk Hope, Drayton Hall and the Governor's New Keblesworth, it had been fashioned by a loving hand and an eye for simple beauty. It's square frame whiteness was devoid of columns. A heavy polished walnut door under an intricately carved lintel opened on a small stoop, the twin curving stairways of which had wrought iron balustrades. Weeds were rank in the oval, oyster-shell drive and an atmosphere of neglect prevailed even in the appearance of the wondering black people Elizabeth could see huddled in groups at a distance.

O'Dwyer was a short powerful man whose muscles rippled under his tight coat. Stubby, brutal-looking hands, in one of which he clutched a soiled, soft black hat, hung beneath too short sleeves. His square, flat face had the slackness of habitual dissipation, great pouches hung beneath blood-shot eyes. He scratched his stubbly beard with dirty broken nails and smoothed the wisp of lanky black hair he had brushed over his baldness. He faced Elizabeth and Andrew Rutledge belligerently across the hastily tidied library. Elizabeth, showing a courage and assurance she did not feel, spoke to this unpleasant figure.

"Mr. O'Dwyer, can you account for the disgraceful condition in which I find Whitehall?"

"Whitehall?" asked O'Dwyer.

"Yes, Whitehall. You are fully aware of what I speak. My father changed the name of this plantation when he purchased it from Mr. Cameron, as you well know. You were left in charge of the grounds, fields, and people living here. Well?"

"I will make my accounting to Sir Alexander Cuming," the man replied insolently.

Andrew stepped forward warningly and O'Gilvie moved his feet noisily from his corner near the door. O'Dwyer looked from one man to the other and back to the girl in the chair who was speaking again.

"You will make your accounting to me here and now. I am the owner of Whitehall."

O'Dwyer's insolent attitude turned to sullenness.

"How could I keep this place in condition with no money?"

"You have drawn regularly on funds held by Mr. Rattray for that purpose. From what I can see the kitchen gardens were allowed to grow knee deep in weeds. Mr. O'Gilvie informs me that the people have subsisted on what wild pigs and cattle they could shoot with bows and arrows fashioned after the Indians. What became of the meat in the smoke house, the corn in the cribs?"

Silence.

"I am waiting, Mr. O'Dwyer."

The man still remained silent.

"Very well since you choose not to talk perhaps you can listen. My records show, as Mr. Rutledge will confirm, that my father bought the remaining two years of your indenture along with all the goods and chattels on the plantation. That leaves me the right to fifteen months of your services. Mr. Rutledge will prepare your manumission which you may obtain from him in the morning.

"You will pack your goods and take a horse of Mr. O'Gilvie's selection and be off these premises by sundown. I will sign a paper that Mr. Rutledge will prepare for your protection until you obtain your legal manumission. In view of the state of affairs here I owe you no more consideration. Good day, Mr. O'Dwyer."

34

O'Dwyer, too stunned to reply, turned to the door. As O'Gilvie made to follow, Elizabeth spoke to him.

"Mr. O'Gilvie, you are the new overseer of Whitehall. I shall be very exacting. I expect loyalty and hard work from you. I, in turn, shall treat you with fairness and consideration. Please gather all the Negroes in the quarters together and tell them the same thing. Examine their health and needs and report to me here after dinner. As you advised, I shall stay away from the quarters until tomorrow.

O'Gilvie, as stunned as O'Dwyer could only say,

"Yes, Miss."

In the quiet after he withdrew, Elizabeth looked up to find a twinkle in Andrew Rutledge's eyes.

She crumpled weakly against the cushions of her high backed chair. Her chuckle was almost like Margaret Johnson's giggle.

"I was a bit histrionic, wasn't I? It's a shame Margaret wasn't here to see the show."

Their spontaneous young laughter echoed through the awakening house.

Busy days passed for Elizabeth. O'Gilvie was a tower of strength and under his careful management the plantation began to assume its former well groomed look. The slaves were put to work repairing their own cabins, clearing the rank growth, and cleaning themselves up as well. Clogged ditches were cleared to release water standing from winter rains. Fallen trees and storm broken limbs were cut and piled for firewood, wagon wheels were mended, tack and harness, stiff from disuse, were repaired and oiled. Finding the account books a hopeless muddle, Elizabeth and O'Gilvie took careful inventory, and the tedious task of setting up new accounts made Elizabeth's head whirl. On their rounds they discovered a small building containing about thirty bags of good grade cotton and several sacks of wool. The slaves were immediately put to the slow task of removing the seed from the staple. Each was allotted a certain amount to clean in a week's time, either on rainy days or during the evenings. Spinning wheels took up their busy hum and looms clicked again making durable slave cloth, a combination of wool and cotton thread, to replace the tattered garments of the Negroes. O'Gilvie unearthed a fair cobbler who set to work getting bare feet shod.

The task of bringing order and beauty to the house Elizabeth left in the capable hands of Aunt Vadie who resumed the vigilant generalship she had practiced in her sister's home in London, never noticing the different color of her army. The house slaves recognized her quiet but definite authority and were careful never to be caught short in their duties though no punishment was threatened or given. To Vadie, life was much the same, what difference if on one side or on the other of the wide Atlantic. She was numbered among those rare individuals to whom the ordinary course of daily living is sufficient reward. To Elizabeth, the deadening work, which under happier circumstances might have been a mental and physical challenge, was an anodyne to relieve the pain of her reception in Charles Town, the crashing of all her new found hopes. She fell into bed bone tired every night thankful that the business of the day and the fatigue of the night gave her no time to think. Deep down she knew that she must face a day of reckoning, but for the moment she buried all thoughts of plans for the future under the endless occupations of the day.

An inventory revealed little equipment and less foodstuffs. Elizabeth began to wonder how they would finish out the winter. Andrew Rutledge had applied himself with vigor to straightening out the muddle of Sir Alexander's affairs. His face took on a more serious look as the seemingly endless accounts turned up. The amount of fraud was much more than it had at first appeared. It began to look as if Elizabeth would have little or nothing left if she persisted in her determination to clean the slate. In this she was adamant. She intended to retain Whitehall. Everything else was to go. A fine line of worry appeared between her eyes as the amount of negotiable funds sank to the point where she dared use nothing for purchases.

For several days after their eventful arrival, Gavin was a daily visitor. His visits, however, were professional ones to the many sick slaves in the quarters, and, though Elizabeth accompanied him daily on his rounds, their conversation was limited to causes and cures and to methods of treatment that Elizabeth must learn against the day when she would be called upon to assume the role of physician in a limited way herself. The few doctors in Charles Town were inadequate to attend the needs of the growing town population and the far flung plantations at the end of nearly impassable roads. Each slave owner learned the rudiments of the simple treatments of the day and called on the overtaxed doctors only in extreme emergencies. These visits had no personal element, and, though Elizabeth caught herself listening for the sound of his horse and Gavin watched her with growing concern in his eyes, the time passed quickly and he was gone again with only his tone of voice to tell her of his gladness to be with her. Little by little the visits fell off. Gavin's life became as gruelling as her own when much sickness in town caused Dr. Killpatrick to groan.

"I'm apt to die before I teach Gavin the proper Charles Town bedside manner, what with those who are sick from natural causes and those who are like to die from that idiot Dale's physicking!"

"In the name of Heaven, it won't take long to teach him your manner," laughed his friends, "for you have none." They sometimes wondered why anyone so impatient with the sick had decided to become a doctor. Confronted, however, with real illness he was a wizard, fearless and sympathetic. Only with the vaporings of idle minds, he wanted no truck.

As the interval between Gavin's visits lengthened, Elizabeth felt a tiny flicker of resentment which she endeavored to suppress for she knew his obligations full well. Gavin had worked all his life for what he got. His self education had consumed all the funds he was able to acquire by the various jobs his studies had afforded him the time to do. In his generous agreement with Gavin, Dr. Killpatrick had not only paid his passage to Carolina but also allowed him funds to discharge unavoidable debts incurred during the years at the university. He accorded Gavin a full partnership in his office. All these favors, Gavin, whose sense of responsibility was as deep rooted as Elizabeth's, determined to repay. He began by throwing himself wholeheartedly into his work and relieving his benefactor as much as possible.

Jon Fenwick's time, on the other hand, was largely his own to be disposed of as he wished. He was a constant and cheerful visitor at Whitehall, helping here, advising there. None knew better than he the state of affairs and the difficulties under which Elizabeth was working to repair the harm done by O'Dwyer. With every visit he brought a useful gift. His gimlet eyes missed nothing and he read the growing concern over finances in Elizabeth's eyes.

"Let me send you enough corn to tide you over until you can make a crop," he suggested one day.

"Indeed not, Mr. Fenwick. Your offer is most kind but I cannot accept it."

"Let's call it a sale then."

"How is it you have produce to sell when you do not farm, Mr. Fenwick?"

"My brothers and I own land jointly. A part of my share returns to the pool to recompense them for my absence. What's left I sell on the open market."

Elizabeth looked at him squarely, "I have no funds to finance such a purchase. Pray do not embarrass me further."

"Business is done on credit every day, Miss Cuming. I shall be happy to accept payment in cash or produce after your own crop is harvested.

But Elizabeth would not hear of it though she welcomed his advice in many matters. His approach was careful but much more personal than Gavin's. He would not take "no" for an answer when Elizabeth pled that she was too busy to relax. He brought a fine John's Island mare one day, and Elizabeth, who loved all animals, was lyric in her admiration.

"Her name is Phoenix."

Garbed in a velvet habit as green as the lordly pine trees toward which they rode, Elizabeth was enchanting. She sat her horse well. Her hands encased in fringed gauntlets held the reins capably. Her excellent horsemanship did not go unnoticed by her companion, a member of the family which prided itself on owning the finest horse flesh in the American Colonies. They were approaching a great forest of towering pines which were whispering sibilantly to each other.

"There lies the wealth of your plantation," Jon pointed to the majestic trees, some over a hundred feet tall and three or four feet in diameter. They cast a tent of hunter's green over the forest's brown needled floor that felt under foot like a deep piled oriental carpet. Elizabeth drew rein and gazed in wonder at endless woods. The pines in Scotland were numerous, yes, but never so gigantic.

"Lumber?" she asked finally.

"Yes, lumber, but more important, naval stores. Pitch, tar, turpentine. These trees were neglected last year though you can see the crisscross scars of their last tapping."

They rode on a bit.

"What large bee hives," Elizabeth exclaimed as they came to a group of rounded huts.

"Not bee hives," Jon smiled at her, "but small furnaces for extracting tar."

Elizabeth examined the crumbling gray mounds as Jon explained,

"There are the circular clay floors," he pointed out, "which decline toward a center hole from which these wooden pipes run to barrels set in the ground. Large piles of split, dry pine wood are enclosed in these clay walls with only a small opening left to kindle a fire. The hole is then closed to create heat without flame, sufficient to force the tar out of the wood onto the sloping floor, from where it runs into the barrels. Heat may be tempered by thrusting a stick through the clay walls here and there." He indicated tiny holes in the crumbling walls.

"How ingenious. When does this begin?"

"Do you see the box at the foot of that tree?"

Elizabeth nodded.

"Next month those must be cut in proportion to the size of the tree. Bleeding begins the middle of March."

As they rode on in leisurely fashion with a warm sun on their backs, Jon who would have preferred to speak of more personal matters, continued to point out the splendid possibilities of a well run plantation.

"A thousand trees will yield two barrels and more at one bleeding."

"How long does it take to fill each box?"

"About fourteen days unless it rains. One able hand fills about two barrels a day. Gum is gathered once every fourteen days until frost."

He paused and turned in his saddle to indicate the endless number of forest giants. "So you see, it can be a very lucrative business."

Elizabeth's spirits rose. Perhaps there was a way out of her difficulties. She must find one, for her pride would never permit her to return to her father after all the extravagant and angry remarks she had made. A pleasant path opened up in front of them. "Let's race," she called back over her shoulder as she spurred Phoenix on. Their horses, glad for a chance to stretch their legs in the nippy December air, flew over the ground. When Elizabeth drew up, her eyes were sparkling, her cheeks flushed. She laughed gaily as she patted Phoenix's neck, "She's wonderful!" she cried.

Looking at Elizabeth, Jon determined that he would have her for his own. He decided to play his cards cautiously in the Anson manner for he had seen a look pass between Gavin and the girl that he fully understood. This time he would not underestimate his adversary but would take every advantage, fair or unfair, that presented itself. With Gavin's preoccupation, he had already an advantage and he set about making himself indispensable to Elizabeth and ingratiating himself with Aunt Vadie. He carefully pretended that some of his frequent visits were to her and often did not even seek to see Elizabeth. His gifts, always to Aunt Vadie, were impersonal ones that were sorely needed at Whitehall: a dark red ham, cured after his mother's special method, that he wanted her to taste, a setting of eggs from a sister-in-law's fine broadbreasted Cornish game hens, a small sack of roasted coffee beans. To make it all seem proper Aunt Vadie returned the welcoming gifts of mother, brothers, and sisters with roots of some of the fine shubbery surrounding the house, or some bouquet of early blooming narcissi. These Jon accepted with a grave bow, and dumped them in the nearest ditch as he cantered home.

Elizabeth was not slow to catch on, and she scolded Aunt Vadie roundly.

"Now, Elizabeth. It is only hospitality. To refuse these small tokens would be most discourteous."

"And I suppose that wagon load of corn that mysteriously appeared in one of the cribs is a small token of welcome from Mr. Fenwick's cousin Millicent. It is very strange that these hospitable aunts and uncles and sisters and cousins never come to express their welcome by a personal call." She sank into a chair and burst into uncontrolled weeping.

"Why, Elizabeth. Don't cry, my darling. If it upsets you so, we shall stop Mr. Fenwick's nice little gifts at once," she sighed, "though that coffee certainly is better than the parched potato peel or dried ground saddle leather we have to drink." As Elizabeth rose furiously her aunt said hastily, "Never mind, never mind. I'd rather drink poke berry juice than have you cry so." She pulled Elizabeth's head to her breast and stroked her hair gently.

"Elizabeth, why should you mind that people don't come to call? You never seemed to need companionship in Scotland?"

Drying her tears and trying to control her sobs, Elizabeth spoke miserably, content to leave her head on Vadie's breast, "It's not the companionship Aunt Vadie; it's the —" she cast around for a word, "idea. No one can live in an atmosphere of hatred and suspicion. And then there's —" she sat up and looked at Aunt Vadie flushing.

"Yes, there's Gavin. You do him an injustice if you think he cannot rise above such littleness. If he really loves you —"

"I didn't say anything about love, neither has he," Elizabeth flashed.

"No, but that's what you meant."

"I did not."

Aunt Vadie rose. "Maybe not," she shrugged. "Now Mr. Fenwick doesn't seem afraid of public opinion —"

"Don't speak of him, and don't accept any more gifts! Do you hear?"

40

"Nor does Dr. Killpatrick, nor Andrew Rutledge, nor the Governor and his lady, nor Margaret Johnson," Aunt Vadie continued as if she hadn't heard the interruption. She turned to meet Elizabeth's stormy eyes.

"Yes, Elizabeth, no more presents," she ended meekly.

One cold blustery morning Elizabeth lay in the cosy warmth of her wide bed while one of Blossom's protegees lighted her fire.

"Why, today's the twenty-first of December," she thought. "Four more days until Christmas." She recalled bitterly her father's letter about the gaiety of the Charles Town season. In the few weeks since their arrival in Carolina, the hostile attitude of a close knit society had not abated. Perhaps had Elizabeth not made the mistake of being so startlingly handsome and had she not added to that mistake the still grosser one of restoring so swiftly and with little apparent aid the beautiful plantation of Whitehall to a vestige of its former charm, the citizens of Charles Town would have relaxed and accepted her. The fact that she had managed to cancel almost all her father's accounts helped no whit. That seemed to add insult to injury. A woman who could do all these things was no lady and therefore not acceptable by the dowagers as a fit companion for their daughters. The daughters, indignant over the fact that the dashing Jon Fenwick spent all his free moments at Whitehall and that the eligible though impecunious new doctor did likewise, added fuel to the raging fire of disapproval. Uncle Roy was Whitehall's only contact with the town. He slept, ate, and read during the day and rode out at night to join the gentlemen in the various clubs where a game of loo was constantly in session. He, with his competent playing, was always welcome among men who, occupied with their own quarrels on a larger scale, had no time to indulge in the petty personalities of their women-folk. Elizabeth and Vadie, accustomed to his idleness, thought nothing of the fact that he did little to relieve their burdens. Besides, his forays into society lightened the conversation at meal times and made his chatter highly diverting. He remained a cautious gambler and neither Elizabeth nor her aunt realized that some of the gifts that they attributed to Jon Fenwick could be traced to Uncle Roy.

Elizabeth flung back the covers and ran to stand in front of the crackling blaze. As she brushed her heavy hair she made plans. Today they must attend a Christmas party given by the Governor's wife. Though Elizabeth looked forward to it with dread, both she and Vadie felt that they could not offend the Governor by a refusal. On Christmas Eve she would invite their few friends to supper. She must see to decorating the house and preparing a holiday meal. Her eyes sparkled in anticipation as she dressed hastily and flew to find Aunt Vadie. Their heads were soon together as they laid their simple plans. After breakfast Elizabeth sought out O'Gilvie rather than wait for their usual morning conference in the library. She directed him to send out a hunter to shoot wild turkeys for their Christmas meal. He told her that the fields lying out were covered with quail which would add a delicate touch to the feast. Men were sent out to fish for the succulent crab, crayfish, and oysters. A half dozen strange hams were found hanging in the smoke house, and as Elizabeth turned away in annoyance she heard a familiar whinny in the stable nearby.

"What is that?" she asked sharply.

"Phoenix, the mare Mr. Fenwick left," O'Gilvie replied.

"Mr. Fenwick's mare? Why is she here?"

"Mr. Fenwick was riding on the other day and asked that I stable her until he could send for her, as he did not think he would repass this way before nightfall. I didn't think you'd mind, Miss, seein' as Mr. Fenwick —"

Elizabeth interrupted him angrily. "See that the mare is returned to Mr. Fenwick today if he has not called for her by noon. And in the future, please consult me before you make such a move!"

O'Gilvie stared in amazement at the anger in her voice.

"I'm sorry, O'Gilvie. I did not mean it. I'm overwrought. You did exactly right; there was nothing else you could do. However, see that she is returned today." She stroked Phoenix's nose longingly while the mare pawed and tossed her head in greeting.

"Yes, Miss," O'Gilvie hesitated. "I wanted to talk with you today again about supplies," he stopped.

"Yes, O'Gilvie?"

"There is very little left to feed fifty black people and your family. It will be months before we can make a crop of any kind. I have had searching parties out rounding up cows and hogs. From our closest estimate there should be at least two hundred head of cattle. There's no counting the pigs. The cows we've been able to identify positively number about seventy-five so far."

"Good," said Elizabeth welcoming any source of food.

O'Gilvie shook his head. "They're a sorry lot, Miss. Poor and stringy. We must slaughter some, of course, but they'll make little and poor food. They need to be fattened," he stopped helplessly, "but we've nothing to fatten them with."

"What about the pigs?"

"They are in good shape, those we've been able to round up. They find plenty of acorns to keep them fat. However, unless we find more, they won't last long even if we eat them all, and we need to keep some brood sows and boars."

Elizabeth looked worried.

"Pardon me, Miss. You could sell some of the slaves," he suggested uneasily.

Elizabeth stopped in surprise. She had thought of the Negroes on the place as people it was her obligation to care for, not as goods to be traded across the counter.

"No, I think not, O'Gilvie," she said thoughtfully. "There must be some other way."

"They'll have to be fed somehow," he spoke realistically.

Elizabeth returned to the house much troubled. The atmosphere seemed to have turned suddenly colder. A bit of the joy had gone out of her plans for the Christmas celebration.

On Christmas Eve the house at Whitehall presented a festive sight to their guests. Aunt Vadie had directed scurrying black feet until the holly and evergreen-hung rooms sparkled and shone. The long dining room, fragrant with spicy pine boughs, gleamed in the warm candlelight. The table, beautifully laid with linen and silver from Aunt Vadie's trunks, held a magnificent silver epergne loaded with polished fruits and dripping with rosy grapes that Uncle Roy had borne home triumphantly last evening. From her own pantry Mrs. Johnson had sent priceless spices which Aunt Vadie had directed Blossom, who was a born cook, to fashion into traditional Christmas cakes and puddings. Governor Johnson's cellar produced pipes of the blood red wine they had loaded at Madeira. The cheer and good spirits were contributed by everyone, with cares and worries discarded for the time being. Elizabeth was radiant in a garnet velvet gown which left her white shoulders bare. Her hair was pulled back softly into a low chignon on her heck, a coiffure she had adopted in keeping with the simplicity of her busy new life. The Carolina pearls were her only ornament. Unfeigned admiration shone in the eyes of her guests. The sparkling Madeira caught and reflected the candlelight redly. Dr. Killpatrick and Gavin had not arrived when the dinner hour came around. Elizabeth had watched the clock covertly with increasing disappointment ever since a groom had arrived with an amusing note from Dr. Killpatrick.

"My dear Miss Betsy," it read. "Nature never seems to realize a holiday and a baby is less inclined to wait to be born than a cow to be milked! If it isn't triplets, we should be there before the wine is hot. If it is, we should still be there before the turkey is cold."

Elizabeth rose. "It must have been triplets," she smiled ruefully at her guests. "However, we need not all eat cold turkey." She led them in to the delicious meal which she endeavored to enjoy without inflicting her disappointment and unreasonable hurt on the others. The last bit of pudding had been devoured with relish when the doctors arrived, cold and weary. Jon noted the glad look that sprang into Elizabeth's eyes when she rose to greet them. Feeling that the prize was worth the struggle, he figuratively buckled on his armor and set his unmistakable charm against Gavin's fatigue. Gavin waited his opportunity and drew Elizabeth into the library closing the door after him.

"Elizabeth," she looked at him in surprise as he used her name for the first time, "I wanted a moment to wish you Merry Christmas. I must leave again shortly."

"Leave," cried Elizabeth. "But you've just arrived."

"I know. You must realize that I had rather be here – with you," he added searching her eyes and taking her hand which she hastily withdrew.

"Then stay," her eyes looked into his.

"I am a doctor, Elizabeth, pledged to do what I can to relieve suffering."

"So is Dr. Killpatrick. Let him go this once," she cried unreasonably, fighting tears.

Gavin put both his hands on her bare shoulders and nearly shook her.

"Can't you see it won't just be this once? It will always be this way."

Trembling under his touch which sent little tongues of fire licking through her body, she was afraid to raise her eyes.

"But I wanted to ask your advice," she said casting around wildly for an excuse to detain him and feeling ashamed as she did.

"Can't it wait until tomorrow? I'll be back, I promise."

"I suppose so," she answered slowly trying to smother the tiny flicker of resentment that remained. Had Gavin pressed his advantage he might have completely done away with her resentment – and also his rival – but he now made a tactical error and the bright moment was destroyed. He dropped his hands from

44

his shoulders and turned to leave.

"Good-night, then. Until tomorrow."

She stood without moving a few moments after he had left her. Smothering disappointment struggled with reason. A noise made her lift her head to Jon Fenwick's smiling eyes.

"Merry Christmas! It is just midnight."

"Merry Christmas," she answered automatically. Taking a deep breath of resolution, she faced him squarely. "I shall accept your offer of produce on credit. O'Gilvie says we must either have food or sell the mouths we have to feed."

"Splendid. If you will give me a list of your needs I shall have them sent over the day after tomorrow – Nay, tomorrow. Today is already Christmas."

"Thank you, Mr. Fenwick. We shall keep a careful check on what we receive, also your little gifts to Aunt Vadie," she smiled faintly. "You will be repaid in full. I accept your offer only on the condition that Mr. Rutledge draw up the papers for a loan."

Jon shrugged, "As you wish."

Weeks passed into months and spring came again to Carolina with all its unearthly beauty – and its fevers.

Chapter Three

Elizabeth could see figures moving in the gloom of the tall pines. She dismounted and, turning her horse over to a young Negro boy who had run out to meet her, entered the shade of the trees and stopped at O'Gilvie's side to observe the working men and boys.

"Good morning, Miss." He pointed to the busy men. "Today we're beginning to extract turpentine. I'll admit I'm interested in my first venture."

Elizabeth smiled at him. "I'm certain it will be well done, O'Gilvie. You're a very capable man. How does it happen that you are an indentured servant?" The question had occurred to her more than once, how this efficient and well educated man should be found in such a position. She was sorry now that the question had slipped out. His face darkened and he spoke gruffly.

"Pardon me, Miss Cuming. This is a land of the future, not the past." His apologetic smile blunted the seeming rudeness of his words.

" 'Tis I who should beg your pardon, O'Gilvie. I didn't mean to violate your privacy. What are they doing now?" She hastily changed the subject, pointing to a Negro who, with a joiner's hatchet, was deftly cutting channels one inch deep into the tree. The channels descended obliquely to meet in a point at boxes near

47

the base.

"The bark will be stripped away on the side to the sun," O'Gilvie explained. "The heat extracts the turpentine. The box of a large tree holds two English quarts, the small about a pint."

"Mr. Fenwick says it takes about a fortnight to fill a box."

"Unless it rains," O'Gilvie raised his eyes to the sunny March sky. "Rain condenses the sap and contracts the pores which discharge the gum. If this occurs the tree must be bled afresh."

Elizabeth wondered again at this man as he helped her to remount. He was absorbed, vitally interested in all the plantation work. He seemed content, even happy, in his work, but he must be lonely. She shook her head doubtfully and with unseeing eyes passed the men repairing the furnaces to extract the tar and pitch that would fill English bottoms and travel the high seas to a land once called home. These same bottoms would return laden with arms, ammunition, clothes, and utensils. Her mind was far from such impersonal considerations, and she was almost on the two mounted figures before she saw them approaching. Her eyes narrowed against the sun and then widened with pleasure.

"Why, Mr. Wigan! and Onconecaw! How glad I am to see you."

They turned their horses toward the house and Elizabeth questioned them eagerly as they rode slowly along. The woods they passed were white with drifted snow banks of dogwood. In the gardens around the house azaleas flamed in a riot of color.

As a groom took their horses at the block, Elizabeth remarked on the compact size of her companions' horses.

"They're a breed of the country called 'Chickasaw' from the Indian tribal name," said Eleazar. "They're believed to be descended from Spanish barbs left by De Soto on his fruitless trip through the Indian country in search of gold."

Here again was another paradox. Why was this highly educated and intelligent man content to live out his life in the wilderness with only red men for company? Elizabeth felt confused. She brought her mind back to his words.

"The fine Carolina racing stock is the result of breeding these swift little horses to imported blooded stock." Eleazar indicated the slight young Indian who stood by his side. "Onconecaw brings a message from his people and also a gift."

"To me?" Elizabeth asked in surprise.

"Yes, Lady Cuming," Onconecaw spoke precisely but exactly, though he stumbled over her name. "My people bid you welcome to their country. Your father, the Great Warrior, promised to return and live among them. They await him many moons."

Elizabeth's eyes filled with tears. "Believe me, Onconecaw, he has tried. The King refuses him permission to return."

"This my people do not understand. Your King has told us that we are all his children and therefore brothers, red man and white. If this is truly so, why does a father forbid brothers who love one another to live together?"

"I wish all life could be so simple, Onconecaw."

"My people would have me tell you that the good strong house they prepared for the Warrior at his chosen spot awaits you. They send this horse to carry you thither."

Elizabeth looked at the Indian in amazement. "Do you mean that they would welcome a woman?"

"News travels like the wind among the Indians." Onconecaw lowered his eyes to avoid embarrassing her. "My people know that the white man in Charles Town has not received the daughter of their friend. They would have you know that in the Cherokee country it would not be thus. Unlike our white brother, the red man often accords a position of highest honor to a woman."

Eleazar had watched the color come and go in Elizabeth's vivid face. Incredulity struggled with humble gratitude as she wondered how a people who had moments of such astuteness could have earned the name of savage.

"Thank you, Onconecaw," she replied simply. "I shall endeavor to find a suitable gift and to frame a reply that will express my own and my father's gratitude."

Onconecaw bowed with dignity. Elizabeth's eyes were thoughtful as they left, and all Aunt Vadie's attempts at dinner time conversation received absent minded replies.

The streets of Charles Town filled with traders seeking to renew their licenses for another year. Eleazar paid several visits to Whitehall where he filled Elizabeth's ears with glowing accounts of the country in the Cherokee foothills. Plans for the proposed settlement near the Congaree fort had gone forward slowly. Surveyors were scarce, supplies more so, and settlers willing to cut themselves off from the protection of the sea were few. Governor Johnson was not dismayed, however, and hoped that the demands for land there would soon be as eager as in Amelia Township where Captain Russell had already bought land and moved his family. Other families at the Congarees were becoming discouraged also with the slowness of the movement in their direction and only Trader Thomas Brown's stalwart presence held them there. The settlement needed a decisive leader like Mr. Pierre

Purry whose Switzers were already trickling into Charles Town in hopes of securing choice lands at Purrysburg.

Eleazar raised his eyebrows and fell silently thoughtful when he met Jon Fenwick on one of his visits to Whitehall and saw the easy familiarity of Jon's position. Jon regarded him warily and a slight coolness crept into their usually friendly relations. Eleazar breathed a little easier when he saw that Gavin was on an equally friendly footing. Jon had recently travelled to the Cherokee country with large packhorse trains for Trader Brown's store at the Congarees. He had also been commissioned deputy surveyor and was as lyric in description of the fine Up Country as Eleazar. A growing conviction that he wanted to cast his lot in this new land had been strengthened by an inviting offer from Thomas Brown to go into business association with him.

"I'm getting on in years and dislike any travelling. I need younger shoulders to carry a pack while I begin to rock and relax a bit," Thomas had said. The proposed settlement at the Congarees would just fit in with Jon's plans to make the move attractive to Elizabeth, little knowing that Eleazar's vivid descriptions had already turned her thoughts tentatively in that direction. Jon fully realized what he was up against in Gavin, but he also was realistic enough to take advantage of Elizabeth's conscience. Charles Town, though more relaxed in its animosity, had not welcomed Elizabeth. Gavin's hard work and evident genius as a physician had put him in great demand, a demand that would be the means of his discharging his debts if nothing happened to alter this popularity. Should he marry an unpopular wife, the fickle wind of public favor might easily cease, or blow as strongly in another direction. Though Jon knew full well this would make no difference to Gavin, it would to Elizabeth. Gavin, however, would be as stiff necked in his determination to put himself in a position to support a wife, though this would mean nothing to Elizabeth. So, Jon who ruled, rather than was ruled by, his conscience felt no scruple in using their consciences to his own end. His arrogance led him to believe that he wanted Elizabeth on any terms.

Therefore he set out to help Eleazar paint an enchanting picture of the Back Country, its natural beauties, its healthful climate and its unlimited fertile land. He looked at Eleazar venomously when they were all together on the lawn at Whitehall one sultry summer day.

"There is a great future for doctors in the Back Country, Dr. McBride," Wigan said innocently.

Gavin, whose Scotch soul longed during the damp hot months

when he fought case after case of yellow fever, for the high lands of Scotland and a free cool breeze, sighed and sipped on his cool drink.

"Would that I could avail myself of the opportunity. I am obligated here. I couldn't desert Dr. Killpatrick. He wished some day to return to England and will not do so until he can leave his patients in my care." Jon breathed easily again. Eleazar looked glum.

The deadening summer wore itself out and O'Gilvie proudly harvested a fine crop. Elizabeth somewhat pompously summoned Jon to the library office to make her accounting.

"Mr. Fenwick, I was a bit hasty in my boasts to repay you in full before the year was out. However, I am not ashamed of what we have accomplished. Next year I shall be completely out of your debt."

"I would be glad to cancel the remainder or better still, I suggest we pool our assets – and liabilities," he looked at her meaningfully.

Her smile faded. "What do you mean?"

"You know full well what I mean. Elizabeth," he covered the distance between them in a stride, "You cannot be ignorant of where my heart lies. Marry me, and let's go to that great country that Eleazar has told you of."

"No, no," she cried drawing back.

"No?" he demanded. "Why not? If the idea is so distasteful to you, why have you let me come here constantly? Why did you not refuse to see me. Is it only for my aid that you have accepted my advances?"

"No, Jon. You are unfair," Elizabeth spoke earnestly. "You have made no 'advances' as you say. Had you done so, I would have refused to see you. I'm deeply grateful for all you have done. Without your generosity we could not have remained. Your friendship has been invaluable. This is not the basis of your welcome here, though. I like you, Jon, and have wanted you here."

"Then what holds you back?"

Elizabeth stirred uneasily. "Is liking enough for marriage?"

"From you, it will be enough to start on. You can't help but return a love as great as mine." He took her hand gently in his and lifted her chin with his finger so that his black eyes looked deeply into her troubled grey ones. "You cannot stay here, you've said so yourself. Come with me," he pled.

"Give me time to think," her eyes fell again.

"Is there something else that holds you back?"

Her eyes still on the floor, she hesitated, "No – I suppose not."

Consumed by a hurried passion at her unusual nearness he drew her suddenly and roughly to him. His sensuous lips closed hungrily on her wide red ones and he crushed her surprised body against his own. Something new stirred deep within her and she remembered the pleasurable sensation with shame after she had pushed him away and he had gone with an assured sparkle in his eye.

It was almost Christmas again when Elizabeth received the letter from her father. She read it at first with pleasure, then with dismay.

> *Spring Garden*
> *17 October 1731*
>
> *My dear daughter,*
> *News of your astounding success as a Carolina planter has reached us, and we salute your ability and determination. Your letters reveal your full and happy life which fact is gratifying to your mother and myself. Vadie keeps your mother well posted on the unending round of social activities in Charles Town. These things you must find to your liking.*

Elizabeth blessed her aunt silently for her precious white lies. She read on.

> *Governmental decisions are slowly made and as slowly carried out. My renewed petition is now in the hands of his grace, the Duke of Newcastle, after receiving a favorable report from the Board of Trade. I am informed that his Majesty is very occupied with affairs of state dealing with the war with Spain and cannot give the matter his immediate attention. I am not disheartened however. I feel that my request to go to the Cherokee country at my own expense will receive a favorable reply.*

Her eyes widened as they fell on the next paragraph.

> *Your interest in the back country pleases me. I have*

at hand a letter from Mr. Jon Fenwick requesting your hand in marriage. He informs me that he plans to settle in the new township at the Congarees, and he believes you are not entirely indifferent to his suit. Mr. Fenwick is a splendid young man of fine family and fair fortune. He has offered to make a most handsome settlement, and I am dispatching my approval to him with this letter to you. Your mother, who continues in indifferent health, and I wish you all happiness, and will hope to reach South Carolina in time for the wedding.

The remainder of the letter went unread as it slipped to the floor from Elizabeth's nerveless fingers.

After she had received this letter from Sir Alexander, Elizabeth kept Aunt Vadie as her constant companion to avoid any private conversations with Jon. She tried to set her whirling thoughts in order and also to get a few moments alone with Gavin. When such an opportunity presented itself, however, she could not muster the courage to bring up her father's letter. That Jon had received Sir Alexander's approval of his suit — more exactly, his consent to their marriage, Elizabeth knew, for he had told her. But she pled the many demands on her time and thoughts so near Christmas to postpone her answer. She realized that she could put him off no longer and determined to have a showdown with Gavin on Christmas eve, when the little group of friends met again at Whitehall for dinner.

After another of Blossom's excellent holiday dinners, Elizabeth faced Gavin, as she had done a year ago, across the cozy little library with its crackling fire. They talked of unimportant matters for a few moments while Elizabeth summoned her courage. She tried several times to find a proper opening, but could not. Finally she blurted,

"I've had a letter from my father."

Gavin waited.

"He wishes me to marry Jon," she kept her eyes on the intricate pattern of the Persian rug at her feet.

"You will not, of course," Gavin spoke with finality.

"Is that a statement or a question?" Elizabeth felt her unreasoning anger begin to rise. She had expected anything — anger, protestations — not this quiet certainty.

"It is a statement, Elizabeth," his admiring eyes watched the changing color in her lovely face.

"And why are you so sure?"

He looked shocked, "Because you do not love him."

"Whether I do or not is beside the point. My father has given his consent."

Gavin rose, alarm in his blue eyes. "Your love is not beside the point. A marriage of convenience may have been all right in England and for someone else, but never for you. You have a glorious gift to give your husband, and he shall not be someone you do not love." He spoke with deep conviction and determination.

"What alternative have I?" she had risen and spoke with her eyes on the fire.

He pulled her gently to him and forced her eyes to look into his. "You, as well as I, know what the alternative is. I have not spoken openly to you or to your father because as yet I am not in a position to do so. This you must have understood. I love you, Elizabeth, and I want you for my wife. I want you now," he took her hungrily in his arms and laid his cheek on her fragrant hair. "I have an obligation to discharge first, but it won't be long now."

"Duty, duty, duty!" She flung away from him. "What is your duty to me?" she faced him with flaming cheeks.

"Duty to you? I don't understand. I have worked night and day to pay my debts and to establish myself so that I might offer you a position of honor in Charles Town. What more can one man do?"

"A position of honor in Charles Town? I can't stay here. As your wife, I would destroy any position you might achieve."

Gavin's anger was rising to meet her own. "How long do you propose to let your father's action control your life? You have paid his debts; now forget it!"

"Perhaps I could forget it — the people here will not."

"That is ridiculous. Where is your courage? They've already forgotten. They would try to be friends now if you would let them. With your beauty, pride and dignity you could face anything."

"If I could, they would make it difficult for you. I won't stay here!"

"How difficult they make it for me is my own concern. If I am not afraid, why should you be? Oh, my dear, can't you see that to have you for my own would make any world a beautiful one?" He tried to take her in his arms again.

"I don't want it that way. Can't you see you must walk with your head high, so must I? We would neither of us be content with anything else."

"What do you propose to do then?" he asked perplexed.

The anger died from her dark eyes and she made a step toward him.

"You and I have often spoken of the new Back Country — how we longed to be away from this humidity and heat — back in a healthy climate like that in Scotland. Mr. Wigan says the Assembly will soon order the township at the Congarees laid out. There is land — thousands of acres to be had for the asking. The people will come from Europe in great numbers, the Governor says. They, too, will need a doctor." In her enthusiasm she had drawn near Gavin and laid her hands on his arms. She looked pleadingly into his troubled eyes.

He looked at her without words.

"Please, Gavin. Let's go there. We can sell Whitehall. It's a wonderful opportunity and Mr. Wigan has told you what you could do for the people suffering so far from proper professional care."

"I can't leave here."

"Why not?"

"Dr. Killpatrick is preparing to return to England. It is for that reason he has brought me here."

"There are other doctors who can take his place."

"He is only content to leave because he has trained me and is satisfied to leave his friends in my care. I cannot desert him now."

"I can't stay here," she drew back angrily.

"Why not?" he asked, equally angry.

"I have told you."

Gavin's face was terrible. He towered over even her tall figure as he seized her arms roughly and forced her to face him.

"How long are you going to let your stupid bitterness ruin your life? Nay, three lives? In your selfish blindness you will destroy the happiness of three people, not just your own. What man could live with a woman like you who did not love him? You've no right to do that to Jon Fenwick. He loves you, too, and has the right to at least the honor paid a defeated enemy. You are not God that you can regulate lives to please your own sense of — of what? What are you trying to do?"

"I am going to the Congarees. If you will go with me, I'll disobey my father. I will *not* stay here."

"I cannot go. Elizabeth, my darling. Can't you see? I would rather go. The country sounds as good to me as it does to you. But a man cannot desert his responsibilities and live with himself. I did not question your sense of duty when you set out to pay your father's debts. Neither should you question mine. I am asking you to stay here with me. My life is here and I want you to stay here and share it with me. It won't be long until I will be free of debt and we can be married. Have this faith in me." He still held her at arms length.

"No," Elizabeth seemed to have lost all reason in her furious anger. "If you will not go, I'll marry Jon Fenwick. I would ruin your life."

They measured each other with hostile eyes. Anger at her stubborness overwhelmed him and he shook her savagely.

"You little fool! You couldn't find a more certain way to ruin it than what you propose to do, and along with it you'll ruin Jon Fenwick's and your own." Her face showed no sign of relenting. He continued with more control, his eyes as cold as steel.

"If you are determined to do this to the three of us, I shall see that you suffer as much as Jon and I shall."

He jerked her resisting body to him and crushed his mouth down on her own. A thousand lights seemed to burst in Elizabeth's head and wave after wave of glory consumed her as Gavin covered her face, neck and shoulders with his passionate kisses.

Finally, he released her and thrust her roughly from him into a chair.

"I hope you will remember that every time you lie in his arms," he spoke through stiff jaws into her stricken face.

Chapter Four

The year 1732 was one of beginnings of which the significance of each may not have been apparent at the time. In a small four room farmhouse on the Rappahanock in Westmoreland County, Virginia, a son was born to planter Augustine Washington and his second wife. They christened him George. The first Swiss colonists designated for Mr. Purry's settlement at Savannah Town in Carolina arrived. The first edition of Mr. Thomas Whitmarch's *South Carolina Gazette* appeared on the street of Charles Town Saturday, January eighth carrying this item of news:

"We hear that Whitehall the former Goose Creek plantation of Roderick Cameron was the scene of the wedding of Jonathan Fenwick, Esquire and a Miss Elizabeth Cuming, lately come to Charles Town, a young lady of a variety of talents and a knack for business which could be the envy of many of the opposite sex. Rumour has it that the happy couple plan to bury these talents in the dreamed of (but not yet laid out) Township at the Congarees. Governor Johnson and his lady were present for the nuptials."

Aunt Vadie's face was expressionless. Elizabeth's dusky color gave place to an ivory pallor which matched the pearls at her throat and the gleaming beauty of her heavy silk gown, the same she had worn on her first tragic evening in Carolina. The stage, thought Vadie, was set for a second tragedy. Her efforts to dissuade Elizabeth from another hasty and ill considered action had been fruitless. Even feckless Uncle Roy had had a word of warning when on Christmas morning Elizabeth had told them of her decision to marry Jon.

"Your hasty actions have already caused enough trouble. The step you propose to take is even more serious. This man is not your kind."

"How do you know? He is my father's choice."

Roy shrugged languidly. "You had better make up your mind whether you wish to play the dutiful daughter role or that of the independent woman of the world. The two don't mix. At least try to be consistent in your tantrums."

Blossom's excellent breakfast lay untouched before Aunt Vadie. Her eyes pled with Elizabeth.

"My dear, Roy is right. You must stop giving away to your ungovernable anger." She hesitated before she proceeded. "You have inherited from your father a determination that is admirable if properly directed. Like your father you are allowing it to degenerate into stubborness. It has destroyed him; it will destroy you unless you take hold of it."

Elizabeth ate mechanically without tasting the succulent squab that Blossom had so proudly prepared for their holiday breakfast. Her eyes remained steadfastly on her plate.

"You are making a great mistake," Vadie's voice urged her gently. "Gavin is the man of your choice."

Elizabeth raised stormy eyes. "That is not true!"

"I am not blind, Elizabeth. Neither is Jon. He knows that too."

"If he is willing to undertake it under those circumstances, that is his affair!"

"Then you admit it's true?"

"I admit nothing." Perilously near tears Elizabeth pushed back her chair. "Leave me alone, won't you? I shall marry the man my father has chosen for me." She ran from the room leaving Roy and Vadie looking at each other.

Roy rose and came around to Vadie's side. Dropping a kiss on her golden head, he sighed. "I am truly thankful, my dear, that you are her mother's sister and not her father's. Anger and haste make life too complicated. Well, there's a game at Shepheard's. I think I'll look in on it a bit." He looked again at his wife's stricken face. "Cheer up, my love, you've lived with this sort of thing all your life."

"Yes," she answered bleakly, "but it didn't concern Elizabeth.

You and I, Roy, are among the side-liners of life. For me, I am content that it should be so. But no, no, not for Elizabeth! She is too vital to be a bystander. She should be in the midst of life and love." She laid her head on the table and sobbed bitterly. Roy unused to such extremes of emotion from his wife waved his lace handkerchief helplessly in the direction of her wet eyes, and departed hastily in relief when the tears ceased as suddenly as they had begun.

"Go on with you!" She dashed the tears from her eyes and shooed him from the room.

Friday, the day of the wedding, had dawned clear and bitter cold. Elizabeth had risen after a sleepless night to a day of restlessness. Somehow she had unconsciously hoped that something would occur to stop the wheels of time and that this day would never arrive. Now that it had, a cold feeling of fear lay in her stomach. She felt like a newly caged animal from the wilds, frightened and senslessly pacing back and forth along the bars of its cage seeking a non-existent means of escape. About noon she slipped out unobserved and went to the stables. She was about to take out the little Chickasaw horse when she heard a familiar whinny. Unknown to her Jon had returned beautiful Phoenix to her stable as a wedding present. In spite of herself she was touched at this thoughtful gesture. In the last two weeks since she had promised to marry him, Elizabeth, by observing Jon more closely during his daily visits to Whitehall, had begun to fear that there was little thoughtfulness or gentleness in his makeup. Little actions began to indicate to her that he was completely self centered, and the urgency of his love making, on the few occasions when he had caught her away from Aunt Vadie, precluded any idea of gentleness. This gift somewhat allayed her rising fears. Needing physical action to still her mounting nervousness she saddled Phoenix without summoning a groom and eased quietly out of the courtyard unseen by the busy servants. Only O'Gilvie, returning from an inspection of a prize new heifer, saw her flash by when she was out of ear shot of the house. He shook his head. It was not for him to say, but that Dr. McBride looked like a much safer bet for Miss Elizabeth. He distrusted, without knowing why, Mr. Fenwick's easy grace and charm. For Elizabeth he had formed a devotion that was complete and absolute, and he would have given his life to protect her from harm or unhappiness. He hunched his shoulders against the cold and waited with troubled eyes until girl and horse, both winded and disheveled, crept back to the stable. He helped her down wordlessly and led Phoenix to

59

her stall as Elizabeth returned slowly to the house.

Aunt Vadie fully aware of Elizabeth's nervousness and distress, helped her dress that evening for the wedding. She could think of nothing to say and the two avoided each other's eyes. Finally Elizabeth was ready and faced herself in the long pier glass of her bedroom. Her unusual pallor heightened her beauty and brought out the glory of her hair which Aunt Vadie had insisted on dressing in the French style that she had worn at Crowfield when Jon had first seen her. How long ago it seemed! Now as she surveyed her reflection in the mirror her nervousness left her and she took a resolute breath. All thought of rescue from the consequences her own rash action were set aside, and fully realizing the enormity of the thing to which she had committed herself, she squared her shoulders to meet her new obligations as conscientiously as she had discharged her old. The memory of Gavin's face and the pressure of his lips on her own, she buried deep within her mind in one of those private chambers on which the brave can shut the door with finality.

The gaiety usually attending a wedding was lacking though Elizabeth set about putting her friends at ease. The genuine devotion and flash of joy that crossed Jon's face when he saw her descending the wide stairs on Uncle Roy's arm deepened her resolve to do what she could to keep that joy in his heart even if it could not be echoed in her own. Her answering smile was genuine as he looked down into her dark eyes when they took their vows before the Reverend Mr. Bassett. Governor Johnson had wanted to bring his own vicar from Saint Philips but as both Elizabeth and Jon were of the dissenting faith, the Reverend Nathaniel Bassett had been fetched from the White Meeting House. Even Margaret Johnson's bubbling gaiety was subdued, and Dr. Killpatrick who attended without Gavin was frankly grumpy. Gavin had neither been seen nor heard from since the violent conference in the library on Christmas Eve. Tonight he was attending a number of patients far from Charles Town who were affected with a strange new distemper causing painful swelling below the ears and a clamping of the jaws.

Next morning Aunt Vadie found Elizabeth standing quietly looking out the dining room window over the bleak grey landscape. She turned as her aunt entered and the two women regarded each other silently a moment. Elizabeth's dark eyes were veiled and her voice toneless.

"You were right. I have made a great mistake," she said quietly, "but I'll try to keep it from everyone but you."

Vadie made no answer, there was nothing to say, as the two sat down to a solitary breakfast.

Chapter Five

Early in May yellow fever descended on the Province with savage violence and stalked across the land, gathering in its victims with democratic impartiality. There were hardly enough well inhabitants to bury the daily quota of dead, and fear took hold and ruled the Colony. Governor Johnson was forced to prorogue the Assembly and farmers were not allowed to bring their produce into Charles Town for fear of spreading the infection, though where else it could be spread, since it had invaded every nook and cranny of both town and country, was not made clear.

Jon left early in May on a long trip to the Congarees. His mission was a dual one of handling cargo for Indian trade and of looking over the land in that section and discussing its possibilities with Thomas Brown. The Governor was anxious for a report on streams, fertility, and lay of the land to better recommend to the Assembly a likely spot for a seating of colonists.

The fields at Whitehall had been planted and the rainfall promised a good growing season for large crops of corn, cotton, and the rye which Elizabeth had recommended that they use to replace the wheat which had done so poorly last year. The rye had been planted in the fall before her marriage. Old fields into which she had O'Gilvie drive the laboriously collected wild cows in order to replenish the worn land with their dung had been fenced.

Returning one morning from an early inspection with O'Gilvie, Elizabeth looked forward to breakfast alone with Aunt Vadie. In the months since her marriage they had had little time for private conversation and she now sought out her aunt in pleasant anticipation.

"Aunt Vadie?", she called when she entered the empty dining room.

Blossom entered with a steaming pot of coffee, her face devoid of its usual special smile she reserved for Elizabeth.

"She sick."

"Sick? She was quite well last evening. What could be the matter? Aunt Vadie is never sick."

"Cilly, she sick too down the row. Doan lak it."

"How long has Cilly been sick? What is the matter with her?"

"She don cum in frum de fiel day fo' yestiddy draggin her tail. Her maw thawt twas laziness but she so hot now she cain't stan no kivver."

"Blossom, please notify Mr. O'Gilvie to meet me in the quarters as soon as he has had his breakfast. I'll go to Aunt Vadie now."

"Naw'm. You eat fust. Den you go. I don fix sum leetle fish jest lak you lak um and dey won't stan no waitin!"

"Thank you, Blossom, but I'll be back immediately. Just let me see what my aunt needs."

Blossom grumbled comfortably about, "Folks what don know food has to be et when it reddy to be good," and returned to the pantry with the steaming pot.

Elizabeth brushed the tiny line of worry from her forehead and put on her best smile as she softly entered her aunt's room. Roy raised his head and lifted the cool cloth he had placed on his wife's temples. The two forgot to greet each other as they looked at the angry flush on the fair face they both loved. At the sound of Elizabeth's soft voice Vadie opened her usually clear eyes now suffused and ferrety. Elizabeth tried to hide her shock and mounting horror. Across the bed her eyes met Uncle Roy's in wordless understanding. His face was ashen and pinched with fear. There was no one in Carolina who was not familiar with the symptoms of dread yellow fever even though he had never seen a victim. Elizabeth's throat was dry and she struggled to control the tremor in her voice as she spoke tenderly to her aunt.

"I am sorry you feel so bad, Aunt Vadie. But you need a rest. Just lie quietly and I'll have Blossom bring you a cup of tea."

"My head aches so, the pain, here," she whispered hoarsely touching her eye brows with a listless hand.

Elizabeth hastened to find O'Gilvie and together they sought out Cilly's cabin while Elizabeth told him her fears for Aunt Vadie. A look of concern grew on the overseer's large face as he listened. He made no comment as they approached the tiny brick cabin, identical in every respect to nineteen others which faced each other across the wide dusty row. A skinny, light skinned Negro girl tossed and cried out incoherently on a wooden cot attached to the wall. The room that they entered was small but immaculately neat. The hard clay floor was swept smooth, the coarse sheets on the corn shuck mattress, were rumpled but clean. The shuttered windows were tightly closed and a hot fire burned on the low hearth casting the only light in the reeking gloom. The pungent odor of many bodies was stifling and mixed with the unmistakable acrid odor of sickness. Elizabeth almost gagged as she laid her hand on the girl's forehead in spite of O'Gilvie's move to protest. The skin was burning and the brown eyes that opened momentarily were congested. The heat was unbearable. Controlling a suffocating feeling of nausea, Elizabeth ordered the windows and doors thrown open and the fire extinguished. A look of sullen stubborness on the face of the prune faced woman who was Cilly's mother met these orders. She made no move to obey.

"Did you hear me?" Elizabeth spoke carefully.

"Naw'm, I mean, Yassum. De evil sperrit don got in hyah and I got um doah shet tuh keep out de odders and smother what's got in."

"You'll smother your daughter along with the evil spirit if you don't let in some air," Elizabeth replied acidly.

They left the stifling cabin with orders to ventilate the foul atmosphere, orders which both Elizabeth and the overseer knew would not be obeyed.

When Elizabeth's eyes had met her Uncle's in wordless understanding that morning over Aunt Vadie's bed her first thought was of Gavin. He, with his great, clean strength, capable hands, and certain knowledge, could save the one person who stood between her and utter loneliness. The thought of him cut as if his flashing scalpel had opened her own veins for bleeding. She had resolutely kept her mind away from him since their final stormy meeting last Christmas. The thought now sent the blood tingling through her body in warm waves as if the pressure on a numbed limb had been released.

She went to her room and took up her quill. For a moment her eyes looked blankly through the window over the steaming countryside. She shook herself and dipping the quill wrote hastily —

> Dr. McBride:
> *My aunt is ill and there is another suspicious case in the quarters. Will you come?*

She gazed frowningly at the sheet and added,

> *I need you,*
>
> *Elizabeth*

She scrawled her name and hesitated momentarily before she added

> *— Fenwick*

Later that evening she heard the sound of hooves clattering urgently up the drive. What little blood was left in her lips drained from them and her hand flew to her heart as if to still its frantic beat. After the first moment of panic when she wanted only to run and hide, she drew herself up and fought valiantly for self control. Her face was composed when Gavin entered the room, but she was not quick enough to prevent the flash of joy in her eyes which met no response in his own cold face. The glad light died as quickly as it had come when Dr. Gavin McBride bowed coldly and stiffly.

"Madame Fenwick," he addressed her indifferently.

For a moment she stood in stunned silence. Then the awful, all enveloping anger, over which she seemed powerless, overcame the first hurt and she replied as coldly, her dark eyes flashing furiously.

"Dr. McBride!"

Their personal feelings were soon forgotten however, in the teamwork of their attack on the ruthless killer now threatening Aunt Vadie which Gavin instantly recognized. Understanding it little more than other physicians of his day, Gavin rolled up his sleeves and called for a sheet, a large tub of cold water, boiling water and a bowl. When these were brought he looked at Elizabeth across the bed with the eyes of the man, not the doctor.

"You'd better leave the room."

"Why so?" Elizabeth flashed back.

"This will not be pleasant."

"I did not expect it to be so, Sir. Please proceed."

For a moment their eyes held in hostility; then Gavin became the doctor, cold and efficient who rapped out orders that Elizabeth carried out equally coldly and efficiently. The lancet flashed, angry red blood flowed, cool damp sheets encased the fever racked body, sheets that dried almost instantly in contact with the burning intensity of the virulent disease. At last they straightened their aching backs and Gavin's wide smile flashed in admiration as he spoke,

"Well done!" before he realized that it was Elizabeth whom he was praising. In his absorption he had forgotten her as a person and realized only the perfection of her instant cooperation with his demands as a doctor.

The smile faded. The impersonal manner returned and Elizabeth's capable hands fell hopelessly to her side. They turned to leave the room. Roy remained with his wife. A sibilant sigh escaped Aunt Vadie's lips as she settled into momentary slumber relieved for a short time of racking pain and fever. Slowly and silently the young doctor and the tall girl descended the wide stair to the gracious hall below. The heat was stifling. The candle flames stood erect and unmoving in the sticky air. O'Gilvie rose from a chair against the wall and looked questioningly at Elizabeth. She nodded wearily,

"Yellow fever."

"There are two other cases in the row, M'am," O'Gilvie spoke gravely.

Elizabeth's heart sank and a tremor of terror swept over her that made her almost stagger. O'Gilvie saw her waver and stepped forward quickly. She pushed his hand aside, angry at her sudden weakness.

"We will go to the quarters now. Please call Clem to light our way."

"Shall I call Blossom also, Miss Elizabeth? There is no need for you to go."

"I appreciate your thoughtfulness, O'Gilvie. Nevertheless, I shall go. Please hurry. I am quite sure that Dr. McBride has many other patients to attend."

They stood without words while O'Gilvie fetched Clem with a lantern. Then they passed silently behind the giant Negro man into the oppressive night. Inspection of the quarters took some time and the three known cases were treated as carefully as the one in the great house. When they turned toward the house a deep line of worry cut Gavin's forehead and he did not protest when Elizabeth ordered refreshments served.

"In the library, M'am?" asked Clem.

Elizabeth flushed, "No, Clem, in the drawing room, please. We shall be cooler there." It seemed to Elizabeth that all the tragic encounters of her life were wont to take place in the deceptively pleasant library.

After a brief silence, Gavin spoke. He looked seriously into Elizabeth's troubled eyes.

"You realize, I suppose, Madam," the word sounded pompous and ridiculous to them both, "the seriousness of the situation?"

Elizabeth nodded wordlessly.

"You realize that your Aunt may not − recover?"

Elizabeth closed her eyes and struggled for self control.

"Please, Gavin! Don't let her die! She's all I have −"

"You have a husband, M'am."

Elizabeth's head snapped up. "I beg your pardon, Sir. I was over wrought." She rose, her face expressionless. "I am certain that you have other duties. I am in your debt. Have you any further instructions?"

The worried look returned to the doctor's face. "These are the first cases near here that have come to my attention. There are no doubt many others. There will certainly be more." He regarded her thoughtfully. "There is so little we know of the cause or cure. Keep her quiet, comfortable and try to force liquids down. That's all you can do. Your greatest worry will be fear. You cannot control the disease but you, I believe, can control the fear among your people. Keep them busy." His voice and face softened a moment. "I wish I could do something more for you. But under the circumstances − I cannot." He turned to leave and spoke over his shoulder in a voice muffled with emotion. "Keep yourself rested. I shall always be available, −" and was gone.

Day after lonely, weary day followed in hot humid discomfort overlaid with the ever present spectre of fear. Mosquitoes swarmed in buzzing clouds over the lowland rice lands and deaths increased daily. No communication was permitted between the village of Charles Town and the country where the dread Black Vomit seemed to cut a wide swath with its deadly sickle. Sullen, dirty grey clouds hung like a pall over the usually fragrant and blooming Low Country. Lush growth hung in limp acquiescence to the hopeless despondency that held the afflicted colony in its grasp. Friend feared friend; the streets of the gay village were silent except for the lugubrious creaking of the death carts. On the plantations, fields and gardens grew rank from lack of hands to tend them.

At Whitehall, Elizabeth stayed busy night and day pushing, prodding, encouraging, tending the sick, and quieting panic as best she could. For the first two days after the sickness struck, she scarcely left her aunt's side and would not have eaten had not Blossom threatened to have Mr. O'Gilvie carry her to the table forcefully. Both Elizabeth and Uncle Roy learned to choke down the tempting food that Blossom set before them, hardly tasting it.

On the third morning after Gavin's visit Elizabeth entered her aunt's room to relieve Uncle Roy. He was dozing fitfully in a chair and Elizabeth's sudden cry brought him up instantly. She had touched Aunt Vadie's forehead and found it cool, the hectic red had left her face to be replaced by a faint lemon coloured tinge.

"She's better! Oh, Uncle Roy."

Elizabeth laid her head on her uncle's shoulder and wept with relief while he patted her shoulder absently. Blossom had entered with a cup of tea which she laid on the bedside table. She looked at the motionless figure on the bed and shook her head.

"Bad sign, bad sign. Tsch! Tsch!"

Elizabeth raised her tear stained face and looked blankly at Blossom who pointed at her aunt who was vomiting effortlessly a clear fluid. Elizabeth ran back to the bed and touched her aunt again. The skin was cold and clammy. She touched her wrist. Where was her pulse? There, finally, but how slow and very feeble. Alarm clutched at Elizabeth's heart.

"Dere now – don take on so. Hit do lak dat. Maybe she will – maybe she won't." Elizabeth looked at Blossom in new wonder. From a frowzy, slatternly wench, she had developed into a handsome woman of doubtful age and studied dignity. She was small and, though birdlike, well formed. The stringiness had disappeared with a steady diet, the sulleness, with Elizabeth's kindness. Elizabeth had discovered in her black adorer a depth of strength and calm that was unusual in her race. Even now she showed not the slightest fear and unlike the frightened blacks in the row, continued her daily round of duties without flinching.

"You gwan now foh yoh food don spoilt. Ah'll clean up dis mess and feed Miz Vadie her tea. Gwan!"

"Aren't you afraid, Blossom?"

Blossom's yellowish eyes flickered a second then she returned Elizabeth's look steadily.

"Yas'm," she answered solemnly.

"You don't show it."

Blossom looked adoringly into her mistress' eyes, "Ah do lak

67

you," she said proudly.

Elizabeth flushed, "Thank you, Blossom," she said simply, touching her shoulder.

After her breakfast, she summoned O'Gilvie who entered the room with a glum face. He reported that Cilly had died in torment during the night and another case had appeared. The slaves were thoroughly terrified and refused to open their doors to him. His conversation had taken place through closed doors. Hostile whispers had answered his angry shouts. Cilly's family had fled to the woods and refused to return to bury her. The three other cases were unattended while the able occupants of their cabins also took to the woods because no hospitable door would open to their pleas.

The tiny pulse of anger began to throb in Elizabeth's neck. She rose to her full height and the flash that had dimmed in her eyes these last three days returned with all its fire. O'Gilvie stared in admiration for anger heightened all her points of beauty and emphasized the Latin glow of her heritage.

She jerked the bell cord and when Clem appeared ordered sharply without her usual courtesy,

"Have Blossom give you my riding crop."

O'Gilvie waited, a question in his eye.

"Mr. O'Gilvie, I am certain your predecessor must have owned a bull whip. Find it!"

The question in the overseer's eyes gave way to alarm.

"But, Miss Elizabeth —"

"At once, Mr. O'Gilvie."

A faint smile of admiration crossed his worried face. O'Gilvie, like Blossom, would have staked his last farthing on this tall straight, young woman.

"At once, Miss," he raised his hand in unconscious salute.

Clem's eyes, white rimmed with fear he had not felt in months, followed the two purposeful figures as they strode toward the cabins. They paused under the great farm bell which O'Gilvie tugged. It rang out hollowly in the eerie silence of the deserted row. The two waited. No other sound broke the stillness.

Elizabeth waited no longer. She strode to the center of the row where she rapped on the door of the slave Cato who was a leader by seniority. She stepped back into the middle of the dusty street and called out loudly and clearly.

"Cato, come out immediately!"

There was no reply, but was there a faint uneasy stirring behind the bare plank door?

"Cato, I warn you, I have given Mr. O'Gilvie Mr. O'Dwyer's whip and if you will not come out, he will come in — to your sorrow!"

The instant consternation behind the similar whitewashed doors made itself felt through their solid thickness. Cato's door opened a crack.

"I am waiting — but not much longer," the girl called again.

Cato's frizzy white head appeared, then his shoulders. Finally he shuffled doubtfully out followed by his wife. Just outside the door he stopped and looked steadily at the ground.

Elizabeth addressed him slowly and distinctly.

"Will you call out the rest of your people or shall I send Mr. O'Gilvie for them?"

Cato's eyes slid to the vicious whip in the overseer's hand. Reluctantly the old eyes rose to his mistress' determined face. What he saw there decided him.

"Naw'm. Ah git um." He shuffled from one door to another on one side while his wife took the other and each door cracked reluctantly to their whispered messages. Frightened figures with surly black faces gathered at the edge of the roadway between the two rows of small brick buildings.

"Come closer," Elizabeth commanded. "I have something to say to you all."

Black face turned to black face for assurance. Finally the crowd edged forward. O'Gilvie helped Elizabeth to mount an overturned box from which she surveyed the forty odd expressionless faces.

"Not one of you has felt the lash since I came to live at Whitehall. Not a one of you *will* feel the lash so long as I am here —," she paused and emphasized each word, *"provided you do as I say."* She looked meaningfully into each black face. "We are beset with a dreadful disease that may strike any one of us next. It can reach you in your stifling cabins no matter how tightly you close the door. It can reach you at work in the gardens and fields. Here at Whitehall if it strikes us it will find us at work, not snivelling in a dark corner." While she waited for the words to sink in, her eyes travelled again over dark faces where uncertainty was beginning to replace blankness.

Directing her words to Cato who had raised his head to return her look, she continued, "I, too, am frightened. My aunt lies stricken just like Cilly. I may be stricken tomorrow, or today, just as each of you may be. You cannot hide from the fever and we must all continue to eat. Go back to your tasks, the grain must be harvested, the gardens and stock tended, the fences mended — all

69

these things you must do." She singled out another black man, whose great shining black body made him an obvious leader in the physical sense where Cato lead by diplomatic supremacy, "Take them back to the fields, Herk. Even if we must die it is better to do so in the open than like rats in a trap!"

Herk regarded his mistress with conflicting emotions crossing his broad flat face. Noticing his indecision Elizabeth spoke again quickly looking at the evil whip that lay like a serpent on the ground at O'Gilvie's feet.

"You may go peacefully if you will — but *go you shall.* Mr. O'Gilvie has my instructions to lay this," pointing to the whip, "across the back of man or woman who refuses to work or who makes any attempt to frighten another. Well?"

Elizabeth was magnificent with her colour heightened by anger and determination and her crop raised to emphasize her words. Grudging admiration was evident on each black face. Herk looked to Cato for backing, and Cato nodded slightly. Squaring his shoulders and swaggering a bit with new found authority, Herk raised his great arm in a beckoning gesture.

"Cummon," he bellowed and the line filed dociley behind him.

Day followed hot, humid day while all toiled, rested, and prayed. Elizabeth had instituted strict rules of cleanliness which she enforced personally, passing daily in and out of each cabin. As the long dreadful summer lagged on no new cases appeared and no further deaths occurred at Whitehall, perhaps because there were no rice fields to attract the great armies of mosquitoes, perhaps because of that intangible medicine, morale. Who knows?

The great whip was never far from O'Gilvie's hand but he had no occasion to lift it. He was every where toiling, encouraging, cajoling. Elizabeth rode out every day among the workers and tried to speak a word of praise to each individual as often as possible. Her magnificent courage spurred them on and each evening they congregated at the kitchen door where they bowed their dark heads with her bright one in thanks for another day passed without mishap.

The hours spent at Aunt Vadie's side were frightful ones. The effortless vomiting continued but its character changed within a few days as it blackened from the presence of blood. In the third week of her illness, Dr. Killpatrick came and told Elizabeth and Uncle Roy that the end was in sight, that if the haemorrhagic signs increased it would end in death, if not Aunt Vadie would recover. Elizabeth was vaguely thankful for his testy but kindly presence rather than another taxing emotional encounter with Gavin. The doctor was grave as he looked into her wan face one night, while they rested a moment away from her aunt's bedside. O'Gilvie had told him of Elizabeth's courage and he now took her to task.

"What purpose will it serve if you kill yourself? You have laid down rules for your slaves with the penalty of bull whipping for a refraction, rules which you do not obey yourself. The work rule, yes, but not the rest. Have you considered what will happen if you fall a victim and die on our hands?" The doctor looked at her, his angry expression turning to one of admiration. "By God, what this country needs is more like you." He pulled his ear thoughtfully and his eye sparkled. "I wish I were a young man, you wouldn't be in the fix you are now. I'm not so easily scared off."

"I don't know what you mean, Sir," Elizabeth bridled.

"You know perfectly well what I mean, Miss. Your courage without your hot headedness would not have landed you in the mess —"

"Dr. Killpatrick," Elizabeth sprang to her feet, anger expressed in every line of her body. "You go too far, Sir. You are impertinent!"

"Impertinent, M'am?" The old doctor's eyebrows travelled toward his hair line. "Age has prerogatives, my dear. An old man can hardly be impertinent to one so young as you. You are very young. You will find forever is a long time."

"If you came here to deliver a lecture on my conduct, you are wasting your time." Elizabeth faced him furiously. "If you came here to treat my aunt, I suggest we return to her room."

The old doctor shrugged wearily as he turned toward the door. "You can pull in your horns. I am not so easily frightened, as some young doctors, by your high sounding phrases. You may fool yourself, Miss, and some others, but you can't fool an old man like me."

Elizabeth stood breathless with rage.

The doctor looked over his shoulder at her angry face.

"I suppose your aunt's life is more important than any quarrel of ours. Are you coming?"

The days dragged on with no surcease from heat, sickness, and death. Aunt Vadie's recovery was slow but certain and she lay day after day in listless apathy while Roy read to her or Elizabeth stopped to speak with a cheerfulness she did not feel, of the many farm tasks. The rumors of her courage and the lightness with which the epidemic had struck her plantation in no wise increased her popularity in harassed Charles Town.

Jon returned late in June, his enthusiasm for the healthy Up Country heightened by the tragic conditions he found on his return. In spite of the prohibition he rode daily back and forth to the village and many men talked around his table of an evening. Elizabeth welcomed the diversion and her excitement mounted as she listened to Jon's glowing accounts. Henry Gignilliat, Jacob Satur, Thomas Stitsmith and Dr. Daniel Gibson were constant visitors at Whitehall.

The death of the Governor's wife in July was followed by that of his son William in August and finally Jon determined to take Elizabeth and escape to the higher lands of the Congarees. Land was to be had for the asking and along with Gignilliat, Satur, Stitsmith, and Gibson, Jon secured, on Thomas Brown's advice, a grant of land on the southwest side of the Santee just below Sandy Run. He secured by purchase directly from Captain Russell his deserted piled stone house within the tiny settlement next to Thomas Brown's store. There he intended to house his family until the land could be cleared and a suitable dwelling erected. The other four men, one a vintner, two merchants and one a doctor chose the north side of the river because of its height, in spite of Jon's advice that they could be cut off by high water from communication with the proposed new settlement to be laid out soon near the old garrison site.

It was decided that they should set out as soon as Aunt Vadie could travel, and supplies could be obtained. The need for haste was apparent. Every day added danger of infection to the relentless disease that held the country in its vise. Also land must be cleared. After consultations with his wife and overseer, Jon was content to leave to them the selection of a proper number of slaves skilled in husbandry and certain essential trades. Blossom declared if Elizabeth left her she would disappear into the swamp. Elizabeth assured her that she would sooner leave her right arm. Clem's attachment to Jon grew as strong as Blossom's to Elizabeth. He became Jon's constant shadow. Elizabeth selected another young black to take over Clem's household tasks while Clem took up the duties of his master's body servant.

Finally on the first day of September, the path that had so recently rung with the hooves of the many horses in Sir Alexander's train, the forests that had been brightened by the flash of many elegant coats were again alive with the creak of his daughter's equipage as she advanced her second step into this wild new land. The hearts of all the members of this second train were full of hope and no face turned back toward the fever ridden lowland.

BOOK TWO

THE REALITY
1732—1742

Chapter One

Elizabeth, startled by a sudden tug on her skirt, looked down into a pair of black eyes smiling joyfully into her own. A tiny ivory face crowned with wiry black hair leaned back to survey the fair one so far above his own. Wobbly legs found support in chubby hands firmly grasping Elizabeth's billowing gown. Completely enchanted with the merriness of the smile on the child's face, Elizabeth stooped to bring her face on a level with his own. The little boy fairly shook with delight as he reached for the pearls around her neck. Musical but unintelligible sounds issued from a wide mouth, the color of crushed raspberries. He patted the billows of the voluminous gown and laughed gleefully as they sank like empty sails.

Elizabeth's answering smile died quickly as the little boy was snatched aloft and angry unknown words flowed across her bent head. Taken completely by surprise, she looked up from her stooping position into a dusky well-formed face whose strange beauty was marred by vicious contortions of rage. For a moment the little boy's face was blank, then the inexpressible smile returned in all its radiance as he clasped his chubby hands around the beautifully ornamented braids of the young Indian woman who disappeared as silently as she had come, bearing him in her arms.

Shaking her head slightly in puzzlement, Elizabeth Fenwick arose. The long trip from Charles Town to the Congarees had been a gruelling one that taxed all her powers of endurance. Added to this was her worry about Aunt Vadie. Her worry seemed needless, however, for Aunt Vadie had travelled as easily as an experienced veteran. Never missing an opportunity to observe with vital interest anything new, she managed to sit her horse like an old camel rider, seemingly asleep at times, lulled by the motion of the animal. Her husband was constantly at her side seeking any means to ease her discomfort. Uncle Roy's own fragile frame seemed tempered with iron and to Elizabeth's amazement he apparently enjoyed the trek through the enveloping wilderness. The long distance was covered without mishap, and now the two women surveyed their new home.

The rude stone house next to Thomas Brown's store was small but adequate. Mrs. Russell's gentle hand had pushed back the smothering jungle just a trifle. Signs of her loving efforts to bring a bit of home to this far away corner remained in the tiny but neat garden with which she had surrounded her home. Elizabeth felt a flash of admiration for this woman whom she had never seen, whose home would now be her own. How, in the midst of fear, want, and the gruelling work of wresting the bare necessities from an ungentle land, had she found time to plan and tend this quaint English garden? Elizabeth stooped unconsciously to remove some weeds from the bed. She took up a handful of the rich soil. Her slender fingers closed over its darkness and new courage seemed to flow through her tired limbs. Land! Deeply rich soil hardly touched by human hand. What a grand heritage, what a challenge to build a new and thrilling future on its bounty! The girl turned to look on this new world of hers. Her eyes struck with almost physical impact the great wall of the forests. She felt a moment of recoil as the whispering giants seemed to close in on her ominously. Were they laughing hollowly at her puny courage? She shivered slightly and, trying to throw off the moment of thrall, turned again toward the grateful solidity of the house which seemed to hunch its shoulders against the wilderness.

"Naw'm, you git on out now." Blossom's voice fussed comfortably. "Clem dun lay a cloke fuh you to res' on 'gin dat tree in de sun. G'wan now! Whar Miss Betsy?"

"She's outside. Now, Blossom, I must direct the placing of the furniture." Aunt Vadie's voice sounded thin and reedy to her niece. "Please don't be difficult."

"You de one bein' hard tuh handle, Miz Vadie. Me en Clem kin

76

put all dis stuff jes ez good ez you. Ain much no how. How Mistah Jon think us kin live lak fiel hands?"

"Woman, be kerful whut you say," Clem's rumbling voice came immediately to the defense of his master. "Ah'll give you de bak uv mah han."

"How you tawk! Since you got to be Mistah Jon's man caint nobody speak to you thout dey ask yoh pardon. Get sum uv dem niggahs and git dat stuff in heah."

Elizabeth realized how tired Aunt Vadie must be to let the servants talk so in her presence. Vadie was always meticulous about their conduct and never permitted any altercations within ear shot. She wondered if she should interfere, but lassitude made rags of her own muscles and she sank gratefully to the porch floor and leaned idly against a post. Carefully she avoided raising her eyes to the overpowering trees and unconsciously hummed a childhood melody to shut their interminable whispering from her ears.

"Miss Betsy, cum wash yoh face and purty yohself," Blossom's voice recalled Elizabeth from her thoughts. Glad to have something to do to escape her oppressive thoughts, she ran into the house to prepare herself for luncheon at Thomas Brown's. She had not seen Jon since he lifted her down from her horse some hours ago. When she had tried to discuss plans for unpacking, stabling horses, housing supplies, he had kissed her absently on her hair.

"You and O'Gilvie take care of it, my dear. You are such a fine manager you won't need me. Anything you decide will be right." And with a wave of his hand he had gone off with beefy, genial Thomas Brown to discuss plans for their trade over fiery tankards of unwatered backwoods rum.

Elizabeth turned uncertainly to O'Gilvie, whose eyes encouraged her.

"There's not much to be done, Miss Elizabeth." His eyes swept over the very small area that had been reclaimed from the jealous forests, the hanging door of the palisade gate. "Settling down will be easy. The work will be in trying to stay." He shook his head thoughtfully.

Elizabeth felt a flicker of resentment as she watched her husband's receding back. Of late he had left the management of their plantation affairs more and more to her. Always busy with his many schemes for the settlement at the Congarees and the lucrative Indian trade he hoped to develop with Thomas Brown, he listened courteously to all her plans, complimented her on her ideas, and said with his wide smile, "Go right ahead, my dear. You and O'Gilvie see to it. You don't need me."

"I *must* be tired to feel so gloomy," Elizabeth thought. "Tomorrow after hot food and a bed to sleep in, it won't look so bad." She raised her eyes defiantly to the trees. "After all, you *are* only trees," she said, and jumped when she realized she had spoken aloud.

Her spirits rose a little and her smile was ready when she greeted her host at lunch. The talk around Thomas Brown's board was animated. The Irishman tried to answer his guests' many questions without alarming them and without painting too rosy a picture of life in the Back Country. He wondered how anyone so obviously gently bred as Elizabeth and her aunt could have thought they wanted to lose themselves in this God-forsaken country. Thomas Brown was neither a philosopher nor a crusader. All that mattered to him was the immediate wealth he could amass by trade with the gullible Indians. He didn't like them, he didn't trust them – but he could get along with them. When the source of wealth here ran out he'd move on. It happened to be healthier for him at the moment here in the isolated back woods of America than in Ireland. To the future he gave no thought. What was the future anyway but a longer lease on the present? And leases in America – as in Ireland – could be quickly terminated without notice. At least here he could live as he pleased. A fellow had enough quiet in which to think, even if his thoughts never got beyond his next meal or his next bed fellow.

Elizabeth felt a tug at her knee. The merry coal-black eyes met hers again. With a pleased cry she swept the tiny figure into her arms and held him up for all to see. The baby immediately clutched her pearls and gurgled his strange words. The young Indian woman stood in the doorway, a bowl of venison in her hands. Jon's chair clattered to the floor as he rose, his face terrible. Aunt Vadie's startled eyes were glued to the little ivory face with its illusive familiarity. Roy ate placidly. Elizabeth was so engrossed with the little boy that the moment of tension went unnoticed.

"Who is he, Mr. Brown?" Elizabeth spoke without looking up. Thomas Brown hesitated but a moment, "He is my son. Pakahle here is his mother."

Elizabeth hesitated. She knew that these Indian alliances were not unusual among the lonely traders.

"What is his name?" she asked finally.

"Ah – Billy – yes, Billy. And now let us enjoy our excelent

78

meal. Pakahle, take the boy."

Elizabeth's smile met no answer on the Indian mother's face as she put Billy in her arms.

The rest of the meal passed in comparative silence, the only conversation being between Elizabeth and the Irishman who seemed to find some secret relish in the discomfort of his other guests. Jon excused himself abruptly and strode outside where he waited in a seething rage until Thomas Brown joined him.

"Why do you have her here," Jon asked angrily of his host. "This is an impossible situation!"

Brown looked at his new partner coldly. "It is a situation of your own creation, Sir. Pakahle," he called. "Come out here."

The Indian girl slid silently to his side, her eyes lowered. Brown lifted one of her gleaming braids. Where her ear had been, the angry red scar of Cherokee justice met Jon's horrified eye. "She is safe, perhaps, with me, but have a care on your journeys that Salone does not catch you alone." He warned him succinctly.

Chapter Two

In the winter of 1736 the first bounty settlers under the leadership of Stephen Crell arrived at the Congarees with letters of introduction from Governor Broughton to Jon Fenwick. As was frequently the case, Jon was away on a trip to Keowee, trading baubles and gaudy English woolens for the seemingly endless deer skins. It fell to Elizabeth, as did so many responsibilities of late, to greet the tired and disheartened new comers.

Stephen Crell looked with wonder at the tall beautiful woman whose hand was extended to him in welcome. He was not a particularly modest man, he knew his own ability, but he twisted his soiled beaver self-consciously and wiped his grimy hand surreptitiously on his breeches. After the cold, bitter journey by piraqua up the perilous, icy rivers, this apparition was the last thing he had expected. Short rations, too little protection against the pitiless February rains and winds had reduced his party of hopeful settlers, who had come with high hearts to the tropic shores of storied Carolina, to a pitiful handful of disgruntled, surly Swiss and Germans. These would have turned back had he, Stephen Crell, not reminded them that the Governor had himself signed the bond for their release from the stinking ship whose grasping captain had held them until someone paid their passage. Return to Charles Town meant return to that scurvy infected hold.

He had also guarded their inadequate supplies with a jealous hand and a ready musket, surrendering his vigil solely to his brother Joseph who was the only one he could trust.

To find this graceful woman at the end of the long, hideous voyage caused his numbed spirit to extend its frozen fingers tentatively to the warmth of her smile. But, how could it be so? Why? Why was an obviously aristocratic woman to be found at the farthest reaches of a frozen hell. Who, but those who were escaping from the galling oppression of a country grown old in bigotry, would choose to lose themselves in the pitiless uncertainty of this cruel wilderness? His thoughts flashed across his broad, intelligent face as he extended his huge grimy hand uncertainly.

"Welcome, Mr. Crell. Welcome to you all." Her genuine flashing smile met little response in the miserable huddle of pinched faces. All their disappointment and discomfort seemed to gather and direct itself toward the well, though simply, clad woman who faced them in the chill grey light of a dying February afternoon.

"Mr. Fenwick?", Stephen Crell questioned in his stilted, bookish English. "My instructions were to place my people in his hands. I have a letter from the Governor and others for you, Madam." He loosened his soiled jacket and drew out a water stained leather pouch.

"Mr. Fenwick is away trading with the Cherokees. We had not expected you so soon, Sir. Runners had brought us word from the Governor, but it was understood you would not be sent until more clement weather. I can receive the dispatches in Mr. Fenwick's name, Mr. Crell, and those of us here will help you in any way we can until my husband's return."

Stephen Crell smiled crookedly. "I am afraid, Madam, that supplies are somewhat short in Charles Town, and forty extra mouths to feed may have been instrumental in causing the change in schedule."

Elizabeth thought with dismay of their own meagre supplies. Wresting sustenance from the jealous soil was a job for each man which took all his fortitude. To be asked to share with forty new comers would cause objections and serious problems in the tiny colony which had bravely stuck out the few lean years of clearing, planting, and reaping a small, barely adequate crop. Only this year had the store houses contained enough to look to the winter without unease. Settlers they needed however; settlers they must have if they were to remain and become a successful colony. They would make out somehow. Thank heaven for O'Gilvie, thought

Elizabeth. O'Gilvie, who met every problem with equilibrium and good sense, O'Gilvie whose courage and good humor never failed.

The crowd was growing restive at this exchange of strange words which they did not understand, and Crell turned to them to translate the conversation. Mutters of dissatisfaction and dissent rippled and rose to a clamor. Elizabeth could not understand the words but the expressions and gestures spoke clearly in any tongue.

"Send us out with almost no food to the protection of a helpless woman in the forgotten backwoods of an unheard of country!" The protests rose to a shouting crescendo.

Stephen Crell tried at first gently to still their cries. There were several children skrinking and cowering with cold, hunger, and fatigue. Elizabeth watched them with pity and looked around for help.

She almost stumbled over Blossom, who whispered noisily, "Don worry, Chile. Mistah Roy dun cum in loaded wid fish. Effen sum ob dem wimmen kin quit screechin' and holp me, us'el hab uh prime stew by fus dark. Ain't nuthin' settles uh body lak uh full stummick!"

"Bless you, Blossom." She turned to Stephen. "Have your people build fires and set camp for the night. Let some of the women help Blossom here, and everything will look better in the morning."

When Stephen relayed the message a black silence descended on the shivering group. One voice shrilled out in cockney English,

"What about those houses they promised us?"

The owner of the voice wormed her way to the front ranks. Elizabeth gazed a moment at the somehow familiar face. Finally the puzzled look gave way to a disdainful smile.

"Well, Nellie. How came you here with these folk?"

Stephen Crell, startled at this unexpected development, looked from the aristocratic woman with her air of authority to the dishevelled slattern whose comic look of stunned amazement almost caused him to laugh aloud. The sudden surge of mirth died as quickly as it had come. Crell's face was grim as he thought of the dissatisfaction Nellie had fomented. She had kept the pot of discomfort constantly boiling by her harping and her loose ways with the men folk. Where had she come from anyway, he wondered. He had not known of her presence until the end of the first day's journey. Her name did not appear on his list, nor had he any warrant for land issued in her name. Rumor had it that she had followed handsome Nat Hayne after he had spent a wine-fuddled evening in Pinckney Street. The men laughed coarsely and said Nat must have had something stronger than wine to see any charm in Nellie. Poor Nat, looking sheepish and harassed, had steadfastly refused to answer the lewd taunts, but everyone noticed that he avoided Nellie like the plague.

Nellie remembered how she and this girl had met in verbal combat once before, and how sadly she had been bested in the fray. Her sullen eyes dropped to the ground and her arrogance evaporated. She pushed at a clod of dirt with a frayed boot toe.

"I've as much right here as anyone!"

"Did anyone promise you a ready-built home?" Elizabeth pressed her further.

No answer. Elizabeth looked questioningly at Crell.

"The advertisements circulated in Switzerland were misleading," Stephen replied dryly.

"Put them to work, Mr. Crell, and come in where we can discuss a plan of campaign, you might say." Elizabeth laughed. She was surprised at how glad she was to welcome new companionship. A few Swiss had arrived the year before. They had settled down with comparative ease and were working industriously at the tremendous task of taming a wild new land. There had been some grumbling and a few had openly threatened to leave. With Jon and Thomas Brown often away on trading trips there was no man to whom the others could look for leadership. The role had quietly fallen to Elizabeth. She welcomed it because it kept her mind busy and her body fatigued enough to rest at night. Now Stephen Crell, who was also a natural leader, was surprised to find himself accepting the authority of a strange female as the most natural course of events.

As they entered the cheerfully lamplit parlor of the piled stone house, campfires were blooming like tiny red flowers, and a cheerful laugh or two could be heard over the grumbling. Aunt Vadie had appeared and, clucking comfortably, had herded a flock of bedraggled children from tot to teen into the stuffy haven of Thomas Brown's store. Though most of them understood not a word of her soothing chatter, all caught the friendliness of her tone and followed docilely.

Hours later Elizabeth found her Aunt giving her young proteges their first lesson in English, while the least ones slept, content and dreamless, on broken-open piles of soft cured deer skins.

"Mr. Crell, please don't feel uneasy because a woman assumes so much authority. Governor Broughton has put my husband in charge of the settlement here, and in his absence he entrusts his affairs to me. I assure you, my instructions come directly from him, and he will not be long away."

Stephen colored with embarrassment that his thoughts had been so easily read on his face.

"I assure you, Madam," he stammered like an inexperienced youth.

Elizabeth laughed gaily. "Please don't apologize, Mr. Crell. You would be less than human if you did not find the situation, to say the least, unusual." Her eyes grew thoughtful. "The unusual is the usual in this isolated spot. This surprise will not be your last, I'm afraid." She sighed and turned to the pile of papers on the table between them.

"Now, let's lay our plans. The men are all hunting and fishing today and should return shortly. A storm has been threatening and they thought it wise to lay in an extra supply of fresh meat."

It transpired that the warrants for land were all blank. Elizabeth advised Stephen Crell to have O'Gilvie and Uncle Roy guide the men over the available land so that they might make suitable selections for Jon to survey on his return.

Elizabeth glanced down the list of names: Fridig, Gallman, Backman, Mueller – only a few English names were scattered among the Swiss and German – Hayne, Gibson.

She raised her eyes, "What will you do with Nellie? Who will provide for her?" Noting the question in Stephen Crell's eye, Elizabeth related the incident of her voyage to America and her encounter with Nellie. Her voice died away and she sat remembering – remembering the sweetness of those days of companionship with Gavin, remembering his tall, clean strength, remembering – she shook herself sharply back to the present. She had no right to these thoughts, they were dangerous and disloyal – and fruitless. Since Gavin had come to her in her distress over Aunt Vadie, she had not seen him. She had closed the door of her mind on this incident in her life, so long ago. Resolutely she had set herself to make a new life from which she knew there could be no turning back. She had severed the ties so definitely that only the future lay ahead, and what did it hold? She brought herself up sharply.

"Pardon me, Mr. Crell. I am afraid I had let my mind slip back –" she stopped. She had started to say "home". But where was home? She caught herself up again angrily. What is the matter with me today? Why am I wallowing in maudlin sentiment?

"One so young and vital as yourself should look forward, not back," Stephen Crell's words sounded stilted and didactic, but they seemed to echo another voice down the years. What had Captain Anson said as the *Garland* sailed past Land's End? "The eyes of one so young should look toward the future – not to the past."

Angrily she brushed these thoughts aside and rose extending her hand again to the sturdy man with his frank and open face. It was a good face which mirrored strength of mind and body. He would need both in the uncertain days to come. She felt glad that he was here and hoped that others like him would swell the trickle of colonization to a steady flowing river like the broad Congaree which glided purposefully and boldly past her door.

Hours later the men returned from their hunt laden with three great bucks and a dozen fat wild turkeys. After O'Gilvie and Stephen Crell had inspected the various camps and had seen that each was as comfortable as circumstances would permit, Elizabeth settled down eagerly to read her letters. There was one from Margaret Johnson and one from her father. The bundle of *Gazettes* and the official dispatches from the Governor she pushed aside and held the two letters, one in each hand, like precious jewels. Finally she laid aside Margaret's thick one for the thinner one from her father. She brought her candle to her chair which she gratefully drew nearer the blazing fire that Blossom had replenished before going to her pallet in Elizabeth's room where she insisted on remaining every night in Jon's absence. Her eyes grew thoughtful as she read.

> *Your mother has not been well of late. She has never seemed to recover from her sister's departure, and has grown more listless since our disappointment over not coming to Carolina for your wedding. I am still working on a plan for us to join you, but I do not have the sympathetic ear of his Grace at this time. I cannot understand the blindness of the home government in refusing to allow me to return of my own volition to live among the Cherokee. It could only serve a good purpose. I understand that the Indians are becoming restive again over the dishonest practices of the traders. I am certain that I could set matters on a much more secure basis for they trust me. I have sent a detailed outline of a plan to control the Indian trade to our interest, as well as to the interest of the natives themselves. As yet I have no answer.*

Elizabeth gazed at the red embers of the fire and thought how different this defeated tone was from the usual pompous air of assurance she was accustomed to from her father. What a pity! She knew the bitterness of his wound at being so ignored by the King. She read on,

Your letters are very interesting. There is a new black beef cattle that has recently been developed in our country. They are heavy necked, short legged, and resistant to many diseases prevalent among other cows. They seem able to forage for themselves and are impervious to any amount of cold or heat. You say that though wheat and corn have done surprisingly well on your scarcely cleared land, you wonder what will be a source of income as your colony grows. You point out rightly that the supply of deerskins cannot last forever at the present rate of destruction of the animal. Could it not be that these cows would answer your purpose? The native growth of wild peavine and maiden cane sounds ample for their sustenance, and I think you would find they would sustain their weight quite well during the long drive to market at Charles Town or Philadelphia. I shall have Mr. Fant send up some later on; at the moment I am temporarily embarrassed for funds.

Beef cows! What an excellent idea. Elizabeth rested the letter on her lap as she looked again into the blazing fire. It was difficult to keep milk cows in any condition to bring a fair price in Charles Town after the long trip down. Though the market for butter was good, it was necessary to boil it and pack it in wooden barrels to keep it from getting rancid. The barrels were difficult to make with their as yet limited supply of tools, and fresh butter obtained at closer low country plantations brought better prices. What they needed was a staple that was not perishable. Elizabeth had thought often of the tiny green tobacco the Indians used in their ceremonies. Smoking had become a fashionable practice even among court ladies and the demand for the American leaf was greater than the present supply from Virginia and North Carolina. She had even discussed it with Eleazar Wigan, who said that the leaf grown in the mountains was smaller than that sent to market from Virginia. Could its inferior size mean inferior quality? Wigan had told her that fair fields of it were grown at Cheulah's village of Gusti near the Ninety-Six Creek junction of the Cherokee and

Fort Moore Paths. Jon spoke often of this spot.

There had been some disappointment in the climate at the Congaree settlement; the summers were almost as blisteringly hot as those in the tide water though the winters were cold and the air seemingly free of the endless swarms of mosquitoes. Jon and Thomas Brown had talked by the hour of the possibilities of a settlement near the Ninety-Six Mile junction to command the increasing trade with the Cherokees, and perhaps the Creeks could be added to their list of customers. Jon was even now looking over the land for a possible purchase by the two men to expand their successful trading business. Though Jon had been warned by both Wigan and Brown to walk softly in this part of the country where Salone, Pakahle's erstwhile betrothed, still burned with an implacable hatred, he had never been molested on his many trips, sometimes accompanied only by faithful Clem. Onconecaw had told Wigan that it was only Jon's connection with the daughter of the Great Warrior whom they still remembered with awe and what affection an Indian is capable of that had so far saved his skin.

Elizabeth's thoughts were brought back by the sharp explosion of a hickory limb. She watched the limb fall and crackle merrily as if it meant to tell her some of the pleasant secrets of the great forest from which it had come. She took up the letter from Margaret almost indifferently, her fertile brain still busy with thoughts of new enterprise for her new settlement. She smiled at herself – her settlement! How possessive and sure of herself she was growing. But one could not put energy, thought, and effort into anything and not become a part of it. After the first quivering fright of the enveloping wilderness, she had accepted its taming as a personal challenge.

> *My dearest Betsy,*
>
> *I wish you were here, or I were there, or we were both in London, or something. Hannah says my grammar is terrible, and I ask her how she knows, and now she's huffed with me. I'm lonesome. Henry is away at school, and all the others here are ninnies except Dr. McBride and I can't get more than a pat on the head from him. Uncle James is still in Charles Town but threatens to leave every day.*
>
> *I don't see Andrew often since his marriage. He is the envy of the town. Isn't Andrew just the lion? As if marrying Colonel Hext's widow before the poor old gentleman was cold weren't enough, he's gotten himself*

elected to the Assembly, and even Papa spoke to him with respect. He's quite a land holder, even more land than he got from his wife. It is whispered that he must have something on Nicholas Trott, something he brought with him from Ireland. Good for him, if he has. Anything evil about that old devil must be true.

Christmas was as usual no fun without you. Three holiday seasons without your Christmas eve dinner! It is our first Christmas without Papa and though Uncle Thomas has tried to take his place and wants us to live with him at Mulberry, I feel very deserted. Hannah keeps me from being completely miserable by making me look after Mary's schooling. The boys are with Henry in London and I am surrounded by females. You are the only female I know whom I really like. Do I sound wanton? Poor Hannah. Making a lady of me must be a trial. Your mind is masculine and I prefer the masculine point of view!

Mr. John Wesley preached in St. Philip's last Sunday. Mr. Garden introduced him, and he expounded for two hours. Dry as dust! He came over with General Oglethorpe to help in the settlement of Georgia. They tell me he is devout, but singularly unsuccessful with the Indians whose conversion he desires. I hear he harangued the Indians and preached them Scripture until both he and his audience were thoroughly tired. Finally he was told that they knew very well if they were good they would go up, if bad, down – he could tell them no more, that he had long plagued them with what they in no wise understood, that they desired him to depart the country!

Margaret's merry laugh seemed to gurgle from the closely written pages.

His brother, Charles, on the other hand, has written some beautiful hymns, one of which the congregation sang.

> *O' for a thousand tongues to sing*
> *My great Redeemer's praise*
> *The glories of my God and King*
> *The triumphs of His Grace!*

It was really inspiring to hear three hundred voices booming out. The dignified columns of St. Philip's fairly shook and Mr. Commissary Garden looked a bit sour at the display of so much enthusiasm in his staid old church. He's stuffy!

Elizabeth smiled, glad that in spite of so much sorrow in her young life, Margaret's spirit was still gay and warm and not forced into the rigid mold of the day. She read the rest of the newsy letter hastily, for the cold was drawing in around her shoulders, and, adding a log to the low fire, sought her bed where she lay thinking far into the night. While she had read, the wind had risen, and before she retired it was howling relentlessly about the few cabins huddled for protection against the menacing elements — both natural and human. Along about dawn she was conscious that the wind had ceased and in the icy stillness there was something uncanny. She lay listening for a moment and then rose shivering to investigate. She met Blossom in the livingroom stirring up the cold embers. The Negro pointed to the one glass window the settlement boasted. Peering out, she saw that the pale blue, eerie light of near dawn revealed a swirling pattern of snow flakes sifting down as if to spread a virgin blanket over the dead.

"Oh, dear!" Elizabeth cried out, thinking of the poor men and women in their make-shift camps. Through the falling flakes she saw their fires dotted here and there. "At least the children are safe," she thought gratefully of Aunt Vadie who insisted on keeping them for the first night in Brown's store.

By morning the snow had ceased to fall, but the temperature continued to drop and a thin film of ice covered the several inches that lay already on the ground. Crell's people were so numbed by cold and discouragement that they even neglected to grumble. O'Gilvie found their sullen acquiescence more ominous than healthy complaints. He and Stephen were everywhere, helping, encouraging, and directing. O'Gilvie had the Negroes, whom the Swiss and Germans regarded with obvious distrust, dig great pits in the frozen ground, where fires were lighted and the deer meat hung to barbecue all during the long cold day. The children, to keep them occupied, were given the task of keeping the fires burning while the women basted the succulent meat. Spirits rose at the prospect of fresh meat. A tiny flame of comradeship flickered and grew as the isolated group drew together for comfort and self preservation. Elizabeth found much sickness. She hoped that it sprang only from exhaustion. O'Gilvie shook his head.

"We need a doctor," he pointed out. "We have been lucky so far, but it can't last forever."

"Yes", answered Elizabeth. "If only Dr. Gibson had stayed."

O'Gilvie snorted. "He found the atmosphere too thin for his blood. His ilk could never stand it here. We don't need his kind. What we need is a man, one like —"

He stopped, looking into her warning eyes, "Excuse me, Miss. I'll just see to this fire. The children have deserted it." He left her hurriedly.

Several days later Elizabeth was answering her letters in the cheerful *parlor,* as Blossom loved to call it. She was interrupted by the noise of angry women's voices and running feet. She sprang to the door and flung it open. Like a frightened animal a figure flew by, into the cozy interior. Glancing over her shoulder she saw Nellie crouched near her own favorite chair by the hearth, her face ashen with fear. Quietly she closed the door behind her and faced the angry women.

"Please, what is it? What's wrong?" Her clear voice rang out and stilled the tumult of their voices.

"Thief!" cried one.

"Husband snatcher", another screamed.

"Leech!"

"Please!" Elizabeth pled again. "I do not understand. Where is Mr. Crell?"

Someone understood the word "Crell" and ran to fetch Stephen, who soon returned breathless.

"Mr. Crell", Elizabeth turned to him. "These women are very angry with Nellie and she has run from them into my house. Will you find out for me what is the trouble?"

"I regret the outburst, Mrs. Fenwick, but no treatment is too hard for that woman."

He turned and spoke with one of the women in German and listened respectfully while she answered with many excited gestures.

"As you know, this woman has come without permission, warrant, or supplies. Apparently she expected the men to take care of her as they have done in the past. She reckoned without a knowledge of frontier justice. Last night she was caught trying to enter Hayne's tent and today she was caught stealing red-handed. They intend to run her out of the settlement."

"Alone?" asked Elizabeth with horror.

"Yes."

"But you can't do that!" She turned to the women congregated at the foot of the steps and spoke to them, her hands outstretched in a gesture of appeal.

"A woman alone in this wilderness would meet certain death by some wild beast, or captivity and slavery by a savage. This is no country of closely knit towns with wide open roads for travel from one to another. We are alone — *alone,* do you hear? We *must* stay together to survive." She looked for sympathy in their stony faces and found none. "Mr. Crell, you cannot permit this."

Stephen hesitated, looking from Elizabeth's beseeching face to the angry ones of his women folk.

"What is to be done with her? She has caused nothing but trouble and to feed her we must rob our own mouths. I, for one, will not do so."

"If I offer to be responsible for her, will you let her be? I give my word that she will bother no one. If she does, I myself will find a way to send her back. Please, Mr. Crell. It can serve no purpose —", her voice died away. They all waited.

Crell relayed her message reluctantly and there was much talk. Finally they nodded assent, glad really to be relieved of a responsibility with no blood on their consciences.

Elizabeth turned back toward the house. "Now, what have I done? What on earth shall I do with her? How can I promise them she won't cause more trouble? She'll have to go back with the first pack train. Heaven guide me until then!" Her face was cold as she faced Nellie cowering by the fireside.

"Why have you come running to me, of all people?"

"They would have killed me", snivelled Nellie, pushing back her frowzy hair with dirty-nailed hands.

"And why shouldn't they?" Elizabeth's eyes flashed.

Nellie swallowed convulsively, her adam's apple bobbing painfully in her skinny neck. In spite of the cold, sweat was pouring down her face. Her clothes gave off an evil smell. She watched without speaking, the girl towering above her. Suddenly Elizabeth shrugged and the fury left her slate-grey eyes. She looked contemptuously at Nellie.

"I have gone your bond, so to speak. I am responsible to Mr. Crell for your conduct — you are responsible to me. If you give me cause to regret my pity for you, I shall not only turn you over to their vengeance, but shall help them drive you out. Do you understand?" The grey eyes flashed steely sparks.

"Yes, Miss", quavered a new Nellie, her arrogance gone.

"Can you weave?"

"No, Miss".

"What can you do?"

Nellie's eyes fell, "Nothing, Miss. The only trade I know ain't no use to me here."

"Well, you'll have to learn to do something. Blossom," she called, "take this woman and show her where she can clean herself up. She's about my size. Give her my grey wool dress to wear."

Blossom spluttered in protest, "Why, Miss Betsy, ah ain't gon let nobody tech yore purty clothes much less dis heah —"

"Blossom, do as I tell you. Her name is," she paused, looking at the bedraggled, cringing woman, "Miss Nellie," she finished on an inspiration.

Nellie raised her eyes to Elizabeth's in unbelief. No one had ever addressed her as "Miss." She drew up her shoulders and followed Blossom with new purpose in her step. At the door she turned,

"Thank, you, M'am," she whispered.

Chapter Three

Elizabeth awakened to find Jon bending over her bed calling her name urgently.

"Why, Jon." She struggled to sit up.

"No," he pushed her back and held her down, his fingers gripping her shoulders until they hurt. "No, lie still. Let me look at you. How beautiful you are with your glorious hair loose on your pillow!" He stroked her hair and his hands became more urgent as they travelled down her throat to her firm young breasts. Elizabeth struggled to control a desire to recoil from his seeking hands.

"Blossom?" she reminded him.

"I sent her away. Oh, my darling, how I've ridden to get to you. I've missed you so. It's been too long since I've held you. Elizabeth, my love," he cried out in anguish and his open lips crushed down on her startled mouth.

Stilling an impulse to struggle, she forced her arms around Jon's neck and prayed for help to give him what he wanted, what he needed. She wondered if he were drunk. Usually he was more gentle with his love making and gave her more time to adjust herself to his mood. This wild passion was frightening. But no! She could smell no rum.

"Jon —" she tried to cry out in protest, but his hungry mouth closed on her cry. He gave himself up to his passion, seeking a something that his soul needed, must have, forgetting to bridle the ruthlessness in his nature that would hurt even the thing he loved most.

Finally when he lay back exhausted and sleeping at her side, another face swam across her reeling consciousness, other words echoed faintly from the past: "I hope you will remember that every time you lie in his arms!" Blessed oblivion swirled nearer and closed in.

When she awakened next morning, Elizabeth found herself alone in their small bedroom. She heard no sound as she dressed quickly and hurried into the livingroom. She stopped short. Jon stood calm and handsome, his back to the stone mantel his eyes expressionless as they looked at his wife.

"Jon —" she stammered in her surprise.

"Good morning," he greeted her cooly.

She started, taken aback. "Is that all you have to say?"

"What more is there to say?"

"After last night —"

"Exactly." he interrupted. "After last night there is nothing more to say."

"But I don't understand!" Elizabeth was on the verge of tears.

"No, you don't understand!" He strode toward her furiously and caught her arms in cruel fingers as she stepped back involuntarily. "See! Even now you draw back in revulsion, though you tried not to. Yes! You are a very dutiful wife! My God, who wants a dutiful wife? Have you no feeling in you? Are you a stone?"

His voice was rasping with emotion and Elizabeth stood wide-eyed not knowing how to answer.

"Of course, you don't understand!" He almost flung her from him. "You wouldn't understand what it means to be set on fire at the very sight of you, to be consumed with agony when I touch you, to ride mile on dreary mile with your haunting face constantly before me. If you can't return it, why can't you free my mind of you?"

"Jon, my dear. Listen to me." Elizabeth fought to control her trembling. Her voice was husky with sadness. "You are being unfair."

"Unfair?" He turned back to her stricken face. "Can it be unfair to seek a response to the fire always eating at my vitals?"

"I did not deceive you when I married you. You were so sure

96

that my liking was enough. Now you have no right to reproach me." She paused wondering what to say to this man who was her husband, for better or for worse. "We have had a good life so far together. Until last night you were always gentle and understanding. Why can it not be always so?" She sought to touch his arm, but he drew away.

"I like you, Jon — nay — I love you. Perhaps I cannot give you what you asked last night, but I am your wife and you have my loyalty and affection."

" 'Why can it not always be so?' " he echoed her words savagely. "This is why! I have always wanted you as I had you last night, but for your sake I held myself in check. For four years I've waited patiently while my desire for you has grown instead of lessened. That could not go on forever. I am only human."

"I, too, am human, Jon." She could think of nothing more to say. What was there to say?

With a shaking hand she laid the packet of official papers before him and tried to speak sanely of prosaic matters.

"You are back just in time. The settlers with Mr. Crell have made their choices and are ready for you to survey their grants." She fingered their papers. "The Crells have chosen Tom's Creek; the Gallmans — he has nine children — selected a site between the creek and the river just below our own. Nat Hayne likes the other side of the river. He wants to grow rice. Thomas and I advised him that he might be cut off from the settlement by rising water — " her voice trailed into silence. Jon was not listening. It all seemed trivial to her, too.

"I'll tell Mr. Crell you are home. He will be thankful to take his affairs out of female hands and turn them over to a man." Her attempt at lightness met no response. From the door she spoke tentatively to his back.

"Jon, I'm glad you are home. It has been very difficult. I needed you."

He stirred slightly but did not turn. She sighed heavily as she pulled the door to behind her.

The little town of Saxe Gotha buzzed with industry and activity. The settlement had received that name from Governor Broughton in honor of the marriage of the Prince of Wales to Princess Augusta of Saxe Gotha. Each settler was given a half acre lot touching on Front Street, which followed the Congaree River for nearly a mile. In addition farm land, fifty acres for each member of a family, was allotted to all. The German and Swiss immigrants, after the February snows had melted and their first disappointment had worn off with regular meals, had set to with a will to clear their land, raise their log houses, and prepare for the spring planting. The trees posed, as always, the most serious problem. Cutting, notching and carrying enough logs to build a house was slow work and the snows had already delayed them. An air of frenzy prevailed. They must be ready to plant! Elizabeth watched their snail-like progress with growing concern.

One day while she was watching the men at work, she looked up to see Eleazar Wigan's rabbit-like face grinning at her. His face and his jerky gait had earned him the Cherokee name of Cheesto Kaihre, the Old Rabbit. Close behind him was Onconecaw, who was already gaining a position of importance in his tribe. He had attained the rank of warrior and with it a new name — Chuconnuta, the White Owl. An air of dignity and growing authority sat well on his slight shoulders and shone from his intelligent eyes. Ever since his trip to London he had worked assiduously to conquer the English tongue and though he now had a fair command of it, he extended his arm wordlessly to Elizabeth. Across the arm lay a shawl of the most exquisite skins that Elizabeth had ever seen. She looked up, a question in her eyes.

"Take it for you, Lady Cuming." He had never addressed her in any other way. Though she had corrected him, he pretended not to understand the English custom of a wife assuming her husband's name.

"Onconecaw! How very beautiful! The court ladies in London would envy me now." She caressed her cheek with its softness. Elizabeth thought she had forgotten her love for the elegance of fine garments. She had had no new gown since she left Charles Town and had had Aunt Vadie to remove the hoops and much of the yardage from her voluminous skirts to adjust them to frugal frontier life. The change had made them even more becoming, even though it accentuated her height; and the richness and durability of their quality would make them last for many years to come. Now all the love of luxury swept over her again as Eleazar placed the shawl around her shoulders.

"It is the kind they make for their chiefs," he smiled at her girlish eagerness.

Again her eyes filled with tears of gratefulness, as they had years ago at Whitehall when Onconecaw had presented her with the little horse as a gift from his people to carry her to that "good strong house" they had built for her father.

"How kind you are to me! Why?"

"My people do not forget the great warrior who was your father. He was their friend. He was not like other white men. They again ask you to come among them. The house still waits."

Elizabeth stroked the richness of the skins. She had often thought seriously of this spot high up the Saluda River that had fired Jon's enthusiasm, where bubbling streams honeycombed the wide fertile plains. Would this be an answer to Jon's insatiable seeking — seeking for what? What was the demon in him that gave him no rest? She could not believe that a man of his ability and strength could find ultimate satisfaction in passion. No, it was not that. But they had already left the security of one life for the uncertainty of the frontier. They had yet to conquer this spot, so moving on to another would not still his restlessness.

Elizabeth smiled at the two men, one red, one white.

"Thank you, Onconecaw. I must see your country one day. I have heard stories of its cool, clean beauty. Some day, I shall come."

They watched the workmen for a while. Elizabeth spoke of her anxiety. They needed shelters quickly to protect them from the spring rains and to free the men for the fields. Onconecaw listened carefully, but made no comment. She finally left them with an invitation to dinner, and turned home, hugging the warm shawl gratefully.

Jon was in from his surveying and greeted her cheerfully. The night after their quarrel he had come again to her room and stood looking down at her. She held her breath and prayed silently and involuntarily, "No, not again, not tonight!"

Interpreting the alarm in his eyes correctly, he touched her cheek lightly.

"Don't be afraid. I shan't hurt you again. I just want to be near you."

He took her gently in his arms and cradled her head against his shoulder.

"I'm sorry," he whispered gently into her fragrant hair.

Now she returned his smile with genuine affection and proudly showed him her gift. His face darkened.

"Keep away from those filthy Indians!" he ordered peremptorily.

Surprise at his curt tone showed in her eyes. He had never spoken to her thus, nor had he ever given her an order.

"But —" she opened her mouth to protest.

"There is no 'but' about it. On this matter, you shall do as I say."

The warning pulse of anger beat in Elizabeth's throat.

"Onconecaw is not a filthy Indian. He is my friend."

"Do not argue with me, Elizabeth. Return that shawl!"

Elizabeth drew herself up. "I shall not return the shawl!" Her eyes flashed. "You are my husband and have a right to command me when there is a reason. In this matter your position is unfounded, and I shall not accept your authority."

The two glared at each other. Elizabeth's color, heightened by anger and the February cold, made her startlingly handsome. Jon's face softened and broke into his wicked smile.

"How beautiful you are when you are angry. You look just as you did at Crowfield the night I first saw you."

He strode to her and caught her in his arms.

"How I wish I could capture your spirit," he said after he had kissed her soundly.

The next day at luncheon, some of his truculent anger returned when he saw that Elizabeth planned to seat Onconecaw at his table as a guest. Only a warning flash in her eye kept him from protesting. She wondered why he hated the Indians so. She was under no delusions about them herself. She was fully aware of their unpredictable savagery, but she felt no personal dislike. Elizabeth realized the importance of their friendship at this crucial moment in the settlement. An ill-conceived move on their part might easily sever the fine thread of friendship that existed between the races.

Next morning the Common, as the new Saxe Gothans called it already, was filled with a silent group of oiled red bodies. At a word from Onconecaw they disappeared into the forest where they deftly and silently fell to cutting and notching the great logs and carrying them effortlessly to be laid into tight sturdy cabins for the new Carolinians. Jon's anger boiled anew, but Elizabeth touched his arm and smiled into his dark face.

"It would be foolish to refuse their help," was all she said.

Three days they toiled, then disappeared as silently as they had come, leaving a score of new thatched cabins to be plastered with mud by the women, while their men turned to the fields.

Chapter Four

"It's my turn!"

"No, it ain't!"

"'Tis too."

"You've had three turns and you shan't have another!"

Slap! The screams of anguish and anger brought Aunt Vadie to the door sighing with exasperation. Rolling and tumbling in the dust, tearing at each others' hair and clothing were two little boys. A small group of delighted spectators was cheering either one or the other.

"Git him, Jacob," squealed one tow-headed lass.

"Knock his teeth down his throat, Billy," shouted a hulking youth taller than the others and with a bully's face.

"Run," hissed another, pulling at Jacob Gallman's heavy boot, "here comes Frau Vadie!"

Too late. Aunt Vadie reached through the swirling dust and emerged with two struggling youngsters by the scruff of the neck. One grimy face was streaked with tears, the other grinned widely, black eyes flashing.

"I bet he has pink toes, he's so sissy. Yeh!" Billy spat disdainfully.

"Now, Billy," Aunt Vadie shook Billy Brown, "You said you'd be good today. Have you forgotten the red cap I promised you if you'd stay out of trouble while I am busy?"

Billy's smile disappeared. He thought longingly of the bright red cap Aunt Vadie was knitting. It was the most beautiful thing he'd ever seen. Was it worth it? He guessed so.

"All right, Aunt Vadie. Just give me one more chance," he begged.

"Very well, Billy." She shook her head as she turned back toward the house. Billy was a problem, but the most charming child she'd ever known. She supposed he could stab someone in the back and be quickly forgiven when he said in his deceptively contrite voice punctuated by the merry smile, "I'm sorry."

Yesterday had been a day, she thought. After lessons, which Aunt Vadie, at Elizabeth's suggestion, conducted every morning for all the children in the little colony, Billy had pushed Blossom against the new Dutch oven she was grumblingly trying to learn to use, grabbed up a flaming knot of pine, and marched triumphantly through the house with Blossom and Vadie screaming behind him. When the tumult from that episode had subsided and Aunt Vadie was knitting peacefully on the red cap, Billy had stolen her ball of yarn and crept in and out around the furniture until the room was cobwebbed with scarlet threads. When Aunt Vadie had pulled on her ball and found the tangled mess, Billy was seated at a tiny pump organ inherited from the former occupant of the house, playing and singing at the top of his lungs, "At the cross, at the cross —", his black eyes snapping. For this defection Aunt Vadie had soundly boxed his ears, and, immediately remorseful, had promised him the cap if he would behave.

Thomas Brown had asked Vadie why she put up with his errant Billy, and exhorted her to make him stay at home. But Billy Brown had become a fixture in the Fenwick household and none had the heart to turn him away. His idol was Jon, whom he would follow to the ends of the earth, but who paid him little attention. With Elizabeth he was on his best behavior, and with Uncle Roy he fished the hours away, drinking in every word of the marvelous stories of adventure that Roy told in masterly fashion. If Uncle Roy omitted any detail, Billy stopped him with,

"Now, Uncle Roy, you go back and tell it right!"

It was Roy who, noticing his interest in the wheezy old organ, taught him to play some simple hymns. It was Aunt Vadie who read to him by the hour in the long evenings from her worn Bible. Though Billy steadfastly refused to study the simple lessons that Aunt Vadie outlined for the other children, he could quote long passages of the Scriptures which he loved to hear over and over again.

Yes, Billy was a paradox, but a lovable one in spite of his mischievousness.

Soon another storm from outside interrupted Aunt Vadie. She hurried again to the door and called sharply, "Billy!"

Billy stopped pulling a tempting yellow braid, and looked from the coveted red cap in Aunt Vadie's hand to the inviting braid. The wicked smile split his ivory face.

"Aunt Vadie, you just keep that cap," he called and giving the braid another vicious tug he flew around the house leaving a weeping fraulein for Aunt Vadie to comfort.

Dashing through the underbrush Billy ran headlong into a man. The shock threw him on his back on the leafy ground from which he looked up into the ugliest face he had ever seen. A shiver of unaccustomed apprehension ran over Billy's lithe, seven-year old frame.

"Who are you?" Billy demanded pulling himself cautiously to his feet.

"I, young Sir, am a wanderer, a troubadour from a foreign land across the wide ocean."

"What's a troubadour?" Billy wanted to know, drawn by the beauty of a deep, resonant voice emerging from the hideous face. The stranger was little taller than Billy.

"Sit down, young Sir, and I'll tell you about it. Would you share my simply repast?"

Billy sat down, drawn by a fascination as strong as that of the legendary rattlesnake that had lured Manabozho. From an ample bag slung over his shoulder, the ugly little man drew out some hard biscuit and cold, fried fat back. As the two, man and boy, munched comfortably, the man's scholarly words and elegant manners made it seem a banquet fit for a king, partaken to the tune of those wandering minstrels' songs about which he proceeded to tell the fascinated child. Deftly, the stranger slipped from telling to asking. Soon he had a clear picture of the settlement at Saxe Gotha, its proximity to the nearest Indian village, its vulnerability, its feeling about its savage neighbors whose blood the man had already surmised ran in his young companion's veins.

Uncle Roy came on the two as they talked and stopped, instantly on the alert.

"Billy," he called. The boy came back to reality as if from a pleasant dream. He ran to Roy's side and caught at his hand. The stranger was quickly forgotten as he admired Roy's heavy string of fish.

"Oh," he cried in disappointment. "Are you through fishing? I wanted to try my new cane pole you made for me. Gee!" eying a particularly fine carp.

Over Billy's head Roy gazed at the strange little man. His face was broad and frog-like. A vicious ill-healed scar made two separate mountains of his bulbous nose and drew up one corner of his mouth evilly. He was almost a dwarf with huge knobby hands and oversized feet. Fanatic eyes, dark and sharp, the eyes of a dreamer, returned Roy's hostile gaze.

Bowing elegantly the stranger spoke, "Christian Gotleib Priber, Sir, at your service." Roy was amazed at the cultured voice, speaking perfect English, which emerged from the crooked mouth.

"What is your business here?" Roy questioned him rudely.

"I come, Sir, from Amelia Township where I found life, shall we say, a trifle difficult. I am the proprietor of a saddlery shop next to Mr. John Laurens in Charles Town."

"If you found life difficult in Amelia, an older settlement than Saxe Gotha, why do you move on toward the still more primitive and dangerous frontier?"

The little man shrugged. "Perhaps I feel a missionary zeal toward my red brother. Shall we leave it at that? Don't be alarmed, Sir. I have no intention of stopping in your primitive, as you call it, village. My destination is the Cherokee hills. However, you can hardly deny a Christian," he chuckled at his pun, "traveller asylum for a night." The three turned toward home.

Weeks later from the Cherokee hills news of the machinations of Billy's ugly little friend reached the settlement at Saxe Gotha. Eleazar Wigan looked grave as he discussed it in the Fenwick living room one cold evening in December.

"He's a madman", said Eleazar, "playing with fire. He has settled at Tellico after spreading his seditious ideas from Gusti to the hills. He wants to establish a confederation of all Southern Indian tribes against both the English and the French."

"Do the Indians listen to him?" asked Elizabeth.

"They eat his words up! He already speaks their heathen tongue better than they do themselves. He gained their sympathy by teaching them the use of weights and measures to protect them from unlicensed, thieving traders."

Eleazar turned to Roy whom he knew to be a great reader. "Do you know Plato, Sir?"

"Plato?" Roy asked in amazement. "Of course I do. Why?"

"What is Plato's *Republic?*" Wigan pressed.

"Well," replied Roy, "Plato was a Greek philosopher who wanted to found a — a socialistic state — do you understand what I mean?"

"You mean where everything belongs to the government and is divided equally among the citizens?"

"Exactly."

Wigan scratched his tousled grey curls. "Women, too?" he looked up at Roy from under bristling grey brows.

"Yes. What's all this sudden interest in philosophy, Wigan? What has it to do with a crack pot German missionary?"

"That *Republic* you're talking about," he pointed a bony finger for emphasis, "is his Bible and I reckon that fellow Plato must be his god. He's got no other, that's for sure."

The ugly little man seated crosslegged on the ground was barely distinguishable from his oiled red companions. Hair dressed in the Indian fashion, he was naked, except for skin shirt and breech flap. Between intermittent puffs on a magnificent clay pipe ornamented with a rattlesnake skin and bright feathers, he harangued his spell-bound audience fluently in their own tongue.

"The English — and the French", he added as an after thought, "you should keep at a distance. Only then can you remain free. Seek an alliance in New Orleans. Then the English can no longer cheat you as they do with short measure and high prices." Only the sighing of the wind in the great oak trees broke the silence as the little man puffed.

"Above all, guard your land!" the captivating voice reached clearly to the outer circle of enthralled listeners.

One young brave could no longer restrain himself and sprang forward to the center of the fire-lit circle. Raising his tomahawk above his head he struck it wildly into a nearby stump.

"I am for the war path. Wet the trail of the white dogs with their bright red blood! Let us block their path to our hills with a red sea as wide as the wide water over which they came in their great birds to destroy us! Several grunts of approval answered this sudden outburst.

For a brittle moment, Priber smoked in silence. Then his impressive voice, now filled with contempt, travelled through the starlit darkness.

"Salone of Estatoe is a foolish hothead. War is folly. The white man crossed the fabulous western ocean many lifetimes ago. What makes you think he cannot cross a puny ocean of his own blood?

In war you will certainly be destroyed. Let there be no more such talk!"

But a smirk of satisfaction cracked his evil visage later in his wigwam when he sharpened his quill and wrote precisely and beautifully under the heading "Government in Paradise."

A few days later Stephen Crell looked with dismay at his fine fat hogs senselessly butchered and lying useless in their frozen gore. The meat had been so thoroughly defiled that even the buzzards refused it.

Thus appeared the first tarnish on the bright chain with which Sir Alexander had joined his red friends to their great white Father, George II King of England.

Chapter Five

That same year a dozen disgruntled immigrants under Herman Geiger's leadership came from the New Windsor township on Savannah River, and twenty-nine hopeful families arrived with John Jacob Riemensperger from Toggenburg, Switzerland. O'Gilvie eyed the former group with many misgivings and expressed his opinion that the New Windsor settlers must have considered their departure a good riddance. He told Elizabeth privately that he was glad they chose to settle above Martin Fridig, who had already anglicized his name to Friday. Friday, with an eye toward future expansion, had settled two miles up the river at the falls, a good spot for a ferry someday. The Riemensperger group chose land below the Crells' land on Tom's Creek, and a few English names appeared on plats about Savannah Hunt Creek. Thus the little colony widened out and took new courage in numbers, which was well, for the whole Province was now visited with a series of disasters that shook the hearts of the most courageous, and only the strong survived.

With the supplies allotted to the Riemensperger group, Governor Broughton announced that the bounty fund was exhausted and further immigration from Europe was discouraged.

The spring planting season passed auspiciously. Fine fields of wheat, oats, and rye waved gently next to straight rows of sprouting green corn. Neighbor congratulated neighbor. The world looked good. Saxe Gotha housed nearly seventy-five families, and had been promised a representative in the Assembly when the number reached one hundred. Yes, the future looked rosy in the spring of 1738. In January the inhabitants, along with those of Orangeburg, New Windsor, and Frederick's Burg, had petitioned the Assembly for horse paths to the market at Charles Town to facilitate the transportation of their hoped-for crops. If only wagons could pass up and down the long, narrow trail it would ease the farmer's prohibitive expense in employing enough horses and packhorsemen to take his crop to market. A committee of the Assembly recommended two hundred pounds for this purpose, and, though debate had been postponed, the Saxe Gothans were not disheartened. Joseph Crell was talking of a grist mill. Yes, things were certainly easing up on the isolated frontier.

Then came the rains.

Late in April Elizabeth was awakened by the slash of water against the glass window. When she and Jon had retired, the sky was full of stars and a pleasant brisk breeze filled the velvety night with the fragrance of the roses climbing tumultuously over the little stone house. Night insects so filled the air with their industrious buzzing that the ominous croak of bull frogs went unnoticed.

Some time during the night the wind had shifted and was buffeting the sturdy walls with angry impotence. Elizabeth lay for a while listening, thankful for the protection of her cozy walls. Drawing the light coverlet closer over Jon's deeply sleeping frame, she snuggled deeper herself to let the sound of the rain lull her back to sleep. But sleep would not come. Soon she realized that a penetrating chill had replaced the April balminess. Shivering a little she sought more cover. Half way across the dark, breezy floor, she stopped, listening. The tone of the howling wind was ominous. From a roomy chest she took a fluffy down quilt which Nellie had made for her and climbed shakily back to bed. She lay, keeping still with an effort, so as not to disturb her husband. Finally she could stand it no longer.

"Jon," she whispered.

"Huh?" he grunted.

"It's raining."

No answer

She shook his shoulder.

"It's raining, I say."

"Raining? Why shouldn't it rain? Go to sleep."

"But I don't like the sound of the wind – and it's cold."

"For heaven's sake, Elizabeth. We need the rain. Why wake me up to tell me that?"

"I'm sorry, Jon. I know you were weary after your long trip –" she settled down again tentatively, "but I'm worried. We don't need so much at one time, and why is it so cold?"

Jon shifted his long body wearily. He patted her shoulder absently and his lips brushed her hair lightly before he relaxed again into dreamless slumber.

Toward morning Elizabeth slept again fitfully. She dreamed that she and Sir Alexander stood, like Noah, on the top of a mountain while turgid flood waters swirled around their feet. The suspended face of Christian Gotlieb Priber grinned mockingly at them while Jon swam away on the little Chickasaw horse, calling repeatedly and hollowly over his shoulder, "You don't need me, you don't need me, you don't need me –." Elizabeth looked around for a means of escape, but in her case, unlike Noah's, there was no ark.

Ten days later it was still raining relentlessly. Once or twice it had ceased momentarily, but only to gather strength for another heartbreaking deluge. The mighty Congaree, fed by jubilant and joyous mountain streams, finally burst its banks and swept out over the flourishing fields of grain while the stricken members of the recently hopeful colony looked on helplessly. With one of those lightning changes peculiar to the middle and back country of South Carolina, the sun split the boiling rain clouds, a purposeful breeze chased them out to sea, and summer was upon the province.

The corn was a ruin.

The wheat? Well, maybe, if the water receded quickly.

Gathering its waters back into its banks, the Congaree swept on, mysteriously carrying on its swollen bosom the remnants of Nat Hayne's lonely cabin and his hopes of raising rice. He appeared at Elizabeth's door, soaked and miserable. Elizabeth looked at him wordlessly. What does one say to a man whose whole plan of life had been swept away with his home, his bounty tools, and stock? He could not look to Charles Town for replacements. The inhabitants of Charles Town were busy with disasters of their own. Late in May the Assembly was again prorogued against another scourge as virulent and as ruthless as the yellow fever plague of 1732. Aboard a slave ship from Guinea a case of small pox was belatedly discovered. Too late was the ship placed in quarantine, for several slaves had already been sold on the block and passed to the great country plantations, taking with them the deadly infection.

Chapter Six

Three men smoked their pipes glumly in the stuffy little cabin of the British man-of-war. Only the lonely creaking of the ship's timbers as it rose and fell on the gentle swells broke the silence. Gravy from a succulent mutton roast congealed untasted on magnificent china plates. A perforated copper lantern straight from the bazaars of Constantinople cast eerie shadows on first one serious face, then another, as it swung back and forth to the rhythm of the sea. They were good faces, these three, one aging and sad beneath thinning grey locks, one young and strong with clear blue eyes now deeply troubled, one broad and stern above a gossamer china silk shirt, torn open to expose a sweating chest to what little breeze was stirring over Charles Town harbor this steaming late May evening.

Mr. Mowbray's shiny patent boot struck the floor with sharp decision and his pounding fist made the plates rattle.

"I say let's try it and to hell with the goddam Assembly!"

The other two men eyed him a moment without speaking. Finally the older man spoke to his companion.

"What do you say, Gavin?"

"It's for you to decide, Sir."

"You realize what will happen if we fail?"

"Fully, Sir."

Dr. Killpatrick tamped his pipe thoughtfully.

"What would you do if I were in London and the decision was solely yours?" He watched Gavin sharply.

There was no flicker in Gavin's steady blue eyes as he replied without hesitation,

"I'd try it."

Dr. Killpatrick smiled briefly but proudly at his young associate. He spoke to Mr. Mowbray, the ship's doctor, who was pacing back and forth wiping his damp bull neck with a fine linen napkin.

"The people of Charles Town will never consent. I don't believe we could find enough volunteers to make it worth while." He chewed on his pipe stem. "We might even be termed heretics."

"Faugh!" Mr. Mowbray almost spat his contempt for the people of Charles Town. "Had these lily-livered bastards rather die in the foul misery of the disease or live in the greater misery of pox-marked hideousness?" He jerked his chair out and straddled it while he drove one fist in the palm of his other hand to emphasize his words.

"I've seen it used successfully in Constantinople. Lady Mary Montague, a dainty woman and a great lady, was not afraid to be inoculated herself during a plague when she was there. She even taught its practice to Dr. Mead, the King's own physician, and it's now widely used in England. What's there to lose? How many cases have you attended today? Your own son died in agony yesterday. You've no right not to try to save other sons when you have the magic in your hand!"

"That's just what it will be called if it works. We'll be murderers if it fails. The colonies with all their belligerent ideas of progress and independence are still very primitive in their ideas of providence and God's will."

"God's will! My lord, man, would you worship a god who would will this scourge on mankind? Humans can't shift to God the blame for the pestilences they bring on themselves by their way of living. If He hadn't meant for us to use the cures we spend our lives hunting and perfecting, why would He let us find them?" Mr. Mowbray gulped a great mouthful of wine noisily, and spoke more calmly. "That was a long tirade for me. Forgive the dissertation on theology. But seriously, Sir," he rested his hands on the table and spoke to Dr. Killpatrick, "Cotton Mather and his father, Increase, both witch hunters themselves, championed the use of inoculation in Boston seventeen years ago. Boston, mind you! And they both died a natural death."

112

There was silence again. The watch's thin voice rang from Fort Johnson,

"Ten o'clock and all's well!"

"Surely, Dr. Killpatrick, you are not afraid!" The ship's surgeon looked at the old man with angry, incredulous eyes.

Dr. Killpatrick shook himself and laid down his cold pipe. He rose stiffly and tiredly, "Not for myself, no, Mowbray. I inoculated myself, my wife, and my two remaining children this morning. For Dr. McBride, here, —"

"You have no need to be afraid for me, Sir," Gavin interrupted. His eyes fell guiltily, "I also inoculated myself this morning without your knowledge."

"Gavin, you dog. Behind your own physician's back. I ought to lash you." Nervous laughter released the tension in the hot cabin. The three doctors looked at each other.

"Where do we start?" Gavin asked matter of factly.

"On the London frigate that brought the disease. Hurry!"

They grabbed up their tricorns and dashed out talking at a great rate in very professional language.

On June first the *Gazette* screamed:

> *We don't hear that small pox spreads much in this town . . . but several, being fond of having it, have been inoculated, and probably the distemper has been propagated more that way than it would have been trusting to Providence. . . ."*

Lieutenant Governor Bull, numbered among those inoculated by Dr. Killpatrick, appointed a Day of Fasting and Humiliation. The *Gazette* shortly after admitted:

> *Distemper is becoming more epidemical,*

but hastily attributed its spread to inoculation.

A separate list of deaths among those inoculated was properly placed so that these deaths were easily distinguished from those who died of the natural course of the disease. That the latter list was much, much longer escaped comment by those in the anti-inoculation camp.

The frightened village of Charles Town was split into two warring factions, one headed by Dr. Thomas Dale who used propaganda against inoculation to add fuel to his personal feud against Dr. Killpatrick. The death of Miss Mary Roche was laid directly at Dr. Killpatrick's door, who wrote to Elizabeth:

As to the case of Miss Mary Roche, this physician, Dale, abused my practice on this occasion very ungenerously and objected to the want of blister . . . The truth of the matter is that that fool, when called in by her addle-pated mother to supercede me, moved the child, a hale, plump girl, and a hoarse pipe for an infant, during a rain from the main house to a leaky out building, and the poor thing died of pneumonia, not small pox. I have finally called Dale to account for his attacks on me in the Gazette. His reply has been indefinitely postponed because both he and his son are sick of the pox. Pardon me while I laugh!

The duel between the two acrimonious doctors furnished a comic side line to the tragedy being enacted in the crippled Province. Again the *Gazette* spoke, this time the contemptuous words of the old doctor goaded beyond endurance by his egotistical colleague,

There is a material difference between the grimace and the practice of Physick, as a trade, and the exercise of it as a profession . . . I might leave the judicious, impartial reader to finish the contention and present the one who deserves it a long-eared cap which every one is fond of shifting from himself . . . the very Pliny that I lent him to assist him in the compilation of a natural history is surborned to face me down in the title page, that I murder for experience – !

The feud and the pestilence rode on rough shod over the quivering, frantic population. Not satisfied with the havoc it had worked in the Low Country, the dread spectre uncoiled its deadly tentacles and reached far up the Cherokee path to the very heart of the Cherokee Nation itself.

For Uncle Roy, fishing had replaced the fascination of gambling. A hot summer day found him propped comfortably against an overhanging tree, book in one hand, pole in the other. Elusive fish, too well fed by the debris in the still swollen river, glided indifferently by his tasty bait. He cared little at the moment. The volume was engrossing. A twig snapped. He looked up immediately on the alert, reaching for his musket.

"Billy! Welcome. Come join me. I'll let you use my pole. The fish aren't biting today, and the water's still too deep to use Indian baskets." He paused, looking at the little boy closely. The usually merry smile was not there. Suddenly without a word Billy's body became rigid, his eyes rolled back and he fell headlong on the leafy ground.

Roy sprang up instantly and turned the child over on his back. He touched his forehead and found it burning hot. The lips fell back in an ugly, slack grimace. His eyes rolled hideously. Gathering Billy into his arms, Roy ran stumbling toward the cabins. He went first to Pakahle's hut next to Thomas Brown's, but when he kicked open the door and tried to turn the little boy over to his mother, she fled screaming to the woods. Roy looked around helplessly. He placed his light burden on a mat of deerskins, and turned uncertainly to the door. His scalp and arm pits prickled. Hadn't the courageous colony suffered enough without this? Already some families were threatening to leave. Forays by the Indians on their poultry, cattle, and hogs, added to the complete loss of the corn crop, had made their cup of bitterness overflow. They were ready to move on. Where would they move? Anywhere, anywhere away from here, they cried.

From Dr. Killpatrick's letters to Elizabeth, Roy suspected this was small pox. Through Eleazar Wigan they had news of the plight of the Cherokees. Among the red men, unacquainted with this product of the white man's civilization, the small pox spread like wild fire, killing, maiming, and defacing. To the proud Indian, death was preferable to hideous scarring. The chiefs and the Beloved Men of the nation, dividing the blame unjustly between immoral practices of their youths and more justly, the coming of the white man to their once happy land, punished their youths by making them lie in the fields, their chests bare to the night dews. When this brought only death, the conjurors suggested alternate sweating and plunging into the icy streams to chase out the evil spirit inhabiting fever-wracked bodies. The effect was instantaneous. They died like flies.

Upon the white man, they visited their wrath in increasing raids and even left a bright red tomahawk cleaving the innocent head of a daring settler above the Geigers on the Saluda River. Panic was spreading. The members of the Assembly in Charles Town, prorogued and harrassed with their own problems, left unheeded the urgent pleas from the frontier for a fort and rangers to protect them. Elizabeth, in desperation, sent word by Eleazar to Onconecaw to ask him to visit their settlement to discuss the hostility of his people. Jon was furious when he learned of this act of Elizabeth's which precipitated between them one of their ever-increasing scenes.

Roy brought his thoughts up sharply. He covered the little frame gently and went in search of his wife. When Jon heard the news he steadfastly refused to allow any member of his household to go near the little hut.

"He is not your responsibility," Jon said positively.

"Whose responsibility is he?" replied Roy, dryly, draping himself indolently over a chair and looking up at his nephew-in-law through narrowed eyes.

Aunt Vadie held her breath.

"He will be cared for," said Jon, striding out of the house, banging the heavy wooden door on his heels.

Jon flushed Pakahle out of the woods somehow and she stayed dead-faced but faithfully by her son through his long illness. Jon returned to face his wife.

"I understand you have sent word to that sneaky Indian to come to see you," his words were a curt question.

Elizabeth looked at him steadily, striving to control her anger.

"What sneaky Indian?" she asked coldly.

"You know very well whom I mean!"

"If you are speaking of Onconecaw, "he is not sneaky and he is my friend, which is fortunate for you," the words slipped out and she regretted them instantly. She turned a seemingly indifferent back on him and fussed aimlessly with a bowl of summer daisies on the table.

He reached her in a single stride and flung her around to meet his face, terrible with anger. She gasped.

"What do you mean?" he shouted.

"Just what I said!" She tried to loosen his fingers. "Let me go, you are hurting me." He still glared at her without releasing her from his brutal grasp. "You should realize that our very existence depends on amiable relations with the Indians at our back door. Should they become enraged they could wipe us out in a few hours. Since we have no fort and no soldiers to protect us, our safety will depend on our wits and our ability to get along with Onconecaw's people. I have tried to promote good relations by my friendship with Onconecaw. That's all that I meant," she finished weakly.

Dubiously, he let her go.

"In the future, consult me before you make such a serious move. I am technically in charge here." He stalked toward the door.

Anger at his egotistical stupidity flared again in Elizabeth. Her voice, low and shaking, followed him. "If you are supposed to be in charge here, stay here and assume your responsibilities. I am sick to death of them!"

She thought for a moment he would strike her. As he looked at her flashingly beautiful face, his fury died within him and left the cold lost feeling he always felt after one of his towering rages. He closed the door too quietly after him as he left without another word.

Completely spent Elizabeth sank into her favorite chair and stared blankly into the great stone fireplace, now cold and filled with fragrant evergreen branches.

"What must I do?" she wondered dully. "This cannot go on. It is becoming intolerable." Since the night two years ago when, casting all pretense aside, he had made love to her so savagely, his moodiness had increased. Elizabeth had even noticed that he had been drinking occasionally. Jon had always been a moderate drinker and she had never known him to be in his cups. However she began to notice that his eyes glittered dangerously and on several occasions he tried unsuccessfully to bait Uncle Roy into a quarrel. Vadie watched with new admiration as her husband nonchalantly parried his threat and escaped an open clash by going fishing in the daytime or disappearing definitely behind the pages of his book in the evenings. Aunt Vadie with misery in her heart, watched Elizabeth's changing face. Neither ever mentioned the fact to the other and tried to make their unhappiness vanish by ignoring it. The wide chasm between Elizabeth and Jon was transmitted to the kitchen, where Aunt Vadie pretended that she didn't hear Blossom mutter darkly about "stobin in de bak" and Clem counter with the veiled threat that the Indians weren't the only ones who knew how to use a scalping knife.

One day when Jon's anger could find no target but Blossom, she answered his complaints rudely. Flying into a rage he berated her roundly and ended with,

"And if it happens again you and I will have to part!"

Blossom, arms akimbo, a heavy iron skillet in her right hand, answered boldly, "Whar *you* gwine, Mistah Jon?"

When he had departed in a huff, the heavy skillet barely missed Clem's head and cut a long gash in the soft pine door.

"An dat goes fuh you too. Git outta hyah."

Chapter Seven

"I've sent for McBride."

Elizabeth's fork clattered to the floor. She stared incredulously at Jon's dark head bent determinedly over the hot corn meal mush that he despised, a fact Blossom well knew.

"Well?" he raised his head and searched her hastily composed face.

"We need a doctor, certainly, but why Dr. McBride?"

"I've a great deal of respect for Dr. Killpatrick. From his letters to you I gather he sets great store by this inoculation thing. He is too old to make the trip, so I've asked for his assistant."

"I see." Elizabeth examined her husband's face covertly. Was this some devilish trick to hurt her, or was it as simple as he said? Would the demon within him that gave his soul no rest goad him to such cruelty, to bring her face to face with a man she hadn't seen for over six years? What romantic fancies for a settled woman of her age! At the moment her twenty-six years sat heavily upon her. She felt old and tired and discouraged. Looking at her searchingly, Jon saw a beautiful face richly colored by exposure to the sun. It was scarcely older than the radiant one he had first seen at the Governor's ball so long ago in Charles Town. The years had matured it, yes, but the spirit behind it had matured also and was reflected in the solemn grey eyes which returned his look steadily.

Between the heavy brows was the only true evidence of the passing of time. Tiny, twin furrows cut the smooth brow deeply, left there indelibly by staunch efforts to stem a sometimes overpowering desire to weep. Elizabeth rose stiffly.

"Perhaps the coming of a doctor will quell the rising panic. But do you suppose these people will submit to inoculation?"

"Have you not always found a way, my dear? I have never seen anyone who could escape your influence."

Elizabeth turned surprised. In his tone there was no sarcasm, only admiration. A tiny glow of almost forgotten friendship passed between them. At the moment they were no longer two people, a man and a woman, absorbed in a personal struggle, but a team fighting together a common enemy. Elizabeth smiled.

"Thank you, Jon," and placed her hand lightly on his shoulder. For a moment his sunburned hand covered it and a fleeting sensation of peace made her fling off her mood of heavy depression.

"How is Billy?" she asked.

Jon shook his head. "It's dreadful and something I hope you will be spared witnessing. The eruption has started and is spreading rapidly. His little face is covered." He paused thoughtfully. "It's strange. The fever has gone and he seems in less pain —"

"Have you seen him?" Elizabeth asked incredulously.

"Yes. Only to assure myself that his mother is caring for him. I thought it wiser to take their food to them to avoid too much outside contact with the infection. So far no new cases have come to my attention, but there are bound to be more."

"Why, Jon. How thoughtful of you. Couldn't you have sent someone else?"

"The Negroes are all frightened."

"Aren't you afraid?"

"Yes," he answered shortly. "Aren't you?"

"Yes, terribly. I should like to run and never stop — but where is there to run?"

He smiled his old jaunty smile.

"Well, there's no need to be morbid. The reality is not like the dream, is it, Elizabeth?"

"No, it isn't."

"I don't suppose it ever is," he spoke with rare insight.

Gavin McBride arrived bearing a characteristic letter from Dr.

Killpatrick.

The company of Killpatrick and McBride is in such bad odor at the present that it needs only one man to handle the infrequent patients! It looks as though the junior member will soon have to seek new fields of endeavor. Seriously, my dear, inoculation is God's blessing. I know your courage and determination and wish you luck. You will certainly need it.

Elizabeth schooled her face, for she knew that Jon was watching her. The shock of seeing Gavin again had struck her like a blow in the stomach, taking away her breath for a moment. She had tried to prepare herself, but all the hours of discipline were swept away with one look at the beloved face. "This is out of all reason," she told herself sharply. "How can a man I have not seen in so long, whom I really knew so little, have this effect on me? I am disloyal, even wanton." But deep in her heart she knew it was not disloyalty but the tragic frailty of human nature. To such a woman as she, love can come but once, and when it came, it was absolute and forever. Now she greeted him with rigid self-control.

"Welcome, Dr. McBride. You have not come too soon. There is need for haste, so I suggest that we begin at once. There will be time later to renew acquaintances." She felt the need for immediate action to quell the fluttering within her.

"You are quite right, Mrs. Fenwick." There was nothing in his face to betray that his thoughts echoed her own. He was cooly polite and glad to see them all.

"Jon," to address him as Mr. Fenwick seemed too obvious. The two men had shaken hands warmly as if nothing had happened to mar their friendliness. "Is there a mild case in the settlement from which I can obtain the serum?"

"There are only two cases that we know of. The Mathias child, so I'm told, has not been so ill as Billy Brown; but you shall judge for yourself." The two men, of a height and age, one fair and broad, one dark and slender, walked away, talking animatedly with no further word to Elizabeth. She felt very alone and went to the kitchen to talk to Aunt Vadie, who was lovingly preparing broth for Billy Brown.

Aunt Vadie looked up quickly. Examining the face she loved so well, she saw reflected there just what she had feared. She said nothing. To cover the ache in her heart, she fussed at Blossom without heat, and Blossom fussed back affectionately.

An hour later Jon and Stephen Crell addressed the entire colony assembled on the common. Jon explained Gavin's presence and left Stephen to coax his protesting people. All hung back and muttered uncomfortably. Elizabeth looked at Jon. He nodded encouragement. She stepped forward and rolled up her sleeve. Gavin hestiated almost imperceptibly, then taking her arm in his left hand, he scratched the surface deftly with a sharp knife. She walked away trembling.

From the crowd came a loud guffaw. A dirty, bearded man in a soiled and battered beaver strode up to the table baring a filthy arm.

"Danged if I'll let no female git ahead o' me. Scratch away, Doc." It was the only contribution Herman Geiger ever made to the settlement at Saxe Gotha. A reluctant line began to file past the improvised clinic.

Billy Brown retained his merry smile and the unquenchable fire of his gay spirit, but the ivory beauty of his face was destroyed. From the first day of his release from the stifling hut, he was Jon's faithful shadow and slave. The two were inseparable. On the little Chickasaw pony which had been Onconecaw's gift to Elizabeth, and which she now gave to an ecstatic Billy, he explored every back woods path, carrying the chain when Jon was surveying, helping to care for the horses when it was a trading trip.

Other cases of small pox appeared at Saxe Gotha, there were some deaths, but the inoculated escaped to a man. Word continued to reach them of the dreadful havoc the plague had worked on the Cherokees. Nearly half the nation perished, and many warriors who recovered, shamed by their deformity, committed suicide.

In September the Assembly in Charles Town passed a law prohibiting the practice of inoculation in and about Charles Town.

The people of Saxe Gotha, glad to take their minds off the small pox, prepared hopefully to harvest the grain that had survived the flooding April rains. To dull their disappointment over the loss of their corn, Elizabeth had determined to take a fling at tobacco. Again she turned to Onconecaw who had brought her a small quantity of the tiny green plants loaded under damp moss and drawn on deerskin sleds similar to the travois widely used by French Indians. O'Gilvie had the tobacco carefully planted on the ruined corn land and gave plants to any adventurous soul who was willing to try the new crop. Some of the staid Germans considered it the devil's weed and all who smoked it the devil's henchmen, so on the whole it was not popular.

On the eve of their first day of harvesting, the air was still and oppressively hot. Dirty orange clouds were gathering on the horizon. Eleazar Wigan eyed them and shook his head. Elizabeth, busy with other matters, had not noticed. Now her eyes followed his troubled ones.

"What is it, Eleazar? What does it mean?"

"Wal, it could mean nothing, just nothing at all." His nervous hand made his long nose wobble. "But I've seen a wind come up sudden like that out of nowhere. Gits mighty fierce sometimes. Can't nothing stand against it." His eyes swept the golden fields of grain.

About four o'clock that afternoon Elizabeth heard a roaring in the distance as from a thousand crickets. She ran to the door. Her skirts were caught and whipped around her legs; dirt stung her eyes. The tornado tore across the land with lethal fury and when it subsided as suddenly as it had come, nothing remained but the small green tobacco plants. The grain was a shambles.

This blow was too much. Discouraged families moved out of the buffeted and cringing colony to the more established settlements of Orangeburg, Amelia, and New Windsor.

Chapter Eight

Desperately Elizabeth drew the dwindling colony around her. Personally and through Stephen Crell she tried to encourage the men and women numbed by one killing blow of fate after another. Vainly she pointed out that anywhere they went they could expect unfortunate years with poor crops. Their plight in Europe had certainly not been one to be envied. She tried to awaken their pride in pioneering, to point out the beauties and the unlimited scope of the great country they had chosen. Of course, the first years must be hard, but think of the fruits for those who persevered!

Completely embittered, the Saxe Gothans cried out against all their other trials which they had been willing to forget in the flush of hope over big, fine crops for the first time. Crops to bring them the means to establish schools and churches for their young, growing up in ignorance and paganism. They cried out in disillusionment against the assembly in Charles Town which had promised them so much, and given so little. They needed roads to the markets, courts of their own to save the long dreary journey to the Low Country for any legal business, forts and rangers to protect them from their savage neighbors raiding and killing from their mountain fastness. All this they needed and more, and who would listen? Did they themselves not form a wall of protection for the fine ladies and gentlemen of the Tidewater who made the laws that governed them, laws in which they had no say so . . . and on and on went the bitter cries and complaints.

Bone tired and completely discouraged Elizabeth rested her head on her arms and tried not to think.

"Why do you do it?" a compassionate voice spoke gently. "What does all this mean to you?"

Without raising her head she answered Aunt Vadie with a question of her own.

"Would you have me give up, run like a cowardly dog with its tail between its legs? What happens to cowardly dogs in the end? They starve to death or somebody shoots them because they are useless."

"What would you be giving up?" Aunt Vadie pressed.

"What would I be giving up?" Elizabeth raised her head and gazed beyond her aunt. "The great lofty trees, that I used to fear and now love in their majestic dignity, the wide clear streams, the sweet smelling earth to be had for the taming, the clear cool air, the gay mocking bird whose song can even shame the elegant nightingale. Why, Aunt Vadie," she seemed surprised at herself, "I love this wildly beautiful land that offers freedom to anyone who has the will to be free."

"Free from what? Are you free?"

"Yes," Elizabeth said slowly. "I am free." She looked straight at her aunt. "You, of course, are speaking of my marriage." She broke her rule of never mentioning her private life. "You forget that I made my own choice, a freedom I would not have enjoyed in Scotland. Freedom also brings obligations, Aunt Vadie. It does not entitle one to escape the consequences of his own mistakes. But, thank you, you darling." She sprang up and kissed her aunt lightly on her fading hair. "You made me count my blessings, of which you are the greatest, when I needed to most." She pinched Aunt Vadie's cheeks lovingly and looked down seriously into her face. "But, my obligations are not yours. You are free to leave at any time."

"Me, leave you?" cried Aunt Vadie aghast.

Elizabeth laughed gaily.

"Now that that's settled, let's see what's for dinner. I'm hungry!"

Each year Elizabeth had been invited to witness the celebration

126

of the Green Corn Dance in Cheulah's village. The festival beginning at the first new moon in which the corn became full eared lasted eight days and she had never felt she could be away so long. This year she decided to make the trip for a threefold purpose. To strengthen diplomatic relations between the colony and the restive Indians, to try to bridge the widening gap between herself and her husband, and to fulfill her promise to Onconecaw to visit his country, Elizabeth rode with Jon up the narrow path along the Saluda River to Ninety Six, as the junction of the Creek and Cherokee paths was now widely known. Two days good riding brought them to the village of Gusti after a stop at Saluda Old Town to survey a grant of a hundred and twenty-three acres for Major Hugh Butler. Thomas Brown was along, for he and Jon had at last determined to sew up what they considered the future center of Cherokee trade.

They were received at Gusti with mixed emotions. The little village had been decimated by smallpox. Cheulah had sent a delegation north toward Keowee to discuss possible amalgamation with another village farther from the widening fan of white colonization. To Elizabeth they were cordial; with Jon they were warily watchful but not openly hostile, for Thomas Brown, whom they respected, gave an odor of sanctity to the little mission. Darkness had almost fallen when they spread their bed rolls on the clay floor of the crumbling cabin that had been built for Sir Alexander. Elizabeth leaned tiredly against the door frame as she watched the red glow like a garnet ribbon that outlined the lofty, deeply blue mountains. How splendid they were! She didn't realize how intensely she missed the hills. It was so long since she had been able to see out, to look over a beautiful world. In Scotland the wild moors had ended suddenly in the cragginess of vast mountain heights cut by frothy streams as gossamer as a bridal veil. In America the mossy trees had smothered her in the humid dampness of the flat low country. At Saxe Gotha though the ground was undulating, the crowning, monstrous trees shut off her view of the azure Cherokee hills that now confronted her in the fading, steel-blue light.

With the dawn she arose filled with a strange excitement. The air was exhilarating. Dew laden leaves flashed like diamonds in the rising sun. The atmosphere was so clear that each tree stood out separate from its neighbor on the lofty beckoning hills. She wondered if King Arthur could have stood here when he saw the smallest stone on the farthest hill. Elizabeth drew in a deep breath of the winey air. What a glorious view to wake up to every morning! Could anyone ever be discouraged in this place? What of sorrow, or hatred or fear could follow one here? How could the Indians, with such a birthright, pillage, murder and burn? Perhaps that was why. Love of this beautiful country made hatred of the white interloper so intense that the Cherokee would stop at nothing to defend his mountain kingdom from the defiling feet of the Englishman.

She wondered if she could slip away unnoticed to explore the fascinating path. No one in the little camp had stirred. Today they were to watch the young braves at their games and fishing. Another time perhaps. Today she must be the appreciative and honored guest of a people who saw in her the image of her father, their friend. With the awakening day the mountain heights seemed to recede mysteriously. With the morning, clarity gave place to fuzziness behind shimmering walls of heat; she sighed. Perhaps they would be back with the evening coolness.

Perhaps Eleazar would join them today. She had advised him of their plans and while admiring her tact and diplomacy, he was a bit uneasy when she told him Jon would accompany her. Though Jon had no relish for the Indian festival, he was anxious to run off his new claim at Ninety Six. So he decided to humor his wife in her desire to become a diplomat, as he laughingly chided her. She accepted his taunts with good grace. She was ashamed of her feeling of relief when Eleazar promised to join them on his way to Charles Town from Keowee.

"Lady Cuming," she turned startled, by the hoarse voice, "I, Kanoona the Bull Frog, am sent to request that you break fast with Chief Cheulah."

Kanoona stood straight and tall. He had not looked at her as he spoke parrot like words.

"Why, thank you, Kanoona. My husband and I will join Chief Cheulah shortly."

Kanoona hesitated a moment then turned abruptly with an indistinguishable grunt of approval or disapproval, Elizabeth knew not which.

"Jon," she touched his sleeping shoulder lightly and spoke to him gaily. "We have an invitation for breakfast with Cheulah. I feel as if I were to attend the king's levee. Hurry!"

"Eat with those stinking red skins? Indeed I won't. It's enough to have to suffer them at my own board to satisfy you. This goes too far."

"Come now," Elizabeth chided gently, holding on desperately to her good humor and the thrilling feeling of the dawn. "We are their guests. We can do no less than accept their hospitality graciously."

"Save your graciousness for the halls of Windsor," he replied sarcastically; "you don't need it in these God forsaken wilds!"

The warning pulse began to beat in Elizabeth's throat but before she could reply Thomas Brown rolled over and stretched himself like a great bear. Scratching his wildly disordered red hair, now heavily sprinkled with white, he growled.

"Stop bitching, Fenwick, — pardon me, M'am," he apologized half heartedly. Pushing himself to an upright position, Brown caught at his back with one hand. "God, but I'm old!" He squinted at Jon with a jaundiced eye. "If I were that little woman of yours, I'd stick a knife in your ill tempered gullet before some savage beat me to the pleasure." There was no heat in his words, but Elizabeth beat a hasty and tactful retreat after one glance at the annoyed look on her husband's dark face.

To her surprise Elizabeth found the strange food delicious. The famous Powhicora, a white oily milk concocted from ground acorns, hickory nuts, and walnuts was served as a drink flavored with the ashes of burnt straw with dried turkey breast as bread. Jon ate nothing, a fact which did not go unnoticed, though Elizabeth talked brightly to cover up his truculence.

They witnessed a fast game of Chunky before seeking the creek for the fishing. A young brave cast a discus like stone of polished quartz. Bevelled on the edge it was concave on both sides with indentures for thumb and forefinger. Other young men, their shapely bodies glistening with bear's grease, cast ten foot poles after the chunky. The poles carried several marks and the score was determined by the vicinity of the bowl to the marks on the pole. There was much laughing and happy shouting among the contestants whose skill was amazing.

Failing to draw Jon from his heavy mood, Elizabeth found herself wishing Eleazar would appear. Though everything was done to please her, she noticed several sidewise glances at Jon from the cross legged Beloved Men of the village. But in the excitement of the fishing, she forgot her husband and found herself laughing and applauding as if she were a carefree child again.

The stream, called by the traders Ninety Six Creek, had been expertly dammed to make a deep fishing hole. Two oblique dams from each shore above the main dam lacked a few feet of meeting in the center. At a signal from Cheulah a score of screeching lads dashed down the stream from a point a distance above the trap and drove the teaming fish before them into the pool. Stopped quickly by brush, the oblique dams formed a barrier to prevent any canny fish from returning upstream. From the reservoir the youngsters now dipped hundreds of great carp, herring, trout, bream and bass. When they had retrieved all but the most agile, one of the watching men dumped a concoction of walnut shells into the clear water which immediately became cloudy. A moment later the remaining fish rose gasping to the top of the poisoned water and were quickly picked off by the fishermen to be eaten a short time later in all their roasted succulence.

Elizabeth turned to share a smile of appreciation at native adroitness with Jon and found that he had gone. She started up in alarm but was restrained by a blunt, beefy hand.

"Don't worry, Lass," whispered Thomas Brown. "Let him go. He's better off alone."

"But he may be —"

Brown shook his head in mock dismay.

"I don't know why you should be concerned, Lass, but I don't think they'd harm him while you're around." He looked admiringly at her face still glowing with the excitement of the game, "If I only had a face like that to worry about me —,"

She patted his arm and smiled her thanks at his gallantry.

Later that evening they were again gathered around Cheulah's great camp fire for an important feast. Bark platters were laden with whole roasted pig surrounded by juicy sweet potatoes baked in the coals. It was delicious and Elizabeth was eating heartily of the rich meat when it occurred to her to wonder why the Indians who ate no pork were serving it during such an important festival.

"The meat is delicious," she commented to Cheulah. "What is it?"

"Dog," replied her host and Elizabeth gagged.

Noticing her distress Cheulah hastily added, "Fear not, Lady Cuming. We eat not the flesh of our friend but another series of wild dog which does not bark."

Elizabeth trying desperately to control her heaving stomach, smiled weakly and turned desperately in search of a means of escape. She met Eleazar Wigan's amused eyes.

"It's not funny," she whispered furiously. "Get me out of here before I disgrace us all by being sick!" Her mouth watered painfully. Perspiration stood out on her forehead.

"You'd laugh at me, too, if I looked like that," he whispered back. Then more kindly, "Take it easy, Miss Betsy. Tain't no dog. Haven't you ever tasted possum before? It's good for what ails you providin' you don't take too much too often. From the way you were tuckin' it away when I first saw you, you've had enough for this season already!" Unable to control himself any longer he burst into great gales of laughter at her miserable face.

Embarrassment and annoyance both tempered her gladness to see Eleazar and settled her stomach. Her appetite was gone, however, and she pecked daintily at the rest of the feast. From that night on she approached with caution any strange new dish.

Long sunny days followed filled with displays of skill and feats of strength and courage interspersed with sacrifices to Yaweh, the one god. After the fire ceremony in which the women threw chunks of fat as an offering to produce good and avert evil, one of the war women danced around the canopy under which Elizabeth sat with the chief and poured a lap full of colored stones that to Elizabeth's amazement looked like amethyst, ruby, and aquamarine. Jon's acquisitive eyes snapped.

To Elizabeth the Green Corn Dance itself was a thing of breathtaking beauty. The glistening painted and feathered bodies moved in wild, savage rhythm to the sound of stiff fingers on clay pot drums stretched with wet deer skins. The finest choreographers of Europe could not have produced anything so fantastic and expressive of the thought of thanksgiving. Elizabeth sipped her Yapon tea without noticing its bitterness, so enthralled was she with the manly grace of the performers.

Races in forty foot long poplar canoes manned by fifteen men occupied the morning hours of the final day. These canoes hollowed by fire and European tools were surprisingly light and flew through the water with the swiftness of a frightened hind. The crowning hour of celebration started in the early afternoon. Children eight to ten years old demonstrated their skill at killing game birds with the sarbacan, a hollow cane through which a small dart was blown. Even the swift partridge was not proof against their skill. Next, the hunters came forward with their great bows seasoned in bear's oil and strung with bear's gut.

Cheulah announced in his loud, flat voice that their visitors, who had just arrived from the north, should participate in the contests. A small group of tall brown men stepped forward and flexed their bows.

"Nottawegas!" hissed Eleazar in Jon's ear.

"Who are they?" asked Elizabeth who had overheard.

"Hush!" cautioned Wigan. "They are troublemakers from up Canada way, claim they're cousins of the Cherokees. The Cherokees are afraid of them though they won't admit it. Watch."

A boy cast a burning pine knot high in the air. Necks craned. A bow string sang and the knot split neatly in two. A low sigh of applause swept over the group. Jon started up and nudged Eleazar. He indicated a group of three shackled Indians slinking in the back ground. Eleazar started when he recognized the three. They were a trio of the despised settlement Indians who lived a lazy, leech-like life on great low country plantations employed by the planters at various tasks.

"Sekakee! Sooreh! Akonettee!" cried Jon under his breath. "All Eveleigh's men."

Wigan nodded. "But hush, you're attracting attention." But before Eleazar could restrain him Jon had risen his face livid with anger and stalked across the contest ground to the three cowering slaves.

"What are these men doing in shackles?" he demanded haughtily turning to face Cheulah who had also risen. The two men, one red, one white, eyed each other with mutual hatred. The natural dignity of the red chief was enhanced by the angry rigidity of his arrow-like body.

"The white man forgets himself!" the chief's voice was coldly venomous.

"I demand to know why Mr. Eveleigh's people are taken into bondage by you," Jon fairly shouted.

"Here," the jesture was sweeping, "is the red man's land. In it the white man has no authority. He cannot demand."

"You thieving rascal," Jon threw the last vestige of caution to the winds. "Those men must be turned over to me instantly for return to their rightful owner!"

Eleazar sprang foward and tried to reason with Jon, to explain to Cheulah.

"Silence, Old Rabbit!" the chief spoke loudly. "This is none of your battle. Let this Anoah Ookproo —" he spat the epithet for renegade, the worst insult in the Indian tongue, "save himself this time. He has known the protection of a woman's skirts too long. Stand back." He swept Eleazar aside. The Nottawegas, understanding only Jon's belligerent attitude, closed in menacingly.

"Chief Cheulah owes you no explanation. These," he paused indicating the three slaves and searching vainly for a fitting name of contempt. He found none and made an obscene jesture that was adequate. "Our worthy cousins the Nottawega will take them as hunters and burdeners on the long trek north. There they will be disposed of fittingly." He raised his hand commandingly to silence an interruption. "You today have laid claim with your chain to lands that belong only to the Cherokee – not to your King George. Tomorrow you will find your stakes burned. With their going you must go, never to return!" He pointed to the south.

Elizabeth, who had sat frozen with horror through the episode now rose on trembling legs, and approached the menacing group around Jon.

"Chief Cheulah, please stay your anger. My husband's action was hasty and ill considered. Please let us go on with the contests." She attempted to draw Jon back to his seat with her. He jerked his arm from under her restraining hand and struck her full across the mouth. She staggered and looked at Jon, her eyes wide with disbelief. No one stirred but Eleazar, and Elizabeth stepped quickly in front of him as he sprang toward Jon.

Jon turned and strode off toward their camp.

Elizabeth walked as if in a dream to her seat under the canopy of State.

Cheulah stood before her bowing his body, an honor that an Indian seldom accorded any man.

"You are worthy of the name Great White Warrior given by my people to your father. What a pity we can no longer be friends." The ominous words cut into her confused consciousness as her trembling hand touched the angry red finger marks appearing on her white cheeks.

Eleazar would have killed Jon later had Elizabeth not warned him, as Cheulah had warned Jon, that he was invading territory in which he had no right.

"This problem is strictly my own. If you wish to help me and to continue our valuable friendship, you will forget what you saw."

Eleazar agreed reluctantly that the quarrel between man and wife was sacred but that the over all effect was much more far reaching.

"Why did the goddam fool have to stir up a stink over a trio of 'eaters of swine and dung hill fowl', as their own kith and kin call them. Even their names given long ago by their parents show they are worthless, Turkey Buzzard, Grass Hopper and One Eye! They are certainly no loss to Eveleigh." He snorted disgustedly and belabored his nose. "I don't know what to do next."

"I am certainly a miserable failure as a diplomat," Elizabeth said ruefully. "But surely, Eleazar, you don't believe they'll hold a personal grudge against a whole nation."

"It's more than that, Miss Betsy." Eleazar spoke more thoughtfully than was his wont. "You see, Jon represents to them all the wrong and injury they feel they've suffered from the white man. They fear, but they also hate deeply, implacably. Their friendship is only an expedient. Some day they'll quit quarrelling among themselves and fight us all together in one last death struggle. I'm sorry, Miss Betsy," he looked at her pityingly, "but it's men like your husband who'll bring it on. Goddam their souls," he cried bitterly as he left her to her unhappy thoughts.

After their meagre supper Elizabeth heard Eleazar's angry voice berating someone loudly. She went in that direction and saw to her dismay that Jon had released the captive Indians and intended to fight for them if necessary.

"You bloody idiot," Eleazar shouted, "Are you willing to sacrifice us all, even your wife, whom heaven knows you don't deserve, to your stupid vanity. These bastards aren't worth the powder and shot it would take to kill you."

"Shut up, Wigan, and leave my wife out of this. Don't forget I'm in charge here. I carry the justice of the peace commission, not you."

"Justice of the Peace!" Eleazar roared. "That's the most tragic joke I ever heard. And as for your wife, it's too bad you didn't think of leaving her out of it yourself. Her life was sanctified with these lunatic, red devils until you got hitched with her. Now her scalp's worth little more than your own, thanks to you."

Elizabeth retreated undetected and lay on her bed roll pretending to sleep while her thoughts raced frantically.

"What can we do now? How will it all end?" She asked herself.

Much later she was awakened from fitful slumber by Billy's excited whispers.

"Miss Elizabeth, look!"

She sprang to her feet and looked toward the village. The sky was aglow with a hundred pyres, the funeral pyres of the Cherokee village of Gusti which its inhabitants had put to the torch as they slunk into their mountain fortress, hatred burning in their savage hearts. The wild strange harmony of the war song floated back over their oiled and painted shoulders to the tiny group of white men listening, alone and inconsequential like ants in the loneliness of an uninhabited land.

Where'er the earth's enlightened by the sun,
Moon shines by night, grass grows or waters run,
Be't known that we are going, like men, afar,
On hostile fields to wage destructive war;
Like men we go to meet our country's foes,

Who, woman like, shall fly our dreaded blows;
Yes, as a woman, who beholds a snake,
In gaudy honor glisten thro' the brake,
Starts trembling back and stares in wild surprise,
Or pale thro' fear, unconscious, parting flies,
Just so these foes, more tim'rous than the hind
Shall leave their arms and only cloaths behind,
Pinched by each blast by every thicket torn,
Run back to their own nation, now its scorn.
Or in the winter, when the barren wood
Denies their gnawing entrails nature's food,
Let them sit down from friends and country far,
And wish with tears they'd never come so far.

Chapter Nine

Life went on. Not as usual, but it went on. Elizabeth often wondered how it could – but it did. The little colony, unaffected by Elizabeth's personal tragedy and untouched by natural disaster, took hope and grew strong. The woods rang with the sounds of many axes cutting back the possessive trees to enable wagons to carry the bumper crops of industrious Swiss and German farmers at Saxe Gotha to market.

The settlement of Georgia had added fuel to the smoldering feud between England and Spain. The governor at St. Augustine published orders that all runaway slaves from English colonies would be freed and protected. A number of Negroes escaped from Port Royal and reached St. Augustine where they were received with open arms and employed for wages. The resultant unrest alerted the Low Country but had little effect on the tenor of the lives of the more spartan Up Country inhabitants. Constantly on the alert against a potential red marauder, the Saxe Gothans had no time to pause in their labors to feel more than a fleeting sympathy for their aristocratic Tidewater brothers now beset with a black menace.

The first wagon train from Charles Town brought the Reverend Christian Theus and letters from Margaret Johnson. After the grateful population had bowed a thankful head for the first time with an ordained minister of God, Elizabeth turned him over to Stephen Crell who was to house him temporarily until adequate quarters could be provided. From Elizabeth's front porch the Reverend Theus had raised his hand in blessing to the eager crowd who gathered around on the ground below. The weather was fine as yet but there was a warning nip to the October night air. Elizabeth wondered where the new minister could gather his little flock, hungry for spiritual guidance. Her own little, piled stone house had the only large room in the settlement and it was inadequate. The great house that Jon had planned had never become a reality. Elizabeth sighed and supposed they could meet in Thomas Brown's store during the cold winter months. How thankful she was to have someone to relieve her weary shoulders of the weight of the personal problems of others. Since hers were the only sympathetic ears, she was constantly consulted and asked for advice. She felt her inadequacy and welcomed the guiding hand and broad shoulders of the obviously kind and courageous man.

She turned to Margaret's chatty, newsy letter. Though her words seemed to be spoken from a dream world, they took Elizabeth's thoughts for a short time from her own problems.

Betsy, My dear,

At last I have entered the dignified state of matrimony. It is wonderful and such fun to be the wealthy and much sought after Mrs. Henry Izard. Even Hannah stands in awe of me! The wedding was necessarily very simple because of the depression. Henry says we must have a new money crop, for over production of rice has been the cause of the pinch. Henry says the rise in freight rate and insurance is crippling. Henry thinks you are a very smart business woman. The tobacco you sent to Mr. Laurens for sale was an excellent and unusual quality. Henry says he realizes that your crop is as yet too small to warrant the expense of transporting it so far over tortuous, dangerous paths even in the ingenious horse drawn hogshead your carpenter contrived. He is willing to dispose of a small crop locally for you. He and Mr. Laurens talk constantly of the possibility of cotton.

The town is swarming with soldiers and all the young men are being called up for military duty. I suppose you have heard of the riots at Stono. A great Negro named

Cato gathered together a group of disgruntled slaves to lead them to St. Augustine where they were promised a regiment of their own, fine uniforms, and regular army pay. They entered poor Mr. Godfrey's house and murdered him, his wife, and his children, then set fire to his house. They found some rum, imbibed deeply and marched on singing and beating drums toward Jacksonborough forcing all Negroes in their path to join them. Mr. Bull was on his way from Beaufort to Charles Town and observed their peculiar behavior. Unobserved himself, he rode off the path and hurried to Charles Town where he gave the alarm. Mr. Golightly, on his way to church at Willtown, saw the rioters, now thoroughly intoxicated, dancing in a field. He rushed to the church and returned hastily with all the men, who go armed by law to church. They engaged the Negroes and quickly dispersed them. The leaders have been hanged but we do not sleep as heavily as we used to.

Henry says England will soon declare open war on Spain and then we will be isolated from home. The high seas are dangerous enough in peace time.

I see I have prattled on for pages about 'Henry says'. You will pardon a dutiful and devoted wife, I'm sure, for being so dotingly boring. The man who brings you this it the brother of Jeremiah Theus, the portrait painter who is the current rage in Charles Town. The ladies think he is fascinating, and simper like bleating sheep! Henry and I stood for our portrait and I think he's marvelous. He made me a raving beauty and my grandchildren will point with awe at their granny and will never know it doesn't look a bit like me!

I miss your letters. The few you've written lately are short and not a bit like you. Are you sick?

Elizabeth let the letter fall into her lap. She laid her head back and closed her eyes. The miserable events of past months paraded before her mind's eye.

After their return from the ill-fated trip to Ninety Six, Elizabeth tried unsuccessfully to make it seem as if nothing had happened. Jon sulked and drew completely into himself. He came and went, eating his meals in surly silence while Elizabeth endeavored to draw him into the conversation. Only to Billy and Clem was he friendly. Aunt Vadie bustled and chatted with a

139

cheerfulness she did not feel. She watched Elizabeth without comment and her heart was heavy. She made no effort to find out what had happened. Eleazar, finding one excuse after another to linger in Saxe Gotha, also respected Elizabeth's privacy and told her aunt nothing. Uncle Roy retreated more often to the river, taking his lunch with him.

After a particularly painful dinner, Elizabeth took her courage in her hands and spoke to Jon.

"Jon," her voice was low and husky. "This can go on no longer."

"And what do you propose to do?" he demanded, his voice heavy with bitter sarcasm.

"I? I can do nothing more. I have been willing to forgive your unpardonable behavior at Gusti. But you – you act as if you are the offended – I, the offender."

"Are you, then, in your pristine white tower guilty of no offense?"

"Guilty of what?"

"What right had you, a woman, and my wife to intervene in a matter where you had no place as if you were the nurse maid to a naughty child?"

Elizabeth looked at this angry man who was her husband. She realized that in her fright she had been presumptuous, overbearing and might have hurt his stiff pride. Engrossed in the narrow confines of his own ego, he was only concerned with what affected himself. Broader visions would have no meaning for him. His life was purely personal.

"I'm sorry, Jon. If I offended it was because I was so frightened for you."

"This is only one incident. Everyday in some manner you point out my inadequacy!"

"That is untrue! You are unjust," Elizabeth cried out.

"Unjust! There again I am at fault!"

"Oh Jon, Jon! Why must we quarrel so? What has happened to our marriage? Why we have not even met our least obligation," she spoke sadly.

"What do you mean?"

"In eight years of marriage we have no children."

"And, I suppose, there again the fault is mine?"

Stung to anger by his insulting tone, she flared, her cheeks blazing.

140

"No, the fault in this matter is obviously not your own."

"Obviously?"

"Billy —" she would have called her words back if she could have. Anger died in her. She looked at Jon. His face was drained of all color, his eyes incredulous.

"How long have you known?" his voice was almost inaudible.

"For years," she replied dully turning from him. "The resemblance is unmistakable."

"And yet you stayed." There was wonder in his voice.

"Stayed? Of course, I've stayed," a little of her spirit returned; "What else could I do?"

He stared at her back a moment before he crossed to her and placed his hands gently on her shoulders. She did not move. Drawing her back against him he laid his cheek on her lovely hair.

"I guess some where I lost the way. Will you let me try to find it back?"

"Yes, Jon," a tremulous sigh wracked her body. What else was there to do?

That year Frederick the Great of Prussia and Maria Teresa of Austria joined Louis XV of France in the ranks of the Grand Monarchs of Europe. Completely absorbed with their efforts to outdo the grandeur of Louis XIV's Versailles they let pass unheeded, like the gentle rustle of the first summer cicadas, the insidious awakening of that vague power, still blind and ignorant, the common people. Those grand monarchs, led by Louis XV of France, were themselves too unlettered or too absorbed to notice the seeping poison of the prolific literary men of the day: Swift, stern and lumpish; lovable Dr. Johnson in England; in France, Voltaire, that supreme mocker of all time, and Jean Jacque Rousseau sentimentally absorbed in idealizing nature and freedom. The disease of independence, slow and crippling to monarchy, spread to America and found fertile ground. What toiling, laboring, fear ridden pioneer had thought to give to the silks and satins and pampered pompadours of European kings? If they gave them any thought at all, it was with a derisive snort that such pimps would last in this rugged frontier land about as long as a lump of suet on a hot skillet.

For a time a new relationship founded on the gentleness of the first years of their marraige existed between Elizabeth and Jon. Elizabeth threw herself again wholeheartedly into the development of the now flourishing settlement and the cultivation of their own land. Margaret's mention of her husband's and Mr.

John Laurens' interest in cotton fired her imagination and she wondered if here was not the new crop of the future. The success of her tobacco had been too mild to warrant increase in its production. The lovely muslin gowns such as those she had brought with her were finding great vogue with the ladies, as were cotton cambric shirts among the gentlemen. The little cotton that she grew to mix with wool for the durable slave cloth made lasting garments for the white women of the frontier also. But the slow tedious work of extracting the seed limited the useful amount one could grow. She talked it over with Nat Hayne who had become a proficient and valuable carpenter.

Nat had finally married Nellie, not too reluctantly. Nellie had taken well and quickly to respectability. Removal of the chronic layers of dirt had revealed a handsome bold face with snapping eyes. Regular meals had filled out her crow-like figure. Her wild spirit, brought within bounds, became a boundless energy with which she bustled the live long day. No house was better run than the tiny one room cabin Elizabeth had ordered built for them near the overseer's quarters on the plantation below Sandy Run. Nat had supervised the construction, and the little cottage, as Nellie nostalgically called it, had fine features which had not as yet appeared in other rustic pioneer abodes. The hand hewn floor was in itself a luxury. But when Nat spent the long winter evenings sanding its splintery surface to a satin smoothness and rubbed it to glassy glossiness with beeswax of his own concoction, it was the wonder of the colony.

After Nellie caught the knack of weaving, she had Nat construct a larger loom on which she began to weave colorful rugs. Her fame even travelled to the Cherokee country and her more gaudy rags went into rugs which began to take their place as valuable articles of barter. Elizabeth felt a personal pride in their success and a little envy at their quiet content. Nat spoke little while Nellie prattled on over the busy clack of her loom during these evenings when they worked, each at his own task. Well fed, his every comfort attended, Nat was a picture of complacent well being.

For Elizabeth's tobacco, Nat had constructed a large barrel with an axle which was attached to shafts like those on a carriage. In this manner one horse could carry easily a hundred or two pounds of the leaf to market provided the hogshead did not strike a sharp stone in the narrow path and burst open, spilling its fragrant contents.

Now Elizabeth showed Nat a letter from her father describing a contraption called a Churka gin which he had seen in use in India many years ago. Nat read thoughtfully and then shook in his head.

"This wouldn't work, Mrs. Fenwick."

"Why not, Nat? My father says it has been in use in the East for centuries."

"Yes, M'am, but just look. Here, let me show you." They were standing in the shade by Elizabeth's fine stand of cotton which had just burst its first bolls and was spilling its snowy whiteness. Nat plucked a boll and pulled at the fleecy down. It held on to the tiny green seed tenaciously.

"See? It says here," he tapped the letter, "That the Indian machine is so constructed that the boll passes through rollers. That might do fairly well on the smooth black seed you brought here first from Charles Town to plant. It would never work on this upland cotton."

Elizabeth rubbed the sticky green seed between her thumb and forefinger. Their first crop had failed miserably and Elizabeth had not known why. Eleazar Wigan was the one who had shown her why. On his return from a long trip beyond the Catawbas he had brought her a handful of a dark seed completely unlike the ones she had grown at Whitehall.

"From Virginia," he said laconically. "Found growing wild there. The man I got 'em from said the kind you tried don't grow nowhere except near the sea. Try them."

She was touched by his thoughtfulness. In all her enterprises he had stood behind her either tacitly or actively.

"Why?," she had asked him once after a particularly thoughtful gesture.

"Wal, you are sort of a private experiment of mine." His eyes regarded her merrily from under his untidy brows. "I ain't never seen a woman behave like you. It's an improvement on the species. I just want to see if you'll last."

Elizabeth laughed gaily as he had poured the seed into her hand.

"With friends like you, I believe I'll last," she countered warmly.

The new seed produced a fine crop but it took one hand a week to clean four pounds of fibre from the seed. Nat looked thoughtful.

"I don't even see how this Churka thing works too efficiently."

"Maybe that's why cotton fabrics are still so expensive and their coolness only within the reach of the wealthy." Elizabeth sighed. It had seemed such a good idea.

"May I keep the letter, Mrs. Fenwick?" She thought she detected a quickening of interest in his voice. Had his fertile brain perhaps caught on an idea?

"By all means, Nat. It looks like large scale production of a substance which weaves into garments of such comfort and sheer beauty would have a great future in a country as hot as this," Elizabeth's voice had a wistful note.

"Perhaps, Perhaps." Nat's voice sounded as far away as his thoughts as he walked away slowly, clutching Sir Alexander's letter in his hand and forgetting to say goodbye.

Chapter Ten

Billy hung around the kitchen getting in everybody's way. He poked his finger into the bubbling muscadine juice being boiled into the ruby goodness of firm tart jelly. Screeching loudly he ran pitifully to Aunt Vadie who poked the blistered member impatiently into a jar of goose grease and demanded crossly.

"What is the matter with you, child? You've been underfoot all morning."

Hurt at the sharpness in Aunt Vadie's habitually gentle voice, he ran outside and soon had the chickens squawking amid flying feathers as they tried to escape his dead-eye aim with sharp pointed acorns. Nellie, who had taken over many of Aunt Vadie's duties and who had learned to marshal her forces as ably as her instructor, soon quieted the fracas by promising to box Billy's ears soundly if he didn't lose himself. Eyeing her respectfully but with obvious distaste, he retreated to the carefully tended garden where he painstakingly gathered a bouquet of varied blossoms with inch long stems. Proud of his civilized behavior he went in search of Elizabeth who, to Nellie's disgust, thanked him profusely.

"That boy is old enough to do his share of the work," grumbled Nellie. "He's always stirring up trouble. You're spoiling him rotten!"

"Now, Nellie," Elizabeth's eyes twinkled. "Hasn't Billy run his legs off this morning carrying water for you? Are you one to gainsay the healing effect of kindness?"

Elizabeth turned to Billy who with the years had grown almost as tall as she. He was as slender and straight as a sapling. His wiry black hair was close cropped above his piquant face whose startling resemblance to Jon had been effaced by deep pox marks. He looked at her solemnly, undecided whether to laugh or not. Elizabeth shook her head in mock dismay.

"You are too old for your naughty tricks. You are almost a man and must begin to behave with manliness. Tomorrow I shall give you regular employment — but, today," she smiled, "let's go hunting. I need some exercise."

The merry smile broke again, black eyes snapped. He dashed around the house.

"You shall ride Phoenix," she called. To Billy this was the perfect gift. He loved the little Chickasaw horse but to him Phoenix was a princess to be curried and combed reverently until her copper coat shone. With the passing years her gait had slowed but the aristocratic tossing of her magnificent head had taken on a stately dignity.

Gaily they trotted off up the path toward the Saluda River. Above the Geiger's was no man's land to Elizabeth. To her, whose friendship with Onconecaw had lessened her fear of his red brothers, the restriction was galling. She longed to be free to roam the beautiful forests now clothed in the brilliant garments of fall. Until today she had respected firm orders from both Jon and Eleazar. The noon hour found them at Herman Geiger's door.

"Good day, Mr. Geiger," Elizbeth called amiably.

She had never forgotten his gesture on the day Gavin had arrived to vaccinate them. His friends were few; he was regarded with distrust by all. His unruly tongue with its strong language kept him in constant hot water with his devout neighbors. Elizabeth privately thought that a little strong language might be as purging as a good spring tonic and had at times been tempted to try it. She suppressed a giggle when she thought of the reaction such conduct on her part would certainly elicit. Now the ill clad, unruly haired man came to his door. Twin brown rivulets ran from the corners of his mouth around his shaggy black beard. What few teeth he had showed yellow in the smile that broke the sourness of his deeply lined face when he recognized his visitor.

"Well, if it ain't, Miz Fenwick. It's right neighborly of you to call."

"We're just passing, Mr. Geiger, and stopped to ask how you are faring."

"Passing? You an thet boy surely ain't goin' no farther alone."

"Don't worry, Sir. We are both armed, and we shan't go far. We brought a nice lunch and want to go on an adventure, don't we, Billy?"

Billy nodded. He didn't like that smelly man much.

"I'd be proud if you'd share my pore fare with me. Tain't much for show but there's plenty."

"How very nice, Mr. Geiger, but we'll go on today. I promised Billy we'd lunch by the river. I see you're curing venison. Is the hunting good?"

"Just fair, just fair. The wolves is a nuisance this year. If you won't stay, wait a bit."

He hurred into his hut and returned quickly with a hot corn pone wrapped in a soiled rag. Billy eyed Elizabeth with unbelief when she accepted the gift as graciously as she had the fine fur cape from Onconecaw.

Geiger held on to the bridle a moment and spoke seriously.

"They's been some of them savages gliding up and down just off the edge of the path lately. They got no business here, and they ain't here for no good. Better not go fur."

Gratefully Elizabeth thanked him for his genuine solicitude and promised to take care. Herman Geiger scratched his bottom thoughtfully and spat expertly at a stalk of golden rod.

"There goes a woman!" He spoke with conviction and all the admiration his narrow soul allowed.

Elizabeth rode astride, a fact which annoyed Aunt Vadie and caused unflattering comment among the buxom women of the colony. Spending so much time on horseback observing the work in the fields, she found the heavy folds of her riding habit too restraining. One day, to the frozen horror of her aunt and the obvious admiration of the three men present, Jon, Eleazar, and Roy, Elizabeth had appeared ready to ride in a pair of Jon's breeches.

"Very sensible," commented Roy and retired precipitately to the river, his usual destination when he scented a controversy.

"Very becoming!" Jon and Eleazar said simultaneously.

"I declare, Miss Betsy. If I'd met you fifty years ago, neither you nor I would be in these hinterlands!" Eleazar guffawed loudly at his own humor.

Aunt Vadie recovered slowly but surely from the shock of the sight of her neice's slender figure with all its firm curves revealed so unashamedly.

147

"Elizabeth! This is disgraceful. I have put up docilely with your highhanded manner for years, but this I will not endure. Go at once to your room and attire yourself properly! Jon, you are outrageous to encourage your wife in such shameless conduct."

Elizabeth opened her mouth to protest.

"Elizabeth!" her aunt warned.

The tall girl, even taller seeming in her mannish garments, turned meekly and retreated to her room.

"It's a shame to waste all that beauty," Eleazar couldn't resist the taunt.

"Sir!" Aunt Vadie's voice was coldly formal. "It seems you two men are late starting whatever you have in mind for the day."

They retreated in defeat.

But on the return from his next trip far into the Indian country, Eleazar, careful to choose a time when Aunt Vadie was busy elsewhere, presented Elizabeth with a trickily contrived divided skirt of petal soft deerskin, beautifully fringed and beaded. A fringed jacket and soft wide brimmed skin hat drooped dashingly over her captivating face now sparkling with delight.

"Oh, Eleazar, it's beautiful. Where did you get it?"

"Oh, I have a copper colored wench up that-a-way," he waved indefinitely, "who supplies all my needs." He grinned wickedly.

"What shall we do about Aunt Vadie?"

"Don't you worry. I've brought a bribe."

He unfolded a long full skirted robe of the same soft skins. The skirt swirled in proper fashion. Where Elizabeth's riding habit was beaded, Aunt Vadie's robe was worked delicately with dyed porcupine quills concealing the joining of the skins. Its exotic beauty was breathtaking. A wide belt of dyed and plaited thongs was caught in front by a shell buckle.

"Oh-h-h! How lovely!"

The instant flare of disapproval in Aunt Vadie's eyes died quietly when Eleazar waved the gorgeous robe before her eyes.

"Well, all right," Aunt Vadie murmured weakly. "I'm getting senile and I always was putty in your hands. You're beautiful," she added as she watched the radiant face above the new outfit.

Jon added high, soft, red boots from Charles Town and Elizabeth was a colorful figure as she went abroad in her strange but striking attire.

Today the ride was pleasant in the brisk autumn air. For a few moments Elizabeth mused uneasily over the news of the slinking Indians. Why didn't Onconecaw come? She had sent word to him by Eleazar since the episode at Ninety Six that she would like to talk with him. Eleazar had never made contact with him. He was always farther up in some other mountain village. Wigan had been forced to send him word, and Elizabeth doubted that he had received it. Her Indian friend made no sign, and she was certain he would have sent some reply. Or, her spine tingled, had he too taken his stand against them under pressure from his tribe? Onconecaw's importance grew daily. Until now he had stood staunchly as an English ally. He was constantly reminding his people that they, now dependent on the colonies for former luxuries that had become necessities, could not strike the hand that fed them. But Onconecaw was still an Indian in whom ran the proudly savage blood of countless ages of wild free men. Blood was certainly a strong tie – but no, she would not doubt Onconecaw. He was honest and would warn her of any change of heart.

"Look!" Billy cried in a loud whisper.

They had turned off the Cherokee trading path at random toward the east and the river. Now in a small opening filled with a tangle of wild berry vines they saw a flock of wild turkeys. As yet unwary they pecked contendedly at dried berries and wild grass seed. Billy raised his musket. Elizabeth touched his arm.

"Wait," she whispered. "They're so beautiful."

The proud cocks strutted and preened their brilliantly colored feathers while dun colored hens ate industriously. Billy shook off her hand impatiently.

"Boom," roared his heavy gun and a gaudy cock twitched and lay still while his companions took to the air with a loud whir.

"Good shot," Elizabeth applauded.

"If these things," he indicated his heavy muzzle loading weapon, "could be loaded faster we could really bring in a batch." He tied the bird to his saddle and they rode on deeper into the woods.

The lunch was delicious, and Geiger's hot corn bread was the high point after they overcame their distaste at the soiled rag. Ravenous hunger, however, made them less fastidious and they devoured it all quickly. After lunch they rested their backs against great tree trunks idly watching big fish basking lazily near the surface of the clean, cold river.

The shadows were longer than Elizabeth realized when they started back. About half way between the river and path Billy sighted a fine buck. Taking expert aim he dropped him with one shot. Too late they realized that the tremendous buck was too large for the two of them to handle and darkness was coming on.

149

So much meat was too valuable to leave to the ravages of wild forest beasts who would soon get the scent of fresh blood.

"Billy, ride back quickly and get Mr. Geiger. He'll help."

Doubtfully Billy did as he was told, leaving Elizabeth mounted with loaded musket to guard their prize. But Herman Geiger, secure in rum sodden slumber, could not be aroused. Billy rode on the additional miles worriedly watching the sky take on the bloody reflection of the dying sun.

Elizabeth heard a sound and turned sharply. A great grey wolf looked at her with lowered head and blood shot eyes. A tremor of horror shook her. Could she detect others of his fellows in the deep gloom behind their leader? With trembling arms she raised her gun and aimed. She was a notoriously bad shot. Jon had spent hours on her, but she couldn't seem to get the hang of it. She fired. The wolf screamed in pain and anger as he shot straight up in the air. Landing catlike on his four feet he chased his tail frantically a moment while his brothers closed in snarling in their throats. Elizabeth now thoroughly frightened tried to urge her mount forward. The horse, himself terrified, stumbled on a sharp rock and fell, throwing Elizabeth against a young maple tree aflame with fall beauty. For a split second she was stunned, her breath knocked out. Gasping painfully she sprang to her feet and tried to reach the horse's reins. Wild with terror he crashed off through the woods.

Looking around for help Elizabeth's eyes rested on the flaming maple. The lowest branch was within reach and she grasped it with her right hand while she tried to retain the gun in her left. With the strength of desperation she threw her right leg over the limb as she had done in her childhood and pulled herself up, dropping the heavy musket in her haste. The hungry wolves closed in on the deer carcass and tore it apart savagely, fighting among themselves for the choice bits.

Elizabeth climbed shakily higher thankful for Eleazar's unrestricting garments. She clung to the tree trying to still her trembling, for she knew her fate should she fall. These gaunt, grey marauders were as heartily feared as the Indian. They roamed the woods in search of fresh meat, killing and spreading terror. Where on earth was Billy? She looked anxiously through he brilliant leaves of her fortress to a patch of fading sky. Darkness came quickly here. There was no long twilights as in Scotland.

Meanwhile Billy and Jon accompanied by O'Gilvie and Clem were dashing back up the path as darkness was closing in. Jon spared no words in berating Billy for their foolish conduct. Tears sprang to Billy's worried eyes and he missed the hardly visible path to the river. They had lost valuable time before he realized his mistake. Elizabeth's frightened mount dashed unseen out of the woods below them and headed galloping for the settlement.

"Surely you didn't come this far," Jon asked angrily incredulous.

Billy shook his head miserably. "I must have missed it."

"You crazy young fool!" Jon exploded and poured such vituperation on the lad's head that he became utterly confused. O'Gilvie would like to have interrupted and calmed the child for he knew that Billy was as familiar with the country as he was with the palm of his hand. Knowing Jon's mercurial temper he knew it was no use and suggested they all halloo as loudly as possible. Perhaps Elizabeth would hear them.

"And bring a whole lurking savage horde down on our necks?" Jon asked scathingly. "If this young idiot is right she is too far away to answer even if she heard."

A quiet figure loomed up below them on the path leading a horse.

"Onconecaw!" Jon cried.

"It's her horse," Billy shrieked.

Jon stared at Billy then noted for the first time that he was riding Phoenix. Fear gripped his heart.

"Where is my wife," he demanded of Onconecaw.

"That I know not," Onconecaw replied with cold dignity. "This frightened horse lamed by a deep cut on the right leg I secured just below here galloping in the direction of your settlement. Hearing your unwary noises, I presumed it was yours." Onconecaw cast his eyes around in the gloom. He pointed. "The animal obviously entered the path from that point."

"Yes," shouted Billy almost weeping with relief. "See that bent dogwood tree? That's the path."

Guided expertly by Onconecaw who noted every broken or twisted branch, they advanced cautiously. The satiated wolves, licking gory lips, lay in a crouching circle around the maple. The great grey leader on his haunches watched his prey for a false move, uttering intermittent throaty growls. Elizabeth staring fascinated with terror into the weasly, blood shot eyes wondered how much longer she could hold on. In the cramped position her legs had become numbed and her weight rested almost entirely on her arms.

Jon raised his musket to shoot but was stopped by a warning from the Indian.

151

"The Lady Cuming must be in that tree. The light fades. If you miss, the shock of surprise may cause her to fall into their midst. If so, I need not tell you what would happen before we can reach her. The leader must be felled with the first shot. The others will then flee, it is their cowardly nature."

While he had spoken Onconecaw readied his bow and arrow. Jon noted with passing surprise that he carried no gun. The Indian looked at Jon with a question in his eye.

"Shoot!" he commanded.

The bow string sang. The slender arrow reached its mark and the great beast collapsed after a wild yell of surprise and pain. In pandemonium the leaderless beasts fled into the covering darkness. Elizabeth slipped quietly to the ground unconscious but unhurt.

Chapter Eleven

The peace that prevailed for a time between Elizabeth and Jon proved only an armistice. Apparently Jon tried valiantly to conquer his weakness, but soon gave up again to abysmal depressions. His outbursts of unreasoning anger were not frequent, but Elizabeth soon discovered she would prefer them to the sullen silences that accompanied his despondent moods. At first she tried to treat them lightly and cajole him into good humor but soon the task was too taxing, and she was content to leave him to his melancholy while she went about her engrossing tasks. For a short while she had thought they might achieve a happiness of sorts. She used all her charm to fire him with her own dreams of the future when there would be good roads and schools, carriages, and fine homes. One day, seeing his mood grow darker, she even suggested they take a trip to Charles Town. The new road would make the journey not too taxing and she would like to see Margaret's new son, Ralph Izard. The town was hastily rebuilding after the disastrous fire of 1740. Margaret's description of the magnificence of the new mansions with their fire proof slate roofs made Elizabeth long for a moment to be a part of almost forgotten grandeur, to escape the primitive wildness that encircled her.

"Why should you want to go to Charles Town?" he asked bitterly. "To secure a doctor perhaps for your beloved colony of stupid Germans and filthy savages?"

Anger flamed within her and she realized that any attempt to take this weak man out of his own little nature was wasted effort.

"If you are so contemptuous of them why do you remain here? So far as I can see you have done nothing to benefit them or yourself."

She slammed the heavy door with finality as she left him. Her anger, which had flared often but dissolved quickly when her common sense prevailed, stayed with her and boiled helplessly within her. What could she do? Jon seemed bent on destroying any hope of happiness for them both. That evening she announced coldly that she did not wish any dinner but would seek her bed early because of a splitting headache. The headache was real enough but she secretly ate with relish the tasty dinner Blossom brought her. Blossom hovered wanting to talk.

"No, Blossom. Please leave me alone. I've got to think."

She tried to read but fidgetted uncomfortably against her pillows. Finally she settled down to an account of the controversy that had been raging in Charles Town. She had had some of it from Margaret's newsy letters. Commissary Garden had cordially invited another roving divine who followed the methodistic ways of the Wesleys to preach at St. Philips. The crowds that young George Whitefield gathered there as well as the mobs who awaited him on every street corner and every stop in his path, had perhaps piqued the commissary's jealousy. Twice he reprimanded the enthusiastic itinerant who paid him polite respect and continued to preach to thousands of bucolic followers without benefit of the *Book of Common Prayer.* Back and forth he roved on foot from Georgia to Maine preaching his gospel in a language the people of the frontier could understand until the enraged commissary had brought the wrath of the Bishop of London on his head and expelled him from the mother church. He hired Andrew Rutledge to defend him, which he did ably. But even Andrew's brilliant wit and clever tongue were not proof against the bigotry of church hierarchy. The day of his expulsion Whitefield was so busy preaching in the field for contributions to support his orphanage in Georgia that he forgot to attend the court. It all sounded sordid to Elizabeth but Margaret had supplied some amusing sidelights.

"In his rage," wrote Margaret, "at the enthusiasm of the evangelist Mr. Garden made a grave error that has caused many laughs at his expense. Taking a text that he forgot referred to harlots (don't let Hannah know I'm even acquainted with such a word. Are you?) and lewd people, he roared pompously, 'Those

154

that have turned the world upside down are come hither also.'
That was too much even for gentle Mr. Whitefield. He immediately
took up the gauntlet and returned the compliment by his text,
'Alexander the Coppersmith did me much evil; the Lord rewarded
him according to his works!' It's wonderful. I haven't had so much
fun in years. Henry says my glee over the controversy is unseemly,
and I replied that I had married him only to get away from such
comments by Hannah. He subsided because he says he thinks I'm
worth the trouble!"

Elizabeth smiled and leaned back on her pillows thinking of
Margaret's piquant, gay face. She prayed that nothing would
happen to destroy that sparkling effervescence. What could
happen? She had a husband she adored; the Elms was a gracious
home, and now they were blessed with a fine son.

A faint sound made her sit up. Her smile faded. Jon stood in the
doorway, his hair untidy, the muscles of his face slack. He swayed
slightly and the heavy odor of rum assailed Elizabeth's nostrils.

"What do you want?" she demanded coldly. She had never seen
him drunk before.

He smiled foolishly.

"What does a man usually want when he visits his wife's
boudoir, my dear?"

"Get out! You have no right here in that condition."

"No right? Can a mere chit tell a man his rights. Aren't you my
wife, or are you? Sometimes I wonder."

He lunged for her and enveloped her roughly in his arms
covering her with brutal kisses and seeking hands. His breath was
almost overpowering. Calling on the desperate strength that had
gotten her into the tree away from the great grey wolf, she pushed
with all her might. Unbalanced already by rum, he fell back
striking his head on the rough log wall. While he recovered from
the surprise and stunning blow, she sprang out the other side of
the bed and slipped quickly into a heavy robe. Before she could
pass to the door, he rose and lurched toward the bed which was
between them.

"You little wild cat! I like you when you're angry but you can
take it too far."

The sight of her usually fastidious husband in maudlin
drunkness was nauseating.

"Listen, Jon. You are drunk. Please get out."

"So now you want to run me off! You've never been a wife to
me – "

"You fool!" Anger conquered her fear for a moment. "I will no

155

longer be a sop for your weakness. I have never denied you anything. We could have had a good life if it hadn't been for the ferment within you that never let's you, nor anyone your life touches, rest. It's not love for me that makes you like you are. It's your own inadequacy that makes you so. You are always seeking something more — you get one thing, you want another. The only real love you have is for yourself." She was trembling violently.

"Now get out, before I call O'Gilvie and cause a scandal. You are no longer welcome here!"

His face was terrible as he stared at her. Her furious words had brought a certain amount of soberness. He understood them and they bit deeply into his soul like a searing hot iron. He turned and left closing her door without a sound.

A freezing chill seemed to take her body and she fell across the bed. She wanted to cry but no tears came. How long had it been since she had experienced the healing effect of weeping? A light hand touched her shoulder. She started up but a soft slurring voice quieted her fears.

"Don take on so, honey. Blossom'll look out fuh yuh."

Oh, dear, she thought. Blossom must have heard the whole disgraceful thing. Shame took hold of her. She cringed, shaking uncontrollably while Blossom, clucking softly, tucked hot salt bags at her feet. Shortly she brought her a cup.

"Drink it," Blossom commanded.

The reminiscent odor of rum struck her senses.

"Take it away," she cried.

"Drink it chile. It works both ways."

Blossom forced the liquid between her reluctant lips. Fiery fingers reached out all through her body. Taut muscles and nerves relaxed deliciously. She slept dreamlessly.

Next morning Elizabeth delayed her appearance as long as possible. Blossom brought her an inviting breakfast and announced without ceremony.

"Dey gone."

Elizabeth looked up, her mouth full.

"Gone? Who?" she asked when she could.

"Mistah Fenwick. He done tuk Clem and Billy."

"Why Billy?" Her eyes were alarmed.

"Don he allus go?" Blossom asked indifferently.

"Yes, but they were not to leave on this trip until tomorrow."

"Dey tuk de Cherokee path."

"How do you know?" Elizabeth's worry was increasing.

"Clem tole me foh he lef."

"Did he say why?"

"Naw'm. Jes say Mistah Fenwick say, 'Git ready en hurry!'"

"Oh, Blossom. He promised not to. He knows what a risk he runs. Mr. Wigan has warned him that there are Nottawegas as near as Saluda Town. They'll never forget what he did at Ninety Six. Their vengeance is awful." She covered her face with her hands.

Blossom looked at her in amazement. She couldn't understand the white mind. Had he been her man she'd already have planted a knife in his guts — and good riddance!

"What you care what happen to him? You know he ain' no good."

"Hush, Blossom," she spoke sharply. "You can't speak that way of Mr. Jon. I wouldn't want anyone to fall into their cruel hands. I don't want that to happen to him. Besides there's Clem and Billy. If anything happens to them it may bring on a war and we'll all be destroyed or driven out."

She dressed hastily and went to find Thomas Brown. If only Eleazar were here. What must she do? She knew the bitter vindictiveness of the Indian mind. The Nottawegas had been lurking nearby ever since the unfortunate freeing of the settlement slaves from their cruel hands. Elizabeth with the aid of Thomas Brown and Eleazar Wigan had finally persuaded Jon that going into the Cherokee country could serve no purpose and might bring bloody wrath on the settlement as well as himself. Thomas and Jon had swapped territories so to speak, Thomas to the Cherokees, Jon to the Catawbas with Eleazar accompanying him as often as he could arrange it. Eleazar shared Blossom's sentiments in a milder version, but for Elizabeth he would agree to almost anything.

Thomas Brown listened to Elizabeth gravely and shook his head.

"Sounds bad. I told that bull-headed young man not to take chances. Maybe the loss of his own skin won't hurt him, nor us for that matter," he said savagely. "But there's scores of folk here that oughten to have to suffer for his stupidity!"

"We must send for him."

"Who would go? You know, Miss Elizabeth, as well as I, that he is little more popular with the whites than the Indians. Who among these people would risk his life for a man who disregards their safety in his own personal pique? I, for one, cannot ask them to make such a sacrifice."

"But, Thomas, we must do something. Don't you see it's my fault that he's gone?" She conquered her shame and natural reticence enough to tell him that they had quarrelled and that she had sent him away. "Think of all the public services he has rendered, the many favors he has obtained from the governor and assembly. It is he who is responsible for our road, our minister, and the fact that we have been promised rangers for protection."

Thomas cupped her chin in his hand and spoke gently but definitely.

"We all know who is responsible for what advantages we enjoy. Though his hand may have written the petitions and his mouth may have made the pleas, we know you dictated them."

"Then do it for me."

"Do you realize what you're asking? Even Jon in his selfishness would not have it so."

"It's my fault that he's gone. If you won't help I'll go alone."

"If you try, I'll shoot Phoenix out from under you." He spoke angrily. "I'm surprised at you. You are not usually so emotional. Realism is the only attitude to take toward the frontier. If one man deliberately gets himself into trouble with the savages, he is expendable!" Looking at her bleak face, he spoke more kindly.

"Any fate he suffers is not your fault. It is the fault of the restless demon that continually devours him. You are over anxious perhaps. We don't know that anything will befall him."

"Eleazar was to arrive today from Keowee," Elizabeth grasped at a straw. "Perhaps he will bring them back."

"Perhaps," said Brown doubtfully. "In the meantime there's nothing you can do."

The day drew out interminably. Just at dusk Elizabeth saw two figures on one horse flying down the path.

Eleazar and Clem! Where were the other two? Why were they galloping? The horses almost ran her down as she rushed out to greet the two men.

"Clem! Eleazar! What happened? Tell me at once!"

Clem was almost speechless with fright. Eleazar looked stern. At the white man's prodding Clem unfolded the grim story.

They had left before dawn and had travelled at breakneck speed until they reached a point some fifteen miles short of the deserted village of Gusti where they paused a moment to rest. There fifteen Indians in full war paint stepped out of the dim woods and surrounded them. The savages were well armed with both guns and bows and arrows and were soon masters of the situation. Relieving the three of their guns and pistols, they mocked and taunted Jon by removing his heavy jacket in which one young brave paraded insolently. When Jon tried to use his hunting knife to protect his cap, which they removed from his head in spite of his resistance, a tomahawk had descended with expert aim on his arm, injuring painfully but not completely maiming. The Indians continued their insults for almost an hour until Jon finally told Clem to drive up their horses hoping they could be used as ransom added to the garments they had already taken, leaving Billy and Jon naked except for thin leather breeches. The Indians indicated that it was definitely no deal and promptly shot the horses so their tracks could not be followed. They then pointed out that the same fate awaited them if there were any more resistance.

Jon tried guile and elicited Clem's release to return to his wife. Clem, warned that any pursuit would mean instant scalping of the two prisoners, stumbled with fright back down the trail after the Nottawegas had driven Billy and Jon off northward on no apparent path that Clem could see.

The story had taken some time and a crowd carrying blazing pine knots had gathered by the time Clem delivered the bloody tomahawk and Jon's neck kerchief into Elizabeth's horror stricken hands.

"Poor Clem" she mumured.

"Miss Elizabeth, I don de bes I cud to keep him frum goin' dat way but he don act lak he crazy. I don know whut got in him. Now look whut don happun," Clem was weeping now with fright, reaction and concern for his master.

"Thank you, Clem. I know you did your best. Go tell Blossom and get something to eat." She patted his quivering shoulder kindly.

For a moment no one spoke while the seriousness of the situation sank in. No one doubted what Jon's fate would be. After exquisite torture, in which the Nottawegas were practiced masters, he would be put slowly to death that they might enjoy his suffering fully. Some had witnessed and all knew by reputation the horror of Indian vengeance. They shuddered. Though Jon was not loved by any, not one of them would have wished such a fate on his worst enemy. And Billy! Poor little Billy, just a pawn in this ruthless game. Everybody loved Billy. What was there to do? Elizabeth put their thoughts into words.

"What shall we do? Eleazar, help me!" She cried out in anguish. "I can't let this happen to him because of me."

"Poor lass," he looked at her proud head now bent in sorrow. "It's a rough game we're playing — and those fellows," he hitched his wiry grey curls toward the north, "play for keeps."

He looked around and finally made his decision. "Get me a fast fresh horse. I'm going to see King Crow at Keowee. I've an idea they headed that way by another route. There were others of their tribe hunting there last week."

"No, Eleazar you can't start out at night alone!"

"It's better alone. Don't want to seem like a war party, just a private diplomat," he laughed grimly. "I'd better get gone before the news travels too far and these Nottawegas take off for home. You advise the Governor, Miss Elizabeth, and try not to worry. I'll keep in touch." He was gone before she could ask him about Onconecaw.

Eleazar Wigan watched the old crone with weary fascination. She must be over a hundred, he computed idly. The face hung in loose wattles like a bag of tripe. Eleazar figured her skin would hold three carcasses as scrawny as hers. She tossed some canes on the fire. It spluttered and flared, revealing the hawk like face of King Crow of Keowee who was smoking placidly, eyes closed to a narrow slit. The four foot long pipe stem was sheathed in a beautiful speckled snake skin adorned with feathers and strings of wampum. He puffed a few whiffs first toward a point indicating the sun, then toward the four cardinal points, then over the breast of his guest after which he handed it to Eleazar as ready for his use. The weary trader puffed as required by courtesy and passed it on to Ludovick Grant on his right. All of two nights he had ridden, and part of this day. At Keowee his relief when he found Grant, a fellow trader equally respected by the Indians, almost overwhelmed him.

"The coat, jacket, and hat were brought in today," Grant told Wigan when he heard the tale. "I recognised Fenwick's hat."

"Where are they?" questioned Eleazar eagerly.

"They refused to reveal their whereabouts."

Now they waited for the chief to indicate that he was ready to confer.

"The Old Rabbit honors us with his presence. We had not expected him again so soon." The mild statement was a question easily translated into Eleazar's own language to mean, "Why in the devil are you here?"

Eleazar spoke, choosing his words carefully.

"King Crow will remember that he and his people are pledged to keep the white trading paths to your nation clean." He paused.

"Well?" King Crow's voice indicated only polite interest.

"Not your people, but cousins of yours, whom you entertain as friends in your country, have abused your hospitality. They hold prisoner two of our people taken on the path two days ago."

King Crow's grunt Eleazar interpreted as meaning, "So what?"

"You must tell the Nottawegas to release them or the Governor in Charles Town will be displeased with his good red brothers."

King Crow was silent so long Eleazar thought he intended no reply. Finally he spoke reasonably as if to a child.

"The Nottawegas are dreadful people. All we can do is ask them to release your friends. I will offer them two scalps in exchange."

Eleazar could not suppress a snort of disgust. He looked to Grant for support.

"If you allow these Englishmen to be harmed the great Governor may cut off your trade. Then what would you do."

King Crow indicated delicately that there were always the French. His face and manner betrayed not the least concern.

Eleazar and Grant held a whispered conference.

"Mr. Grant and I will offer a hundred weight of leathers if you will send a strong party to release our brothers — five times as much to those who should bring him home," he added desperately unable to read the stony face.

"King Crow will stir in the matter — but not until our cousins the Nottawegas who have taken the warpath to the Catawbas have returned." He spoke with finality which no amount of persuasion or threat could change.

Defeated, Eleazar returned to Saxe Gotha leaving the affair momentarily in the hands of Ludowick Grant. Wigan hated to face Elizabeth, but when he did, her face was calm and resolute. If necessary she would go personally to Charles Town to see the governor.

Charles Town
South Carolina
March 22, 1742

Stephen Crell, Esquire
at the Congarees
Sir:

I am very sorry for what has befallen Mr. Fenwick, and the consideration that he was upon many occasions useful and serviceable to his country makes my concern the greater. I am afraid that this affair may have disagreeable consequences by intimidating the people of your parts whose fear of Indians has been but lately dispelled, and there may be also some reason to apprehend that it may embolden these French Indians

161

to venture near our Settlements. In both cases I must recommend to you to keep up the spirits of the people in your parts.

I hope likewise that you will endeavor to comfort Mrs. Fenwick and assure her that nothing shall be omitted for Mr. Fenwick's safety and assure her also that she shall find in me a friend.

I am, Sir, your most humble servant,
William Bull, Lieutenant Governor

Stephen Crell sighed. Words, words! Was this to be the only answer. The people of Saxe Gotha were genuinely alarmed. Had the Indians not taken two of their own with impunity? If the Assembly were as lackadaisical in their efforts to obtain Mr. Fenwick's release, what then was any colonist's hope of protection from a government who did not seem to consider this frontier settlement as one of its integral parts?

Crell wiped his brow and looked at the glassy blue sky. It was unseasonably hot for March. Plowing and planting were already underway. A man, weary with the monumental toil of the day, needed nights free from fear for deep and dreamless sleep. Knowing heads predicted a long, dry summer and were urging haste in order to have a mature crop before the burning drought that they said was in the offing.

Later that evening after a satisfying supper Stephen Crell took up his quill. He chewed its tip thoughtfully a moment before he wrote,

Saxe Gotha
March 27, 1742

The Honorable William Bull
Lieutenant Governor
Charles Town, South Carolina
Your Honour:

Thank you for yours of the twenty second instant. The courier arrived without incident but much exhausted by the speed of his journey. By the same hand I send your Honour this reply.

As Your Honour has taken note there is much unrest here occasioned by the capture and retention of Mr. Fenwick. All efforts by ourselves and the traders have been to no avail and these savages have need of a

162

*stronger hand than ours to restrain them. Mrs. Fenwick,
who has hitherto enjoyed the respect and admiration of
the Cherokees because of the efforts of her father — of
which you must be aware — has been in contact with
the young warrior Onconecaw, now known as
Chuconnuta, who was one of the Cherokee mission to
London in 1730. This Cherokee warrior has been steady
in his regard for the English and in personal friendship
with Mrs. Fenwick whose courage and fortitude he, as
well as her fellow settlers here at the Congarees, greatly
admires. He has promised to do what he can to affect
Mr. Fenwick's release, but we hear that he is himself in
danger of losing the faith of his own people if he
continues to endorse the English cause so strongly. The
incident of Mr. Fenwick's release of Mr. Eveleigh's
Indian slaves is of course only an excuse to harass our
own settlements. We are fully aware here, if you are not
there, that the Nottawegas are in French employ and
were sent south to stir up trouble among our erstwhile
friends, the Cherokee.*

*There is much pilfering of our hogs, chickens, and
stock. Our wheat fields are unnecessarily trampled by
the Indians trafficking at Brown's Store who pretend
not to understand our protests. We have neither men
nor ammunition to do more than protest verbally.
Several days ago thirty-seven Indians stopped at Mrs.
Fenwick's house and stayed for hours. They were very
insolent though she prepared an excellent repast for
them. They took great freedom in wandering about and
several articles were missing after their departure. Mrs.
Fenwick showed courage and tact in handling an
impossible situation. She inquired after her husband.
They professed ignorance of his health and
whereabouts, and pointed out that they had no hand in
his enslavement. Using amazing self control, Mrs.
Fenwick in turn pointed out that he was being held in
their nation and they, the Cherokee, would suffer loss
of face and confidence with the government in Charles
Town. They blandly replied that if Mr. Fenwick were in
their nation they were ignorant of the fact.*

*I respectfully submit that we are in great need of a
fort and a regiment to man it. The suggestion by the
Assembly that we build and man our own fort with*

money supplied by them is hardly feasible. One man cannot build, spy, drill, and work for a living in the meantime. Some of our settlers are planning to remove themselves and families unless there is some immediate show of protection from the government. I am certain that Your Honour, as well as I, will agree that this will be regrettable, for the removal of the colony will mean the removal of the first line of defense enjoyed by the people of Charles Town. Also respectfully, Sir, I submit that for the great service that Mrs. Fenwick has rendered her country in her every effort toward the success of this place, she deserves more consideration.

*I remain, Sir
Your obedient servant*

Stephen Crell

Stephen sighed again as he reread this long epistle. He was more adept, he felt, with his hands than with his words. The new responsibility weighed heavily on his shoulders. He was no diplomat and chafed at the senseless, stilted courtesy of the day. The pompous fools! He'd like to erase all those empty words and rephrase his petition in such harsh language that the well clad gentlemen of the Assembly would sit up aghast from their lolling in delicately carved chairs while the savage hordes above the defenseless settlement at Saxe Gotha prepared to sweep over the countryside, leaving death and destruction in their path. A firm, immediate policy of action might stem the tide –. Useless, dreaming thoughts. He folded the letter impatiently, snuffed out his candle and walked heavily to his hard bed.

Some hours later Elizabeth, who slept now just below the surface of consciousness, came sharply awake. Had she heard some noise? She experienced a strong feeling of alarm. She lay still, ears straining. The spring air was filled with the thin croaking of tree frogs calling for rain. Why had she awakened so suddenly? Under the puny din of the frogs she had heard some noise. She tried vainly to recall it to her conscious mind. One by one the fretful frogs hushed their cries and a stealthy silence drew in. The feeling of alarm grew so intense that Elizabeth rolled over cautiously so as not to cause a rustle in her mattress. She slipped softly to the floor and began to crawl toward the open door. The night was close.

164

The two wooden windows of the bedroom were flung wide to allow a draft through the open living room door. Why was she crawling, she wondered? What was the nameless fear she felt? She stopped and looked over her shoulder toward the window. There it was again! A faint, formless noise. She felt a prickling at the roots of her hair and under her armpits. Cautiously she inched forward, feeling the need for more haste. A stream of moonlight lay on the living room floor and she tried to avoid its brilliance by crawling behind a chair and under the table. Finally she reached her aunt's room and crawled in. Tugging on her light bed covering she whispered into Aunt Vadie's ear.

"Don't make a sound! There's something wrong, I don't know what. Wake Uncle Roy, quick!"

Aunt Vadie awakened her husband who lay unmoving while he listened to her soft explanation. Neither questioned Elizabeth's fears. They all lived subconsciously prepared for that awful night when they would be called from their beds to meet they knew not what savage horror.

"I'll send Clem to alarm the others," Roy was drawing on his clothes as he crouched in a dark corner uninvaded by the brilliant moonlight.

"No, no," Elizabeth whispered. "You'd better go. He would surely be detected!"

"And leave you two here along?" Roy was aghast.

"Go on, Roy. Blossom and Clem can stay here with us. Elizabeth's right. That clumsy oaf would never get there." Vadie looked at her husband a moment. How had this delicate man who loved comfort and ease survived the hard years of life on the frontier? His slight frame had hardened into withe-like wiriness; his eyes were deeply thoughtful. Vadie threw her arms around his neck. "God bless you, Roy."

He held her a moment closely.

"God keep us all, my dear." He was gone without a sound.

Elizabeth had aroused Clem and Blossom. She silenced the man's frightened exclamation by quickly stuffing the folds of the coverlet into his mouth. They crept into the living room careful to avoid the stream of moonlight. Sliding toward the gun rack, Elizabeth heard a slight noise. From her crouching position she raised her eyes to the big door leading onto the porch. The latch was easing its way up. She watched for a split second frozen with horror until she saw the door move a fraction. Without further thought she dived across the floor and threw the whole impact of her flying body against the heavy door. An unsuspecting

165

moccasined foot was wedged firmly between the heavy door timbers and the frame. Before its owner could recover from the surprise counter attack Aunt Vadie, Blossom and Clem had added their weight to Elizabeth's. An unpleasant crunching sound resulted.

"Quick, Clem! Get the axe. Too late for guns!"

Clem, forgetting his fear in action, sprang to the kitchen and returned in a flash with a heavy, two edged axe. Elizabeth grasped it from his hand and brought it down with all her strength on the squirming red foot. A howl of rage and pain rent the still night air. Echoed by a dozen red throats it became the dreaded war-hoop. But the drama of surprise attack and counter-attack was not yet played out. Flinging the door open Elizabeth flashed pass the hopping, howling savage in the direction of the great alarm bell atop a tall cedar post near the gate. Her loose night shift flying behind her, her flowing hair catching fire in the moonlight made her a sight not forgotten by red man or white for a generation. Unconsciously still clutching the heavy, now bloody, axe she grasped the bell rope and pulled with her remaining strength. Whether this wild apparition or the instant musket fire of the aroused Saxe Gothans put the red marauders to flight was a moot question for years to come.

Later, in his florid accounts to anyone who would listen, Clem produced a gruesome relic at just the right point. Chuckling softly he remarked it was as lucky as a rabbit's left hine foot!

Chapter Twelve

The heat was intolerable. Jon strained at the thongs that held his hands, palms outward, extended above his head. That only increased the pain by making the thongs cut cruelly into his wrists. The change in him was startling. Worn by the unbelievable heat of fast forced marches and the unaccustomed half raw fare, Jon's body had melted away to hardened, leathery skin stretched tightly over aching bones. Constant harassment by incidental and preliminary torture had lined his face deeply and his raven dark hair was streaked with white. He tried to wipe the itching sweat off his bearded face by rubbing it against his bare shoulder. The movement tortured his benumbed arms. At the moment, he thought he would even welcome his tormenters. Anything was better than being strung up like a pig to be gutted.

Where was Billy? He tried to look around. The movement brought his neck into painful contact with a thorn studded halter which held his head close to the post to which he was secured. So far their captors had not inflicted any physical punishment on the boy whose merry smile had not returned to his pox marked face after the first "game" he had been forced to witness with Jon as its prize. Thus trussed, Jon had been the target for unerring Indian arrows that flew from practiced bows to strike the post between his fingers or to sear the flesh delicately, wounding painfully but not maiming. When the men had finished their sport he was turned over to the women who cauterized the wounds on his flinching body with flaming pitch covered sticks. He wondered how much more his crippled body could stand. Not much.

He had tried diplomacy at first. That had failed completely. The Nottawegas who were from the north could not be threatened by cessation of trade with the English for they trafficked with the French on the Mississippi and in Canada. They had no need of, and were contemptuous of, the English.

"Then why do you bother with me," Jon pointed out. "I am no good to you as a hostage. You have nothing to gain from my government."

"Should your government stop its trade to the Cherokee they will be forced to enter the French trade. That is our mission," they replied slyly.

"On the contrary, your cousins the Cherokees may become so annoyed if our trade is stopped at your fault, they may take to the warpath against you."

Since this argument was too logical, they pretended not to understand the raving white crow of a man.

Jon had turned from tact to vituperation. He had cried out his scorn and hatred of their whole filthy race. Undaunted by their vicious tortues, he had shouted in anger to hide the cries of pain that welled up. The savages were more impressed by this behavior. Interpreting it as the courage they tried to instill in their warriors they accorded him some extra comforts and even left him free of torture for several weeks, free of all torture, that is, except the hard marches in the relentless heat over cruel stones. His shoes had long since worn out. Now he presumed they were going to start their tortures again.

But no, suddenly he was released and slipped to the ground unable to stand on his numbed legs. Preparations were being made for departure. He wondered at this sudden change of plan. Was someone on their trail perhaps? He felt a faint glimmer of hope. His captors indicated that he was to move. He refused to budge. They forced him up but he immediately crumpled to the ground when they released him. His legs were really useless. He looked at them dumbly. He had meant to fight a delaying action to gain, he hoped, precious time. He had not expected this help from his scrawny legs. He was prodded painfully from right and left then hastily dumped into a makeshift stretcher of skins and the wildly hasty passage northward continued. The blazing, relentless sun struck Jon with the force of a physical blow and he closed his eyes against its molten fury. He either fainted or slept.

Chapter Thirteen

"Do you wait upon the Lord, my sister?"

Elizabeth looked up into the happiest black eyes she had ever seen. They gazed out of a kindly pale face at the young woman lying prostrate on the ground. Elizabeth sprang to her feet and tried to cover her embarrassment. In her misery she had not heard anyone approaching. She had sought the solitude of the forest near by to hide her disappointment at her last letter from the Governor. Months had passed since Jon's capture, months of meaningless messages back and forth up and down the road from Saxe Gotha to Charles Town, courteous pleas on the one hand, empty promises on the other. The latest communication from the governor was now crushed in her hand. It read:

> Madam,
>
> I am sincerely sorry for the unhappy accident that has befallen Mr. Fenwick and you. Be assured that I shall take every proper measure of serving him to the utmost of my power. I have written to all the governors to the Northward and likewise to the French governor should Mr. Fenwick be carried among them. I think you have little reason to doubt but you may see him soon back at his home which I assure you is my hearty wish.

169

In the meantime you may rely upon my firm friendship in everything that I can be useful to you.

Your most humble servant,
William Bull

To Mrs. Fenwick
at the Congarees.

"What do you mean?" Elizabeth endeavored to tidy her dress and hair.

"You seem in deep distress. Do you not know the great words of Isaiah the prophet? 'But they that wait upon the Lord shall renew their strength; they shall mount up with wings as eagles; they shall run and not be weary; and they shall walk, and not faint.' "

The beautiful, resonant voice was so eloquent, the gestures of this austerely clad man so graphic that Elizabeth unconsciously looked toward the sky to follow the flight of the eagle. Such a feeling of peace seemed to creep over her in the stranger's presence that for a moment she forgot to question the arrival of an unknown dusty traveller from apparently out of nowhere.

"Who are you?" she finally remembered to ask.

"George Whitefield, Madam, at your service through our Lord Jesus Christ."

"Mr. Whitefield!" she cried. "Your fame has travelled before you, Sir. But how come you to these isolated parts afoot?"

"Shall we sit down and rest a moment? I think we are both spent, I physically and you spiritually."

"But, Mr. Whitefield, come let me offer you refreshment."

"Nay, later. A moment to relieve my weary legs. They have done me good service today." He looked at them ruefully. "However, they also need encouragement from Isaiah at the moment." He laughed heartily as he pointed to the holes in his thin shoes.

"Now," he said, "can I be of service to you?"

Elizabeth found herself pouring out her story to the sympathetic ears of this understanding stranger in the wilds of the Carolina back woods as if he had been her father confessor for life. All the bitterness she felt toward herself whom she held entirely responsible for Jon's plight tumbled out. She told him how she realized too late the fact that she had failed her husband in many ways, that she might have helped him to over come his weaknesses.

170

" 'Tis true," Whitefield's forceful voice was deep with pity. "We humans fail each other constantly in a world of weal and woe. But you reproach yourself unduly. Each man is responsible in the end for the salvation of his own soul. There are man-made and God-made laws that we all know. If we break these laws we must suffer the consequences. Though one can do no greater service than to lay down his life for his friend, and I am confident you would do this gladly for your husband, he cannot hold himself responsible if that friend knowing the nature of wolves deliberately casts himself among them."

He looked at the lovely face now filled with distress where the fine marks of worry and sorrow were lightly etched. It was a fine face more beautiful in maturity, still, in spite of heavy disappointment, filled with an eagerness for life with all its great adventures. Ah, the wilderness could not hold its own against many such as she, thought Whitefield. Such are the foundation stones of a great nation.

Both felt refreshed by the encounter and soon rose and walked slowly toward the settlement. George Whitefield told Elizabeth of his journey on foot from Philadelphia where he had preached daily to thousands of eager listeners. He was now hastening to his orphanage family in Bethesda, Georgia with the fruits of his labors for their sustenance.

"Will you stop again in Charles Town," Elizabeth asked.

"By all means!"

"But where shall you preach?"

Whitefield's eloquent gesture indicated the molten sky, the great trees, their leaves now limp and lifeless.

"There is a tabernacle on each street corner and under every tree. Did not Jesus himself preach his greatest sermon on the Mount? With no walls to confine him, the little meannesses of mankind dissipate into thin air when there is fellowship."

Rev. Christian Theus welcomed the evangelist with open arms and gathered his little flock to hear Mr. Whitefield speak. They hastily threw up a protection of poplar poles and oak branches against the merciless July sun. Seated on the ground or stumps and leaning against the trees they heard avidly and hungrily the words of hope from the plain man with the beautiful voice and dramatically expressive movements. By parable, as had the Master he followed, he unfolded the lesson he wished to impart. His listeners leaned forward spellbound and followed the progress of the blind man tapping his guiding cane along the sheer precipice. The speaker guided him so realistically near the edge that one of his listeners cried out suddenly,

"Look out! He's going to fall!"

A sigh escaped the tense audience as the man looked around foolishly, embarrassed color mounting his thick neck.

"Just so, Friend," called Whitefield to him, "is the road of life. 'Look out lest ye fall' should be the motto of us all!"

The feeling of hope and courage that Whitefield left with the little colony at the Congarees sustained them through the gruelling heat and drought that dragged on endlessly. On July fifth a large Spanish fleet entered the St. Simon's harbor in retaliation against General Ogelthorpe's abortive attempt against St. Augustine. The news caused hardly a stir in isolated Saxe Gotha. August and September blazed into October burning the crops to a crisp, shrivelling the gushing streams to mere threads and forcing Saxe Gothans to slaughter their cattle for a glutted market to keep them from starving.

Chapter Fourteen

Blurred faces swam into Jon's returning consciousness. Moccasined feet prodded him painfully.

"Go away. Let me sleep. I'm tired."

He wondered vaguely why his bedroom was full of people. That wasn't like Elizabeth. She was always so thoughtful of his comfort. How tired he was. He must have travelled too far in his over anxiety to get home. He tried to turn over. God! What's wrong with my legs? I don't remember having hurt them yesterday. The pain brought him to the surface of consciousness. Indians! What the hell are those filthy devils doing in my room? Now that is overdoing it a bit! He'd consented to let his wife coddle the pilfering fiends by having them dine at his table, but he'd be damned if she could bring them into his boudoir.

A ghastly smile split the death's head lying on the litter in the Ohio woods. The cluster of prodding redskins watched the frame of what had been a man shake with inaudible glee.

A fine line of worry added itself to the myriad wrinkles that made the emaciated face look like the dried, cracked mud in the creek bottoms. Jon shouted for his manservant. Clem!

Billy, watching the ugly scene in stupefied horror, saw the man's lips move and form a word. The cords in his gaunt temples stood out with the effort. For weeks they had zigzagged,

173

unmindful of the awful heat, toward the northwest, forced to carry Jon, now delirious, on the litter. Some of the younger men had grumbled because this retarded their hasty trek toward the haven of French protection in the land around the Ohio. Billy had sat shuddering while whispered conferences took place. Since this shrunken skeleton could afford them no more entertainment, what use was he to them? His scalp would serve as well. Their supplies were exhausted and the parched countryside yielded them nothing. The problem of water became daily more serious. Billy knew that if they disposed of his companion his turn as object of their fury and scorn would surely come. He wondered if the tortures they would inflict on him would be any harder to bear than the slow murder of his idol that he had been forced to witness day after day for months.

"Mr. Jon!" he whispered urgently into the ear of the thing that lay on the ground near him. His captors had left Billy securely staked to the ground while they retired for a conference to decide on their next move. The grumblings of the young men could no longer be ignored. They had reached the Ohio River and a great harvest moon was rising. They were all anxious to get to their villages to prepare for the first hunt. Some day soon this heat must break. There would be rain, cold, and snow. At the rate they were travelling winter would overtake them. They had stretched their luck far enough. Billy edged nearer and put his lips against Jon's ear.

"Can you hear me?" Jon stirred.

"Clem?" he formed the word but no sound came.

"No, its Billy. Please, Mr. Jon, you've got to hear me! It's the river, we're there." He shook Jon desperately, watching the quarrelling group of Indians cautiously.

"Billy!" Billy had to put his ear almost against the cracked lips. "I didn't call you," the whisper was peevish. "Send me Clem to clear out these fool savages!"

With their arrival at the river a hope born of desperation had risen in Billy. At night the Nottawegas had ceased to guard their captives. The man was too helpless to escape, the boy too weak to try it alone. If they could only slip to the river perhaps they could swim or glide far enough to elude their captors. Billy surmised that after the first fury of anger when their escape was discovered he and Jon would not be thought worthy of pursuit. The young warriors, hot to be home, would not hear to it. What they would do for food once they were away, Billy thrust from his mind. To escape was all important. He'd figure something out when that was

174

accomplished.

He now looked with dispair at the raving man beside him. Could he manage him? It looked hopeless, but the thought of leaving him never entered the youngster's head. The desperation in his voice must have penetrated the fog of Jon's mind. His eyes opened and he regarded the boy with a ray of intelligence.

"Yes."

"The river! Could you make it tonight if I helped you?"

Jon tried to touch the boy but the effort got no farther than the thought of it. The attempted smile was ghoulish. Billy's stomach quivered in horror and despair.

"No, Billy. It's too late for me. But you, you must go if you can. Tell Miss Elizabeth —," the veil again fell and the fever clouded eyes looked over Billy's shoulder far beyond into another face.

"Elizabeth —," he whispered. Making a supreme effort he tried to lift his head. He sank back and Billy with tears streaming down his face watched the cracked lips moving wordlessly and endlessly.

Billy eased back to his place and sat chewing his lips despondently. He watched the little knot of savages break up and walk toward them with a purposeful look on their faces.

"No," screamed Billy. "No." He jumped up and dashed toward the approaching Indians forgetting the slave halter around his neck. Reaching the end of his tether in his headlong dash he was jerked back and thrown to the ground, almost strangled by the thong which cut deeply into his throat. Billy lay still a moment while his captors laughed heartily at the tragically ridiculous by-play. He gasped for breath trying to rise. He became entangled in the tether and again fell sprawling, his face striking the dust which rose in a lazy cloud and settled whitely in his long black hair. New roars of laughter rose from savage throats and hands struck thighs in glee as the once ivory, now yellowed, face with its sunken black eyes looked up with tears streaking its dusty grime.

"See, it weeps like a woman," yelled an Indian youth who, hardened and tempered by the sight of tortures, was preparing to be initiated into the brotherhood of warriors. "Faugh." He spat contemptuously.

Billy dropped his head into the dust and lay hopelessly still. The Nottawegas distracted momentarily from their decision to destroy their now useless victim, looked meaningly at Billy. They moved into immediate action. A drum began to beat softly; a pole was miraculously hoisted and a burning firebrand attached to it six feet above the ground. A strong grapevine was attached to the pole trailing about fifteen feet on the ground. Bundles of pitch tipped canes were cast into the fire by the women.

Billy raised his head and, seeing the preparations, recoiled in terror. He looked around like a frightened rabbit and whimpered as he saw a woman approaching, her hands full of wet clay. The boy was in no doubt of the meaning of the sudden activity. After his head had been carefully capped with the wet clay to protect his valuable scalp from the burning brand and the flaming canes, the stout grape vine would be attached to his slave collar. Surrounded by screaming women armed with flaming canes and half crazed by diabolic glee at the antics of their victim, he would run mad with pain hither and yon to the length of his grapevine tether to escape that which could not be escaped.

Billy was almost fainting with terror when they dragged him toward the center of the circle and stripped him of his few tattered garments. On his feet they forced a pair of bear skin moccasins.

Completely absorbed in anticipation of the promised sport, the Nottawegas had forgotten their other victim. The monstrous beating of the drums travelled across the abyss that separated him from the world and pricked Jon's consciousness. That ominous sound could mean but one thing. He subconsciously drew in his skin tightly to withstand the searing canes. Nothing happened; the beat of the drums increased and seemed to enter his bursting head. He opened his eyes.

The sight of Billy being dragged to the stake shocked Jon to full consciousness and the last spark of life in him caught fire and flamed in a final mighty effort. He dragged himself erect, swayed and tightened his muscles. A red hot barrel reserved for the final act of exquisite torture, protruded from the bed of fire. Without further thought Jon sprang forward, a wild figure which might have emanated from the pages of Dante's *Inferno*. Grasping the barrel in his bare hands he swung it about his head wildly, driving back the astonished savages. Shouting at the top of his lungs he dashed about, a terrifying apparition.

"Run, Billy, Run."

Billy hesitated only a moment to see a feathered tomahawk descend and cut off the last wild cry.

"Run —"

Something in the boy's mind snapped and he ran wildly like a forest animal unmindful of the vicious thorns punishing his flesh as cruelly as the flaming canes would have done. Without conscious thought or fear he fled toward the great river and sank gratefully beneath its cooling surface. He forced himself to stay under the water, letting the leisurely current carry him along until his lungs nearly burst. Cautiously he rose to the languid surface. No sound broke the unearthly stillness. The leaning trees pressed down on him and he sank again away from a nameless, formless fear. His head ached and pounded. His ears were like to burst. He rose gasping as his feet struck a sandy finger of land pointing out into the river. He dragged his bleeding body out and crawled onto the burning sand. Without rising from his crouching position he looked up into the glassy sky. The last rays of the sun hanging like a relentless fiery ball struck his aching eyes and penetrated his reeling brain like a hot sword. He shut his eyes and sank unconscious on the blazing sand bar.

Weeks later a terrified, senseless boy was picked up by a trader in the Virginia forests. He was unable to tell his saviour how he had come there; in fact he seemed unable to say anything. He followed the trader willingly, ate voraciously like an animal, and slept unmoving on the dry skins provided for him. No word passed his lips and his black eyes stared blankly from a pinched, yellowed, old face. His fear seemed to disappear with companionship and the filling of his physical needs.

The story of the capture of the South Carolinians by the Nottawegas had traveled from the Floridas to the Massachusetts Colony and the Virginia trader had no doubt who his protege was. He sought to determine the fate of Jonathon Fenwick, Esquire, the well known Carolina surveyor, but his pointed questions elicited no gleam of either understanding or interest from the boy. He stared placidly and unblinking when quizzed on his capture or his companion. Other directions he comprehended and obeyed automatically but an impenetrable wall seemed to lie between the present and the past. All Billy Brown required of the present was the answer to the simple physical demands of his body and a close companion to whom he listened attentively but never spoke. On the first night after he was found wandering aimlessly he was led to a comfortable pallet in the circle of the protective camp fire built by traders on the move as a protection against wild beasts. When the others of the small party had settled down for the night Billy had quietly moved his own bed roll to a place where he could reach out and touch the feet of his benefactor. He followed the same procedure every night following, falling immediately into heavy slumber from which he awoke instantly and completely if the trader made a move to arise. Dumbly Billy followed the man until he complained uneasily to his companions that it was like his guilty conscience punishing him for his sins which God knew were worthy of such a hair shirt! Finally he sent word to Eleazar, with whom he was well acquainted, to meet him at a point designated to turn the boy over to him. Whenever the Virginia trader had attempted to send Billy to the South, Billy had quietly disappeared until the traveller toward the Carolinas could wait no longer. When Eleazar met them, Billy accepted the change with no question and no further thought for the man he left behind as he turned his face toward the South. That night and for every night of the long journey to Saxe Gotha Billy placed his bed roll at Eleazar Wigan's feet.

The strangely sorted pair finally reached the settlement at Saxe Gotha in late October but not before the news of the tragedy had come to Elizabeth officially from Charles Town.

My dear Elizabeth,

This letter is very hard for me to write. There is little that I can say that will lessen the pain or the horror of what has befallen your husband. I only wish that I could be of some service to you and regret that I must only add to your sorrow. If the news were not certain to reach you from another source, I should delay telling you of Margaret Izard's death at the birth of her second child, a daughter who survives and carries her mother's name. I attended Margaret at her lying in, but there seemed nothing of medical skill, at least that I knew, to save her. She had been warned after the birth of her son, Ralph, that another pregnancy might prove fatal. However life, as we both know, is a very strange and cruel thing. Her husband is inconsolable. She spoke of you in a way that makes me tragically certain that she knew her end was near. She asked that I give you her love and the hope that the future may offer you all you justly deserve. Those are her words which she commissioned me on my honour to send to you. Along with them I send another strange message which I do not understand but I am assured you will. A Mr. George Whitefield whom you sent to visit Margaret happened to be at the Elms and wishes me to tell you not to forget the eagles.

Of news, there is little here. The people are eagerly awaiting the arrival of the new governor, James Glen, a

Scotsman. He is said to be vitally interested in Indian affairs and highly thought of by those who know him.

Dr. Killpatrick tells me that he has already written to you of his decision to leave for London before the year is out. He has never forgiven the Assembly for outlawing inoculation and says he has to get out of this stifling atmosphere. He advises me to do the same but I am forced to point out to him that he has taken all my capital by selling his practice to me, and I am now penniless and thus unable to travel.

Please convey my respects to your aunt and uncle. I am certain that you neither need nor desire my advice. Let me add my word to that of Dr. Killpatrick that the frontier in 'this time of great danger and uncertainty is no place for a woman like you alone, especially after the unfortunate accident that has befallen your husband.

Your obedient servant,
Gavin McBride

The news of Margaret's death broke the dam of rigid self control that had sustained Elizabeth during the dreadful months of Jon's capture and the word of his tragic death. Somehow through the thought of Margaret's sweet gaiety Elizabeth had experienced a sense of vicarious happiness that might have been hers — but was not. Now even that bridge to her happier youth had been destroyed and with Margaret, a part of Elizabeth died too. For Margaret and for that bit of herself Elizabeth wept the first tears she had shed in many years. From a sky that was grey to match the sorrow of the young woman who sobbed on the ground, the first rain in six months began to fall and mingle its drops with her flowing tears.

BOOK THREE

FRUITION
1743—1747

Chapter One

The pleasant, moonlight-gilded night was alive with the characteristic noises of two widely different races. On the outskirts of the settlement of Saxe Gotha numerous caravans of pack horses manned by rough drivers, as well as many merely mischievous boys, broke the wilderness quiet with their roistering. Smoke from a hundred camp fires curled above the thick tops of the trees. The woods resounded with the neighing of horses, the barking and howling of hungry Indian dogs. Today a large supply of goods had arrived from Charles Town. Pack saddles down from the Catawba Nation were loaded with skins. Having quickly acquired the art of salesmanship from their white benefactors, the Indians had their wares already spread out displaying their skins and furs to best advantage.

In spite of the darkness the science of barter had begun. In the open air and in Thomas Brown's well stocked trading house were motley assemblies of pack horse men, traders, hunters, squaws, children, and stately Indian warriors. The latter were silent and grave, seemingly uninterested. As Eleazar watched and entered into the loud huckstering and obstinate contending in several barbarous tongues, he smiled wryly to himself at this grand display of false hauteur. Each dignified chief had coached his chosen henchman and schooled him carefully. Swift and thorough would be the punishment inflicted on the miserable fellow if all went not according to plan. The seeming composure was belied by the covetous brightness of the warlike eye which darted from one pile of gaudy wares to another.

Hunters from distant wilds wanted powder and ball; squaws fancied bright colored fabrics for a new petticoat or dress in imitation of the great ladies they had heard of in Charles Town; warriors and old men demanded guns and ammunition; prune faced grandmothers clutched fine white duffle blankets.

An uproar arose from a spot in Brown's store yard.

"Kanune, you thieving devil, how many times must you be told not to bring in such stinking skins," shouted Eleazar angrily.

"Cheesto Kaiehre, Old Rabbit, is mistaken," replied a slender brave slyly. "Kanune's skins are of the finest." He strutted cockily looking around for approval which he instantly received by grunts and gesture. A small crowd closed in in gleeful anticipation. "See, Old Rabbit, your eyes are failing. Kanune's beavers are the heaviest, Kanune's foxes are the longest. Kanune great hunter, very rich man." He struck his breast proudly and stooped to pick up the English goods he had selected from Eleazar's stock. "Kanune's skins are as fragrant as the blooming bay," he added as the crowning touch.

The little knot of savages who had seen the travesty reenacted many times and were acquainted with every line of the drama, turned expectantly to Wigan. A sigh of appreciation went up as Eleazar's great foot descended quickly on one greedy hand. Holding his squirming victim in this embarrassing and un-warriorlike posture Wigan hissed into his upturned face.

"As sweet as the bay, are they?" Eleazar snarled. "Pass that under your insensitive nose." An unrolled skin revealed that neither horns, hoofs, nor snout had been removed from the poorly dressed skin which was crawling with worms and from which a putrid odor rose. "So you would cheat me again, you rogue." Eleazar kicked the Indian's buttocks with his free foot, rolling him over on his back.

"You know the rules and if you ever again bring in hidden hooves and green skins to increase your weight I'll turn you over to another trader who is as skilled in the art of cheating as yourself!"

Wigan scowled down at the deflated warrior.

"Open those skins up. I'll examine and weight each separately."

The well known play over, the crowd turned away and the huckstering began again in loud, flat voices.

Elizabeth smiled at the comical byplay as she leaned against a post of the porch. She sighed. The trading season brought a breath of exotic excitement to the struggling, drab colony. All too quickly the clamor would subside, all too quickly the last bargain would be struck; goods and pelts alike would change hands. Once more the packs would be made up — goods for the Indian towns, pelts for the seaboard market. Everything would again be ready for the trail. The boys would crack their whips and the forests would ring with their shouts and halloos. The pack trains would enter the narrow paths and soon be far on their way, leaving the settlers to the monotony of the wilderness until their next visit. Yes, romance was certainly comparative.

Elizabeth raised her eyes to the smiling face of the moon. How close it seemed! The common and the open fields were bathed in its gentle light. Through the young oak leaves it filtered and cut a lacy pattern on the ground beneath, rich with mould of many centuries of unmolested leaves. How could there be hate and savagery lurking in the moon dyed fastness of the forest? Wasn't there room enough for them all in this great wide land? For centuries the red inhabitants had overlooked the treasures of the fertile soil which covered, heaven knew what other, undelved sources of natural wealth and was in turn shaded by many untouched fortunes in lumber. With Jon's death, Elizabeth's sympathy for her red neighbors had died also. She thought fleetingly of Onconecaw, his intelligent eyes, his young eager mind so like her own. But no! He was not a true member of his race. He was the exception, not the rule. Even toward him she felt a cold wave of enmity. Why had he not prevented the senseless cruelty and tragedy? She had heard that the reason for his failure to communicate with her was that he had so angered the Northern Indians in his attempt to free Jon that he himself had been taken prisoner to Canada. She was unable to confirm the rumour, but neither she nor Eleazar had seen or heard of his being in the Nation.

Elizabeth shuddered in the warm spring air and tried not to dwell on her melancholy thoughts. Bit by bit, in spite of efforts to spare her, she had learned the bitter details of the tragic journey. Once again she turned to work as an anodyne for pain and self reproach. Through the long winter she spent many hours with Nat, urging him on in his hunt for a machine to separate cotton seed from the staple. She had O'Gilvie drive the hands unmercifully to open more land for the new money crop if Nat were successful.

One night in the winter O'Gilvie had looked with concern into the beautiful unsmiling face, slender to the point of thinness. Elizabeth had summoned him to discuss business after a long letter from Andrew Rutledge had arrived advising her that Jon had liquidated all his assets to acquire land, extensive land. With his death, her only source of cash income had ceased with his trading partnership. The need for "hard money" as it was known on the frontier was not great. Each man to survive must make himself self sufficient, but Elizabeth had a great many people both black and white dependent on her for a living. The crops had been bad or short for several years because of unfavorable weather conditions and forays by the Indians. The drought of the preceding summer had been devastating.

Elizabeth laid the facts quickly before her aunt, uncle, and overseer.

"There's always the slaves," O'Gilvie's eyes were troubled. "The market for them is excellent since the Stono Rebellion caused the hike in slave duty to make importation prohibitive. They'll bring you cash and relieve you of their mouths to be fed."

"You suggested that once before," Elizabeth brushed aside his proposal. "I feel now as I did then. I'll sell them only as a last resort. Besides, if we care to look at it in a purely selfish manner, who would work all this land of which I am now the mistress?"

"Elizabeth, this is ridiculous," Aunt Vadie protested sharply. "You cannot stay here now. There is only one thing to do, sell the land and go!"

Elizabeth looked at her aunt coldly.

"Go where?" her voice was heavy with irony.

"To Charles Town, to Scotland, anywhere away from this ghastly place."

"Pray tell me, Aunt Vadie, on what we shall live in Charles Town? Or perhaps we could join my father at the Charter House where he languishes because he is unable to pay his own debts!" Her voice was bitterly scornful.

"Don't speak to me like that, Elizabeth."

"Then don't make inane suggestions. The situation is desperate and I've called us together to solve a serious problem — not to indulge in foolish willful thinking!" Seeing her aunt's stricken face, she was instantly sorry. She sprang up and ran to her, throwing her arms around her.

"Forgive me, Aunt Vadie. I did not mean to be angry, not with you of all people."

"Miss Vadie is perhaps right, Miss Elizabeth," O'Gilvie began but Elizabeth broke in,

"You have none of you considered the fact that all these acres of mine are uncleared land, well chosen as to position and availability of water," she tapped the pile of warrants under her hand, "but of little marketable value. The new settlers have no money to pay and can only accept the King's bounty. The merchants and wealthy planters would buy perhaps, but not at a price that would allow us to purchase a plantation in Charles Town. You and I have no saleable talents, Aunt Vadie," she smiled wryly at her aunt, "and it's a bit late for Uncle Roy to start in as a merchant." She drummed her fingers on the table. "Scotland is impossible now that my mother is dead and our lands are gone."

Elizabeth looked around the table and took a deep breath like a diver preparing for a plunge the outcome of which is uncertain.

"I have a proposition which may solve our difficulties. Please all of you hear me out," she pled.

"Aunt Vadie, I have brought you to this condition. To say I am sorry would be to waste time in idle regrets. If you would like to go to Charles Town, I think we can count on Andrew Rutledge to tide you over until the scheme that I have pays off as I believe it will. O'Gilvie," she turned to her overseer before her aunt could protest, "you have long since worked off your indenture. Now I will have no money to pay your wages." Elizabeth sought through the pile of papers and brought out two which she handed to him.

"These are the warrants for five hundred acres of land on Ninety Six Creek at the junction of the Savannah Town and Cherokee paths. Thomas says the center of trade is bound to move in that direction, and just see the streams! The land is ideal for cultivation and Eleazar says the climate is much better than here. I have seen it myself and the country is beautiful!" Her eyes looked back in memory to the beautiful, cool, blue hills. Resolutely she did not look at the other half of the picture.

"O'Gilvie, I'll give you half the land and a fourth of the proceeds from the lands here if you'll manage it all." Elizabeth ran her tongue over her lips nervously.

"Miss Elizabeth," O'Gilvie spoke quietly and with great dignity, "you don't owe me anything. It is I who am indebted to you. You've no cause to give me any of your land. I'd work for a share of the crops."

Elizabeth eyes misted over.

"I believe you would, O'Gilvie. You have all been such good friends I can never repay you." She cleared her throat and looked at the ceiling, blinking back her tears.

"No, only on these conditions will I consent to go through with my plans."

"Have you thought of the labour, Miss Elizabeth,"

"Yes, I hope I've thought of everything." She laughed. "I've spent many nights plotting!" The circles under her dark eyes bore out the statement.

"Nat and Nellie are willing to go. You will have to take half the Negroes and provide cabins for them. Nat and Nellie can use the house built for my father. It is in bad repair but can be made to serve them and you, while you are there, until they can build something better. You, O'Gilvie, will of course divide your time between the two places and Nat will be in charge there while you are here."

"Elizabeth, listen to me," Aunt Vadie burst out, unable to contain herself longer. "I will hear no more of such wild plans. We would all starve to death if the Indians didn't get us first. I have a letter here from Jamie Glen, our kinsman, ordering us to return to Charles Town at once. He rightly says that women like us have no place here. He says he feels a family responsibility and will see that we are taken care of there."

The pulse in Elizabeth's temple throbbed dangerously.

"Ordered? On what grounds does he order?"

"James Glen is the Governor of South Carolina! He is responsible for the safety of his people."

"Governor Glen may have the power to order the affairs of this government. He does not have the power to order me about personally. You, of course, are free do to as you please."

"Roy, listen to her raving," wailed Aunt Vadie.

Roy, who up to this moment had fingered the pages of a book, making no comment, now closed the book with a snap. He looked at his wife gently but firmly.

"I recall, my dear, some years ago you said to me positively 'We'll go' and we went! Elizabeth in this case is quite sensible. I say to you now, quite as positively, my love, 'We'll stay!' You were saying, Elizabeth?"

Aunt Vadie sat back like a deflated balloon.

"Oh, Uncle Roy, you darling!"

"Elizabeth, my dear, I may be too old to become a merchant but I've long had a yen to learn to plow. You will need an overseer here while O'Gilvie is at Ninety Six, will you not?"

"Indeed I will," Elizabeth cried in gratitude.

Eagerly they laid their plans. O'Gilvie, Nat, and half the Negroes were to leave at once to begin clearing land and building cabins. If the mild weather held, they could do much in a month. In recent years some intrepid settlers had established themselves on the Cherokee path between Saxe Gotha and Ninety Six to live by hunting and farming, and word had reached Saxe Gotha of several warrants for land taken out by men of English name. It was that that had inspired Nat and Nellie to accept Elizabeth's proposal. The new surveys made in the settlement at the Congarees since 1740 were to Germans, and the colony was predominately German in character. The newcomers were not quick to learn the English language and Nat felt that the growing interest in the lands up the Saluda River toward the mountains shown by his own countrymen would make a home there more congenial.

"You'll need supplies, O'Gilvie. Give me a list. Blossom and I will begin to get them together." Aunt Vadie spoke softly and timidly.

Three pairs of eyes turned to the gentle, resigned face under its fading golden hair. Elizabeth kissed her aunt wordlessly while Roy patted her shoulder gently.

News of the pressures being put on Elizabeth to leave the Congarees spread like wildfire after Jon's death. Many families had moved on closer to the older establishments nearer the sea. Those who remained were uneasy and fearfully sullen. On the evening after the decisive conference in Elizabeth's household, Stephen Crell had appeared on the doorstep dressed in his best with something obviously on his mind.

"Why, Mr. Crell. Do come in. I'm so glad to see you. I've something I wish to discuss. Let me call my aunt."

"No please M'am, Mrs. Fenwick. I have something I'd like to say and I'd like to have my say first."

Elizabeth was puzzled. The man was obviously terribly nervous. She wondered what had gone wrong now. Gravely she invited him in and they sat quietly a moment before the blazing fire. Finally Stephen cleared his throat.

"Mrs. Fenwick, we hear that the Governor wishes you to return to Charles Town since Mr. Fenwick's death. He feels an unmarried woman has no place here, am I correct?"

"Yes, Mr. Crell, but —"

"Excuse me, please," he broke in raising hand to silence her. "The colony here has looked to you for guidance; you are a symbol to them of courage and hope." Stephen Crell paused a moment, looking into the fire. Elizabeth waited. When he spoke again he did not look at her.

"My people are frightened and disturbed, at their wits end in fact. We need doctors, soldiers, and schools for our children who are running wild. All these things have been promised us but the promises have not been fulfilled. You are a link to them between here and what they have left behind, a hope that they may enjoy these things in the future. If you leave now," he spoke earnestly, pleadingly, "our little settlement may fall to pieces — disintegrate. For most of them that would be tragedy. They have no money, no land if they leave here —."

Elizabeth started to rise.

"But, Mr. Crell, —"

"Please, let me finish!" He took a deep breath. "I came to ask you to be my wife —," his voice died away. Only the busy crackling of the burning logs broke the peaceful quiet.

Elizabeth sank back, completely taken by surprise. A lump rose in her throat.

"Do you mean that you would do this for your people, for the success of the colony?"

Stephen Crell looked squarely at the lovely face, warmly flushed in the firelight glow.

"It would not be a sacrifice," he spoke gravely and with feeling. "I am not your kind, I know. You are a great lady and I am only a rough man. I can offer you my devotion and protection if that be enough."

"No one could offer me more, Mr. Crell," Elizabeth was deeply touched. "As for our being alike, we are very closely akin in our love for this country, our faith in its future. That's all that counts here. There are no ladies and gentlemen, only a group of human beings with a purpose that must be kept burning."

Elizabeth looked at the big clean man across from her. Here was decency, honesty, and courage, a foundation stone. Any woman would be fortunate who could accept his love and protection. She sighed deeply.

"I cannot accept your proposal, Mr. Crell. You have paid me an honor that I shall never forget. I am deeply grateful."

Stephen Crell rose defeated.

"Just a minute, Mr. Crell. You have not heard what I wished to discuss with you." She was smiling into his troubled eyes.

"I shall not leave Saxe Gotha. Pray, sit down and let me tell you my plans over a cup of hot coffee."

On the heels of this proposal followed another even more astounding. Eleazar Wigan was the bearer of another demanding letter from the Governor. Watching the look of annoyance cross Elizabeth's face as she read the contents whose message he

190

guessed, he twisted his hat self-consciously.

"The name of Wigan ain't pretty enough for anybody as pretty as you, M'am, but it's yours if it'll do you any good.

Elizabeth looked up to laugh with him at his joke. His face was serious and now flushed scarlet as he added,

"There'd be no obligation along with it."

Impulsively Elizabeth hugged him. "Nobody ever had such friends as I. What would I ever do without you?" She smiled mischievously though her eyelids stung. "I prefer to keep you as a friend and never let you know what a nagging wife I'd be."

"Wal," he scratched his head thoughtfully. "I'll still be around if you change your mind."

The day after Crell's proposal, the little colony gathered on the Common. The day was crisp and clear, a tiny wind rattled tenacious brown leaves that still clung doggedly to the great oak trees. It brought a bright color to the plain, broad faces but no sparkle to their eyes. Elizabeth looked at the unresponsive faces. Only the kind face of the Reverend Christian Theus reflected the fire of decision and firm purpose. He smiled encouragement and Elizabeth spoke to the people.

"Mr. Crell has asked me to talk to you. We are all frightened and discouraged. Many of you are planning to pull up and leave."

"Us? What about yourself?" A voice called from the crowd. Elizabeth turned and spoke in the direction of the unidentified voice.

"I am not leaving." She paused. A ripple ran over her audience. Neighbor whispered to neighbor.

"In spite of my misfortune, I shall remain here. I feel that this country has a great future for those who can withstand the trials of pioneering —."

"And what of those of us who don't survive? I don't want my scalp hanging along side of Mr. Fenwick's!"

"Shame! For shame!" cried a woman's voice.

Elizabeth hesitated. The minister's eye still led her on. Crell nodded encouragement.

"Wait!" Elizabeth called out. "Have you thought that you have an obligation to discharge? You all own your own land, your tools to work it. What have you paid for it?"

She looked around defiantly.

"I'll tell you what you've paid for it! Your promise to our King, to our Governor, to open the land and till the soil. Other than that, not one farthing have you paid. You are living on the King's bounty. Does that not entail some responsibility?"

A wild looking young man sprang to a stump and drew the attention of the wavering crowd.

"Don't listen to her! We *enjoy*," he fairly spat the word in sarcasm, "the King's bounty only to protect the ladies and gentlemen of the King's court at Charles Town from the tomahawks of the savage brutes waiting in their high mountains to swoop down on us and cut us down like rats." He spoke savagely into Elizabeth's upturned face. Stephen Crell stepped forward but Elizabeth placed her hand on his arm. Her eyes snapped as she replied to the fanatic looking young man atop his stump.

"When those ladies and gentlemen of the King's court first came to the shores of South Carolina they met the same trials and hardships that we have had to meet. Those that could stand it are now enjoying comparative peace, some comfort and luxury because they stayed and fought. I say, we too have the same opportunity here in a more beautiful and healthful land. This is a land for strong men and women. Our future may not be easy; we will falter many times. Hardship will be the fire that will separate the true metal from the dross. Which will you be?"

Her beautiful voice was filled with emotion, her face full of resolution.

"Leave this place? No! My life's blood is in this land. It is all that I have ever had that is truly mine. With God's help I can make it do my bidding — and I shall!"

Cries of applause arose when Elizabeth's voice died away. Some were still unconvinced. Some had not understood her words though they felt their meaning. Crell was speaking to them in their own tongue.

"Where will you go?" he asked.

His listeners looked blank.

"Back to your own country? You have perhaps forgotten that you left there because you would have died of starvation or been cut down by religious persecution. What is there in the old country for you?"

He paused dramatically.

"Nothing!" He answered his own question. "Here you have a glorious wide land that is yours for the asking, freedom to think and worship as you please. The old country has been formed and set by hands long since dead. That you cannot change. Here some of us will have the privilege of being potters to help mould the clay of a new country after our own ideas! Here our only enemies are ones we can understand, nature and a savage, uncivilized race.

These things a man can cope with; they are constant and ever present, not like fickle prejudice that blows hot and cold with the times." Stephen Crell felt completely spent emotionally and utterly discouraged as he looked at the silent group about him.

Christian Theus stepped forward and raised his hands.

"Let us pray." His resonant voice poured over their bent heads.

"Almighty God, interrupt our concern for ourselves. Awaken us to the challenge of this land as well as to Thy Kingdom. Lead us to accept the experiences that must come our way that we may learn how to make them bear fruit for Thee and Thy glory. Give us wisdom and courage and sustain us, O Lord, when we falter. Guide us to accept our duties and our trust. Make us mindful of the promise of this fair, new land. Help us, O Father, to live joyfully and fruitfully that others seeking the source of our strength and joy may find it. Walk with us through the darkness toward Thy light. Amen."

Knowing the great value of music as an uplifting power to the hearts of mankind, Theus' clear tenor voice broke out in one of the inspiring new hymns Charles Wesley had left in Carolina.

A charge to keep I have,
A God to glorify,
A never dying Soul to save
And fit it for the sky.

The response was instantaneous. The beautiful and heartening words of the young missionary seemed written for the encouragement of this lonely frontier post, and now rose in beautiful harmony toward the clear, blue sky.

To serve the present age
My calling to fulfill;
O may it all my powers engage
To do my Master's will!"

Faces were smiling and alight with a crusading fire as the voices swelled into the last verse.

Help me to watch and pray
And on thyself rely,
Assured if I my trust betray
I shall forever die.

Another furious outburst of quarrelling brought Elizabeth's thoughts back to the present. A gesticulating knot of Indians was protesting loudly. She rose and drew near them to watch. The primitive method of selling watered, frontier rum was always amusing, and she laughed silently as she watched. A great, hulking fellow chosen by the buyers for the out-size of his mouth was on his knees, his head bent back. The buyer held an earthen pot and jealously watched the kneeling man's adam's apple while the seller poured in a tote of rum from his goat skin. The measurer emptied the contents of his mouth into the pot and tilted his head again. Suddenly the adam's apple bobbed. The unfortunate measurer, caught in the act, was dealt such a blow that he fell sprawling, gulping the last drop of fiery liquid.

Elizabeth turned back toward the house. On the steps she paused and raised her eyes again to the glorious spring moon. She smiled as she reentered the house to answer another annoying letter from the Governor. Eleazar had once said that you could measure the progress of civilization by the angle at which you must tilt your head to see the sky. Yes, the angle was certainly not as acute as it had been ten years ago.

The feeling of peace passed as she drew the Governor's letter to her and dipped her quill. Why did he persist? She thought she had made her position eminently clear.

Saxe Gotha
April 20, 1744

To His Excellency James Glen, Governor
Charles Town, South Carolina
Honorable Sir:

In answer to yours of the first instant I wish to express my appreciation of your concern for my safety but respectfully reject your statement that a woman of my sort has no place in these parts. In view of the fact that I am only one of nearly a hundred souls that need protection, I humbly suggest that it would be more feasible for your Honor and the gentlemen of the Assembly to vote the necessary funds to erect a fort at this point and equip it with a garrison. You and your predecessors have received such petitions many times from the inhabitants of Saxe Gotha along with a statement of other very real needs for schools and churches and a court that will eliminate the need for

194

long and costly trips to Charles Town to transact our business and to buy land. We have no funds for such journeys nor can we leave our employment necessary to our very survival. Had your Excellency and the Honorable members of the Council not ignored these petitions, as you did the one I made personally to stop the Cherokee trade after Mr. Fenwick's capture until his safe return was assured, I humbly conceive that none of us would be in need of your personal protection.

The Nottawegas are still lurking about in our forests and causing much fear and loss of crops and stock or I should not presume to trouble your Excellency and also know I have not the capacity to do so. I have become convinced that these brutish creatures who know no gratitude must be kept under control by fear and hot presents.

In that regard you advise me to withdraw from my plantation at Ninety Six, warning me that this land belongs to the Indians. I remind you, Sir, that the land on which I now reside is also to be considered Indian land for that matter. I am not acquainted with any treaty or purchase that gives to the English title to any of the land occupied in South Carolina. Certainly, such a purchase would be of great value to us and to the many British subjects who have come through here from other parts seeking an advantageous point to settle. A Mr. Francis from Pennsylvania has visited us and we hear he is making some improvements at Saluda Old Town.

I recognize your superior wisdom and ability and am grateful for any advice you have to offer as governor or kinsman. Such advice I shall consider gravely and thoughtfully. But, Sir, I respectfully retain my right as an individual to accept or reject it as I see fit. My home is here; I have no other; and here I shall remain.

Trusting that this finds you and your family in good health and happy in your new situation, I remain, Sir,

> *Your humble servant,*
> *Elizabeth Fenwick*

Aunt Vadie was tearful.

"You can't send such a letter," she cried as Elizabeth sealed her spirited message with finality.

"Why not?" asked Elizabeth.

"James Glen is the Governor; one doesn't address a governor in such a manner. That letter is insolent!"

"The letter is not insolent, Aunt Vadie, and I did not intend it so." Elizabeth smiled and her eyes sparkled. "It is positive perhaps; thus I did intend. Perhaps if our kinsman is annoyed he will pay us that promised visit and see the desperate situation for himself!"

"Oh, Elizabeth, my child," moaned Aunt Vadie. "Why are you always so ready for a scrap? Haven't you learned anything with age?"

Elizabeth was instantly serious. She cupped her aunt's chin tenderly in her hand.

"I didn't mean to be flippant, but if I were not a scrapper where would I be now?"

"Back in Scotland, safe and sound, where you ought to be!"

"Come, now, Aunt Vadie. Where is your crusading spirit? Will you let Uncle Roy get ahead of you after all these years?" Elizabeth smiled again.

"Go away with your wiles. You've always gotten the best of me, but someday I'm going to get up enough spunk to leave you alone with your wild ideas."

Elizabeth laughed gaily. "Be careful, my sweet. I'll not be alone. I don't believe Uncle Roy would go with you."

"Oh-h, you —," Aunt Vadie spluttered in exasperation.

The next day Eleazar left for Charles Town with Elizabeth's letter to the Governor in his pouch.

Chapter Two

Mary Glen left the men to their Madeira and the smoke from four pipes curled up comfortably, giving a fragrance and an air of pleasant relaxation to the cypress panelled, informal, family dining room. The long, many paned windows were open to the gentle spring night which was disturbed only by the sibilant whispering of the water in the bay and the far away eerie echo of a sailor's cry. The four men in the tastefully appointed room were widely different in outward appearance and as deeply different in personality. James Glen's keen face struggled between acquired arrogance of position and natural gentleness of birth. His attire was carefully splendid as befitted a colonial deputy of His Majesty George II, by the grace of God, of Great Britain, France, and Ireland, King, Defender of the Faith, etc. His blue velvet coat, trimmed in heavy silver lace, fell open to reveal a silk damask waist coat finely embroidered in a series of exotic and vari-colored plants. Well turned legs were encased in embroidered lisle hose and ended in slender feet in shiny patent leather shoes with high heels and jewelled buckles.

In direct contrast, Eleazar Wigan was perhaps more striking in his simple buck skins. The darkly burned, leathery face was deeply lined but belonged to a man of indiscriminate age. His only concession to the grandeur of the occasion was his painfully slick hair, which effect he had finally resorted to bear's grease to obtain. The lively and far seeing grey eyes were peaceful and content at the moment but had lost none of their piercing quality.

The two younger men represented a different world in which there were also decided contrasts. Andrew Rutledge's attire was less flamboyant than the Governor's but had the restrained elegance of a dandy. Ambition, success, and a naturally acquisitive nature had sharpened his slender face and given it a hawk like alertness. He now took his glass of ruby wine to the window and lounged there a moment, admiring the moonlit splendor of the night.

The other man of the party was by far the most solid figure in the little room. Tall and broad, with gold hair that had lost none of its youthful spring, Gavin McBride looked at his companions with liking. The intensely blue eyes still reflected the heather of his native Scotland and though they were softened with a certain sadness, they added vigor to the mature handsomeness of his face. His attire was plain but tasteful.

They smoked a moment in silence. Governor Glen tapped the letter before him that he had just read to his companions.

"My kinswoman would make an excellent Secretary of State," he commented.

"What a woman!" Andrew's voice was full of admiration. Gavin was silent.

"But what shall I do with her?" the Governor's voice held a slightly querulous tone.

"Pardon me, Your Honor," Eleazar's voice was dry, "I'd say the matter was out of your hands." He pointed significantly to the open letter on the table.

"Why, man, I can't let her stay there in the jungle. It's-it's all right for this-this poor rabble from Europe, but she is an aristocrat, a woman of gentle birth entirely unequipped for such a rigorous life!" The Governor was spluttering in his anger.

"We all know her determination from past experience," Gavin spoke quietly. "Personally, I think she is right." He rose and joined Andrew at the window where he spoke again regretfully as he looked up at the waning moon. "I wish I had reached that conclusion sooner."

Andrew placed a hand on Gavin's shoulder.

"Even in our youth," Gavin went on, "when we came with eyes shining with hope to a great new country where every man would have a fair and equal chance, we, none of us, expected it to be easy. For her, it has been harder than for the rest of us. If she has still the determination that letter would indicate, I would say the

198

Back Country is in good hands. What this province needs is more like her."

"Amen!" Said Andrew fervently.

"Governor, you needn't worry your head about Miss Elizabeth. They ain't a person I know can stand what she has like she's stood it. Those folks at the Congarees look to her for strength, not she to them. If you could get her to leave there, and I don't think you could, that colony would fold up."

Andrew smiled into Gavin's eyes.

"There's one serious need she didn't mention in her letter."

Gavin returned the look with a question in his eyes.

"Doctors."

"Yes, I know," Gavin smiled too.

"Well?"

"This time I don't want to make a mistake. I'll be cautious."

"You've thought of it then?"

"Thought of it? Of course I have. For two reasons. Besides my own personal inclination, there's so little for me here in Charles Town. There's a glut of doctors now who can push pills and practice a charming bedside manner. I can't. Frankly, I'm a failure. I can't work under restrictions that throttle medical science – such as the law against inoculation. Governor Glen, if – ."

"Now, Dr. McBride," the Governor broke in, "don't get me embroiled in that controversy. I've enough problems with the Indians!"

"But, Sir, the Indians are a menace that will be eliminated. Any thinking man knows that they cannot resist the tide of British colonization. But small pox is an enemy that will always be here to maim and kill unless we doctors are allowed to use our weapons against it. To suppress us by legislation is the same as outlawing guns to protect ourselves from a scalping savage. Providence! What idiocy." Gavin pounded the table in the enthusiasm of his favorite crusade.

"Dr. McBride," the Governor spoke coldly, "that is Mrs. Glen's favorite table. If you wish to chop wood with those tremendous hands, I'll call my man to direct you to the block! We are here to discuss another matter."

Gavin smiled ruefully.

"I'm sorry, Sir," he apologized. "I did not mean to be discourteous."

"Sir," Andrew broke in, addressing the Governor. "I have another letter I think it would be appropriate to bring to your attention. It's author is the same and it is a bit personal," he smiled slyly. "However if it will add impetus to her petition I don't think she would object. May I read it?"

"By all means, Mr. Rutledge. I find the whole affair most interesting."

The lawyer read, purposely omitting nothing.

Dear Andrew,
With you I need not waste paper and time with idle pleasantries and inane and unfelt courtesies.

Andrew could not resist a grin at the *Governor,* who squirmed uncomfortably but smiled, unable to resist the humor of the obvious feint in his direction. Andrew Rutledge read on,

To get directly to the point, I need money, cash. As I have already written you we are working on a method of mechanically removing seed from cotton in order to make it a money crop. My venture into tobacco was not successful because of the prejudice of these people against its use, and we need money if we ever plan to get beyond the primitive frontier barter stage. From the lack of interest shown by the government in our need for schools and churches and better homes, I predict we will have to meet these needs on our own. This takes money.

My carpenter is as yet unsuccessful in producing a proper gin for our rough seed cotton so we were unable to increase the acreage in cotton as we had planned. Perhaps next year. In the meantime O'Gilvie tells me that our land near Ninety Six is suitable for excellent production of cattle and I want to try the new black beef cows of which my father has written.

I would like for you to sell the land in Orangeburg, for which I have no use, at the most advantageous price and send to Scotland for as many of these cows from Aberdeenshire as the proceeds will allow. Mr. Fant, my father's former factor, is thoroughly honest and will handle the matter to my advantage. O'Gilvie\ also requests some of the drought resistant lucerne that has been recently imported by Miss Eliza Lucas and grown with success. O'Gilvie plans to plant it in some of the land prepared for cotton that we are unable to use this *year. From what we hear this lucerne will make excellent hay as well as grazing.*

All is well with us. We work from dawn till dark. It would amaze you to see Uncle Roy behind the plow. He returns from the fields a perspiring and dirty farmer, to Aunt Vadie's horror, but immediately becomes, under Clem's deft hands, the suave gentleman he would really rather be though he won't admit it. His work is not done even then, for after dinner (we call it supper behind his back) he works as hard keeping us educated. Aunt Vadie mends or knits while he reads to us, and I do nothing useful but sit and enjoy the sound of his voice. Please arrange for a subscription to Mr. Franklin's new Pennsylvania Gazette *for his fifty-fifth birthday. How times does fly! Deduct the cost from the price of my land.*

One is fortunate to have such a friend as you. Aunt Vadie reluctantly refuses your offer to bring her to Charles Town as Mrs. Rutledge's companion. I trust your wife's health is improving and that all goes well with you as usual.

Your friend,
Elizabeth Fenwick

At the Congarees

The letter was greeted in thoughtful silence. Eleazar broke the silence, his voice paying solemn tribute to heroism.

"Would it not be better, Sir, to make the way easier for such a one as this? If this country is to grow in wealth and extent, others like her, both men and women, will have to come. I am not a diplomat or a scholar, but I can recognize true greatness, thank God!" He sniffed suspiciously as he gave his nose a strenuous work out with his hand. Gavin remained standing at the window, his back to the room. Finally the Governor spoke.

"Getting the House to vote funds for any cause, no matter how worthy, is like getting blood from a turnip." He rubbed his hands together thoughtfully as he walked back and forth in the little room. He stopped and looked beyond his guests into the night.

"Perhaps, I should visit the Congarees and the fine land 'So healthy in its situation, so good in its kind or sufficient enough to support such a number of colonists as may be sufficient as to make themselves secure against the attempts of Indians or other enemies!' "

His thoughts came back to his guests.

"I quote from a letter from a Mr. Turk of Augusta County, Virginia. He tells me that he and others have examined the lands around Ninety Six which the few settlers there tell them belong to the Indians. They among others are petitioning this government to purchase these lands and reserve them for settlers from Virginia and Pennsylvania who wish to move south. Perhaps it's not a bad idea. I could combine a trip of inspection with a friendly visit to the Indians. Then I should know what to recommend to the Assembly."

"That would certainly be better than trying to buy a pig in a poke," Wigan nodded.

During the ensuing discussion the Governor became very excited over the idea which had already grown in his mind into a magnificent journey of State, a highly colorful diplomatic expedition involving the gentlemen of the province and a well equipped army to impress the ingenuous red man with British might.

Andrew shook his head inwardly in dismay. He wondered how the Governor planned to extort the exorbitant amount necessary for such an expedition from a tight fisted Assembly which had so far refused to vote a farthing for desperately needed frontier schools and churches.

The three guests left the Governor's mansion together and sauntered in silence down Church Street toward Gavin's lodgings. Andrew's carriage horses clomped slowly ahead with the coachman dozing on the box in the fine spring night. They parted at Gavin's door. Eleazar leaned out the carriage window and called softly to Gavin.

"You serious about moving north?"

"Never was more serious in my life," Gavin replied with a grin.

"Wal, you'd better hurry, Son. They're standing in line. I ought to know. I stood with them!" His merry chuckle was wafted back to Gavin as the carriage clattered off over the stones. The tousled grey head appeared once more out the bobbing carriage window. "You ain't gettin' no younger, either." He shouted.

Gavin smiled at the annoyed clack of a shutter thrown open in protest by a disturbed sleeper. He looked once more at the sailing moon. Did its one remaining eye wink at him. He felt strangely buoyant as he closed the heavy door softly on the glory of the night. Years seemed to fall away to a long distant night with such a moon on shipboard. He sighed. It had been years. He wondered if she had changed much. From the tone of that spirited letter to the Governor he'd wager not.

Chapter Three

"O'Gilvie," Elizabeth looked at the overseer in horror, "Why didn't she tell me? I would never have let her go!"

"That's why she didn't, Miss Elizabeth. She said she knew you'd keep her here and Nat needed her. She made me promise not to tell you now." O'Gilvie shook his head worriedly. "But she isn't well though she tried to keep it from Nat. I don't know what Nat would do if anything happened to Nellie. Nor the rest of us either. She keeps us all comfortable and clean and well fed. Every day she inspects the Negro cabins, sees that the women tend the kitchen gardens, feed the stock, and leave the men free to do the heavy field work. Without her we could never have accomplished what we have in so short a time." He paused hesistantly, "Pardon me, Miss, but she's a lot like you."

"Why, O'Gilvie. What a nice thing to say! I feel a little like Nellie is my own child though she's older than I. I didn't make her what she is but I did help her to find herself. I'm proud of that. Could she travel?"

"Her time is near, not more than three weeks, Nat says. Her legs," he flushed with embarrassment, "are badly swollen and she has fallen several times."

Elizabeth's face was grave. "Nellie is too old to have her first child. It will go hard with her. When do you plan to return?"

"I need to be here for gathering the corn. It's late already."
O'Gilvie looked worried.

"That's because the cotton did so well. Uncle Roy has done a splendid job." She looked toward the sweating Negroes in the warm October sun. Roy stood, legs wide spread, on a wagon bed directing the bringing in of the last load of fleecy cotton. His wide brimmed hat was pushed back from a tanned face sweaty and streaked with dust. "Life does funny things to us doesn't it, O'Gilvie?"

"Yes, Miss, it does," he smiled in Uncle Roy's direction, "not all of them bad."

Elizabeth waved her hand to greet Blossom whose hot, shiny black face grinned up at her over the full tow sack slung from her capable shoulders. Knowing the strict slave caste system which drew an impassable line between a house Negro and a field hand. Elizabeth had approached Blossom cautiously when the need for more hands arose with the unexpectedly large crops.

"Does ah mine? Lawd no! Pickin cotton is happy wuk, de hottah de sun de bettah!"

Clem balked but Blossom soon pulled his nose out of the sky by pointing to his adopted master working with the best of them.

"Who do you think you is nohow?" she had yelled at him with scorn. "You'll do whutevah Miss Betsy wants if it's clean de privies!"

"I believe Uncle Roy can handle the corn if you give him instructions."

"The corn is mighty important, Miss Elizabeth. We'll need every bit of it if those cows arrive safely. They'll be in poor shape after a long sea voyage. We are fortunate to have Mr. Stack's mill this year."

"Very well, then, I must go without you. There's no time to lose."

"Go where?" O'Gilvie demanded.

"To Nellie, of course."

Completely forgetting his role, O'Gilvie spoke with authority.
"Indeed you will not!"

Elizabeth's eyes were wide with surprise. Could this be O'Gilvie? Seeing her shocked face, O'Gilvie quickly apologized.

"I did not mean to offend you, Miss Elizabeth. But what you propose is preposterous. You cannot go," he added stubbornly.

"You did not offend me, O'Gilvie. I was surprised, not offended. However, I shall go. Nellie would do the same for me."

She turned abruptly to cut off further protest and stumbled

headlong into Billy Brown.

"Oh, dear," she cried righting herself by his outstretched arm which had prevented her falling. Sometimes she almost forgot Billy. He was always there at her skirts, quietly contented, understandingly helpful but always silent, his face blank and impassive. He seemed to understand all that was said to him though there was no light of intelligence in his eyes and he would never answer a question. He had spoken to no one since Eleazar had brought him home though all of them had tried to prod him about his capture. Questions he seemed not to understand; directions he followed docilely. Elizabeth was rarely out of his sight and each evening after she retired he lay on the floor in front of her door. When they had tried to move him forcibly, the sight had not been a pretty one and Elizabeth had let him stay. After that the shiny knife that protruded from his belt had discouraged any further interference. Every one in the household protested to Elizabeth. She admitted only to herself that she felt uneasy.

"What can I do with him?" she countered their protests.

"Send him away from here. His constant snooping presence is positively ghoulish, Elizabeth. How can you stand it?"

"Where could I send him, Aunt Vadie? We have no hospitals for such as he. That's where he should be. His mind must have gone after his frightful experiences. I can't turn him out to starve."

Elizabeth wondered if he were watching her. She finally discarded that theory. What then? Was he seeking protection for himself or protecting her? Finally she gave up wondering and adjusted herself to his vague companionship.

Now she looked up at O'Gilvie as Billy ambled off with his rolling gait.

"There goes my conscience," she sighed.

When it became apparent that Elizabeth fully intended to carry out her decision to go to Nellie's aid at Ninety Six, O'Gilvie remade his plans and, working long and late, made arrangements for Roy to carry on with the harvesting and milling. Aunt Vadie offered to go too, but Elizabeth decided one of them must stay with Uncle Roy. The two women hastily threw together every necessity they could think up while Aunt Vadie moaned that the baby would have no proper clothing. Elizabeth laughed and teased her aunt who was obviously disappointed that she was deprived of the pleasure of making the tiny trousseau. Elizabeth promised her that she would send all that Aunt Vadie could prepare by spring. What the baby wore under necessary swaddling against the piercing cold that swept off the Cherokee hills in winter would not matter.

Three days later they set out in a cutting wind that blew out of the east, chasing grey cloud banks across the bright blue sky. When O'Gilvie and Elizabeth mounted their horses, they found Billy Brown quietly astride a wild looking spotted pony holding the lead ropes of the two laden packhorses. O'Gilvie and Elizabeth stopped short, looking at each other. An angry flush swept over the overseer's face.

"You cannot go," he said sharply.

Billy made no move nor indicated that he had heard. O'Gilvie started to dismount. "Please, Billy." Elizabeth spoke softly and coaxingly as to a child. "Stay here and take care of Aunt Vadie for me." She waited. No sign. "Uncle Roy will read the Bible to you," she pleaded, holding out this prize as a bon-bon to an infant. Billy sat quietly.

"Clem, hold his bridle and hand me the packhorse halters," O'Gilvie ordered grimly.

Clem started forward. Billy's hand slid to the hilt of his shining knife. Clem fell back instantly.

O'Gilvie's face darkened. Again he started to dismount. Elizabeth stopped him with a gesture.

"Let him go, O'Gilvie." She sighed heavily. "We might need him anyway.

O'Gilvie's face was angry as Elizabeth went on. "We shouldn't lose any more time, and I couldn't leave here if we upset anything. I suppose he's better off with me."

The little crowd was silent as the three rode off and were swallowed up in the narrow tunnel of the forest path.

They rode silently with only the slap of the horses hooves on dry leaves and the lonesome sound of the wind in the tree tops to disturb the calm of the vast forest. As they drew near the point where Elizabeth and Billy had turned off on their memorable picnic, the mate to Billy's spotted pony glided out into the path. Astride it sat Pakahle. Elizabeth gasped. Since the day nearly thirteen years ago when she had arrived full of hope in Saxe Gotha, Pakahle had never spoken to her. Her black eyes had gleamed with hatred every time it had been necessary for them to meet. Since Jon's death Elizabeth had scarcely seen the Indian woman. Now as she faced the trio her face was the noncommittal face of an Indian devoid of any emotion. O'Gilvie's hand sought his pistol.

"I go too," Pakahle's voice was flat and toneless. She saw O'Gilvie's instinctive movement. "No need that," she pointed to the glinting pistol in his hand. "Pakahle help, not hurt. Indian know things not known to white man. Medicine cut birth pain like knife." Pakahle made a slicing motion with her hand.

Elizabeth looked suspiciously at Billy's blank face.

"How did you know where we are going?" she demanded.

Pakahle bent her head suggestively. "Indian learn to keep ear to ground; safer that way," was all she would say.

Elizabeth's head whirled in confusion. What would happen next? She was weary with trying to solve all these inexplicable problems, to fix the pieces of this hopeless puzzle together. She felt a sudden desire to turn her horse's head and dash off in the opposite direction away from everything, every problem, fear, and responsibility. The inevitable question arose — where?

Pakahle's voice recalled her to reality.

"We go now, yes?" She pointed to the clouding sky. "Storm come soon. Maybe tomorrow. Need hurry."

"Yes — yes, I suppose so," Elizabeth nodded wearily. She had not realized that the air had grown so cold. She huddled closer into the warm folds of her fur shawl as the ill assorted little caravan ascended the rapidly rising trail.

The next evening they rode, or rather were swept by the tearing gale, into the clearing in front of Nat and Nellie's house. Nat must have heard the sound of the hooves under the shrieking din caused by the storm. He flung open the heavy door which was torn from his hands and banged dully against the strips of wool he had padded around the frame to keep out the seeping chill. Nat was frantic, his eyes wild with fear. He was almost tearfully grateful when he saw the two women.

"Why, Nat, what is it?" cried Elizabeth alarmed.

"She's dying, Miss Elizabeth. It's awful."

"Dying? Come now, Nat. You're upset. It's two weeks till the time, isn't it?"

"No, No! She's been in pain for two days, awful pain. It started at dawn yesterday with the east wind."

Elizabeth groaned. Every bone in her body ached. They had ridden hard for two long days hardly pausing for food. Only when darkness had driven them in had they made camp for the night. She had scarcely slept a wink, what with over fatigue and unease over the motives of her uninvited companions. She felt glued to the saddle.

"Hurry, Nat, help me down and let me see if my legs will still work. Stop worrying. If you stay calm you'll be more help to Nellie." She looked enviously at Pakahle who sprang down from her horse with the agility of a cat.

They entered the ample, stout cabin and Elizabeth looked around in amazement. A roaring fire lighted and warmed a pleasant room whose now heavily shuttered windows were hung with gay curtains of the inevitable slave cloth made colorful with strips of Elizabeth's own old dresses from Nellie's frugal scrap bag. The large room had a hand hewn, sanded floor with Nellie's bright rugs thrown cheerfully about. A bright Indian basket by the huge stone fireplace was filled with fragrant pine cones. The feeling of pleasant surprise was followed by one of dismay as her eyes travelled to the figure tossing on the wildly rumpled bed against the clay chinked log wall. Had she not known it was Nellie, Elizabeth would not have recognized the swollen, pasty face crowned with lank, dark hair. Sweat poured off her forehead. Her arms were flung above her head and knuckles were white from the iron grip of her hands on the crudely carved pine headboard. Nellie's rasping breath made a loud noise in the room, flecks of blood from lips bitten by teeth that tried to hold back the screams of anguish spotted the sheet. Elizabeth's knees shook. What must she do now, she thought wildly. Her thoughts darted about in panic like little white mice trying to escape from a maze. Her eyes found Pakahle who was quietly warming her hands by the fire. She spoke over her shoulder to Elizabeth with easy dignity and commanded.

"Send men out. Billy stay!"

"No, Pakahle. Please not Billy. He's had enough. Someone else."

Pakahle shrugged. "Better Billy stay. Need strong arms."

"O'Gilvie?

"No. Husband need help too. O'Gilvie help him."

Elizabeth stood undecided.

"Hurry," commanded Pakahle swinging a full iron teakettle over the flames. "Much talk, no action she die."

Elizabeth threw off her cape and bent over Nellie. She laid her hand on Nellie's forehead. Nellie flinched and looked at her with pain glazed eyes. The ghost of a smile flashed across her tormented face and she grasped both Elizabeth's hands.

"I don't want to die," she cried out.

"And you shan't," Elizabeth promised stoutly.

Pakahle handed Elizabeth a steaming cup.

"Make drink," she answered the question in Elizabeth's eyes.

A peculiar aroma rose from the steaming concoction.

"What is it?" Elizabeth asked alarmed.

"Herb. Ease pain," Pakahle answered laconically. "Hurry!"

When Elizabeth still hesitated, the Indian woman brushed her impatiently aside and with Billy's help forced the hot liquid between Nellie's clenched teeth. Billy laid her back gently. Almost instantly the tenseness left Nellie's harassed face and her body stopped its fevered tossing. Elizabeth looked at Pakahle in unbelief.

"What have you done to her?" she whispered. She had heard of the potency of Indian poisons. She wondered fearfully if Pakahle had poisoned Nellie before her very eyes.

"Made easy. No woman can born child all bound in fear. Fear closes passage to life. See? No longer afraid. She big woman. Should born fine young brave." Pakahle made a gesture of contempt. "White women all weak. Indian no need such medicine."

Elizabeth could not suppress a flash of humor. "If Indian women 'no need' such medicine why do you know of it? We white women know of no such herb!"

Pakahle busy at the fire made no answer. She brought a large pot of warm water and indicated that Elizabeth was to clean up their patient. Meekly Elizabeth complied while Billy sat near the fire, his back decorously turned to the women. Pakahle threw back the tangled covers and made a thorough examination with a practiced eye.

"Good," she announced shortly. "She not die. Built loose like animal. Should bear many sons."

Nellie smiled at Elizabeth weakly.

"What did she do?" She whispered. "I feel warm and tingling all over. Where is the pain?"

"Never worry," Pakahle snorted. "It come back. Man born in pain to live in pain."

Between the two of them, they soon had Nellie clean and comfortable. She was able to rest a bit between the staggering, ripping pains that returned as Pakahle had predicted. Elizabeth wondered now why Pakahle did not offer Nellie more of the seemingly magic potion. Pakahle shook her head when questioned.

"No need now. She no longer afraid. Fear cause most pain. Too much herb make sleep. That not good. She got work to do before sun rises again. Maybe we give little more later, not much."

Elizabeth sat back now quivering with fatigue and tried to relax her own aching body. Each new onslaught of pain caused Nellie to reach out and cling to Elizabeth's strong hands. But after the pains receded she could smile weakly but gratefully and even doze a little.

Outside the storm was increasing in fury. Much later a great clap of thunder boomed over their heads and brought them all awake. Even Pakahle's stolid calm was shaken.

"Why it's too late for thunder," Nellie said. "Isn't today the first of November?"

"Yes, Nellie. I suppose summer is making one last mighty effort."

The night and the storm wore on. The continual muttering noise of the thunder finally ceased as a torrent of rain descended on the huddled cabins. Finally Elizabeth slept a moment to be brought awake by Pakahle's impatient hand on her shoulder.

"Time now." Nellie was gasping and writhing again. Pakahle got busy with blunt, capable fingers. They worked furiously together. A quite different picture flashed momentarily through Elizabeth's mind of another team who had worked desperately and efficiently together to save another life. The quality of the room was different. Only she and the eternal struggle for the tenuous threads of life were the same. Was she the same person? She wondered.

Again the steaming draught quieted the writhing figure on the crude bed. Suddenly Nellie settled back with a sigh of release as Pakahle held a screaming red mass aloft.

"Man child," she said, proudly handing him hastily to Elizabeth while she went back to finish her job.

Sometime later Elizabeth was startled awake by a movement in her lap. She looked down into a pair of piercing lashless eyes. The tiny mouth was sucking noisily on a clenched red fist. She smiled sleepily into the wizened face.

"It was a long hard journey, wasn't it, little man?"

A cold clear sun had risen on a well washed world when Nellie awakened to see her son in Nat's proud arms. Elizabeth stretched tiredly as she leaned against the soaked logs of the staunch house. Her eyes rested in wonder and a certain peace on the blue heights above her. Every tree stood out separately in the clear, clean air. She drew in great draughts of the winey atmosphere. It would be hard to turn her back again on such a sight. Those beckoning blue mountains pulled at her heart like a magnet.

In the sunny, chill days that followed, Elizabeth inspected the remarkable progress that O'Gilvie had made. Jon had audaciously and characteristically included within his and Thomas Brown's surveys the open Indian corn fields in Cheulah's deserted village. This had given O'Gilvie a decided advantage. These fields he had quickly prepared and planted in row crops — cotton, tobacco, corn and food stuffs while the new land was opened for the proposed experiment with lucerne. Rather than leave the endless stumps to rot and take up profitable space, as was customary on the frontier, O'Gilvie and Nat had carefully counted them and allotted an equal number to each Negro family to burn. To the first family to completely destroy his quota, an enticing bonus was offered. To all who accomplished his task before the last fall plowing and the sowing, five acres of land was to be designated as his on which to plant whatever he chose and from which to reap the profits as his own. This innovation produced a miracle. The stumps dissolved as if by magic. Such consideration had never been shown a slave and such heretofore untried methods proved to be good business. The Negroes worked cheerfully and with a will, not seeming to mind the isolation of their situation.

Before Elizabeth's eyes stretched neat clean fields covered with a pale downy green.

"Splendid, O'Gilvie. How have you done it?"

"Any man needs ownership as an incentive. When I realized what owning my land had done to me, I decided to try it on the Negroes. For a disease called apathy, it's the best medicine I know. The twenty-five acres to the five families shall be deducted from my half of the land."

"No, indeed not. We shall deduct their acreage equally from the two of us. We now appear as joint owners on the land records as I directed Mr. Rutledge to do. However, I think it better that you have your half in your name. Have you looked the land over so that we can make an equitable division?"

"Yes, Miss Elizabeth. I did that at once and taking the streams, timber, and amount of open land into consideration, I have run a tentative line for your approval. Do you feel up to walking it today?"

"The sooner the better, O'Gilvie. I must start home as soon as Nellie is able to have me leave. She insists on staying with Nat." Elizabeth looked worried. She need not have worried for on the day of departure Pakahle announced,

"I stay."

Elizabeth was surprised but vaguely glad. Pakahle proved an excellent nurse for both mother and son. All of them enjoyed her method of cooking which added spice to the stolidity of boiled English dishes. With the long cold winter setting in she would feel better if Nellie were not left alone. She wondered about this strange woman. Why was she doing this? Her thoughts burst out.

Pakahle eyed the white woman without emotion.

"Once we enemies. Now nothing left to be enemies about." Her eyes watched her moccasined toe trace a pattern in the dirt. She spoke again, her head still bent, "Both my men love you." Seemingly angry with herself for such weak sentiment, she turned on her heel abruptly, "All Indian admire courage, that all!"

Billy's spotted pony stood ready with the other two for the trail.

Chapter Four

With the coming of winter, Saxe Gothans stolidly and painstakingly set themselves to separate the seed from the cotton by hand, and to weave and fashion the durable cloth into warm garments against the piercing cold. Huddled companionably before enormous stone fireplaces burning with gigantic logs from the receding forests, they baked in front and froze behind while they thanked their stars that the noises of the conflicts in Europe reached them as only faint echoes. The tussle between Frederick of Prussia and Maria Teresa of Austria had finally erupted into war between France and England, reflected in the Colonies as King George's War. Governor Glen had wished to advance on the mighty French fort at Toulouse in an effort to break the back of French imperialistic expansion, thereby erasing the nearer menace of a Cherokee outbreak instigated by prowling French agents and French Indians. The House of Commons, remarkably hard of hearing when the subject under discussion involved money, turned a deaf ear to the Governor's request and jealously drew the purse strings but a little tighter, thus causing him to write plaintively to the Board of Trade.

"Thus little by little the people of South Carolina are getting the whole administration into their hands, and the Crown is by various laws despoiled of its principal flowers and brightest jewels.

No wonder if a governor be not clothed with authority, when he is stripped naked of power." Reflecting unconsciously the developing feeling of Americans in general and Carolinians in particular that security against oppression is more to be valued than efficiency in rule, he concluded, "but I cannot but make this short, disinterested reflection that though a virtuous person might be trusted with a little more power, perhaps there may be as much as can safely be delegated to a weak or wicked man, and such in all times may happen to be employed . . . "

He signed, dropped his quill, and turned his frustrated thoughts to another avenue for pomp and display. The tentatively suggested expedition to the Indian country to cement wavering Catabaw and Cherokee loyalty had caught the imagination of the gentlemen of the Council, and James Glen was cautiously courting their favor. His genuine interest in Indian affairs was only a little deeper if clothed in pomp and circumstance. Such were the thoughts of the royal governor of South Carolina while in far away Albermarle County, Virginia, Peter Jefferson was guiding his infant son Thomas in his first independent steps.

Elizabeth and her little family sat comfortably around a new stove, product of the remarkably versatile mind of Mr. Benjamin Franklin while Uncle Roy read to them from Mr. Franklin's popular new *Pennsylvania Gazette.* The stove, along with many other small comforts and rare conveniences, was a Christmas gift from Andrew Rutledge.

"Well, I am very thankful for this one, aren't you, Uncle Roy?"

"Hmmm," Roy agreed comfortably without raising his eyes from his book.

Aunt Vadie looked at a letter from Andrew that arrived with the stove.

"And who does he mean by 'we'?"

"His wife, of course."

"Humph! His wife never saw you, nor you her. 'We', indeed. I'll wager she didn't suggest the remark about the garnet gown, nor did that selfcentered Andrew!"

Elizabeth flushed and rose annoyed.

"Now, Aunt Vadie. I have no intention of questioning Mr. Rutledge's gifts. At this point, without two sous to rub together, I shall not look too deeply into the source of any comfort for which I do not have to pay!"

"Looks like history repeating itself to me! I recall — "

"Hush, Aunt Vadie." Elizabeth stamped her foot. "What is the matter with her, Uncle Roy? She sounds like a querulous old maid lately instead of a much loved aunt, doesn't she?"

Elizabeth whirled and left Uncle Roy looking reproachfully at his wife over his near useless spectacles for which he had sent off to Charles Town. Eleazar, entrusted with the commission had reckoned by his own keen eyesight and brought back a fashionable pair of shiny rims fitted with clear glass.

"Was that necessary, my dear? You could be wrong, you know."

"I'm not wrong. Why should Andrew Rutledge take such a sudden interest in Elizabeth's comfort?"

"Because he realizes what straits we are in for ready money. He has always handled her legal affairs. Besides, if he isn't behind these gifts, what does it matter?"

"I don't want Elizabeth hurt again."

"Hurt? How?"

"Elizabeth will never return to Charles Town. You have encouraged her in this stubborn attitude yourself," she added reproachfully.

"So?"

"That doctor will never leave his safe, fashionable practice in town."

"How do you know?"

"He didn't once before, did he?"

"Gavin McBride is a man in every sense of the word. He had made his life and his wife should have been willing to share it with him. You cannot hold him responsible for what happened. Circumstances and Elizabeth's own foolish stubbornness are to blame."

"If you feel she was foolish why do you encourage her to stay here?"

"May I remind you, my love, that was thirteen years ago? Elizabeth is a different woman now. One who has seen what she has seen and fought so hard for existence would never be content in the surface life of a city. Her wonderful energy and capacities would be stifled. She could never live such an aimless life again."

"There, you see! You are agreeing with me. They are too widely separated for their paths to cross. It is better that they never meet again."

"There I do not agree. Gavin comes from vigorous Scotch stock and must also find the life of Charles Town too rarefied for his great animal frame to breathe. Having met his obligations in full, as we learned from Dr. Killpatrick, he himself might wish to shake off the shackles of society that bind his science."

215

"Roy! How can you talk so? You used to be a gentleman who revelled in these so-called shackles you are now decrying!"

"Perhaps I have found something more satisfying than being a gentleman, my dear." He returned to his habitual light tone, "However I still cherish my comfort enough to try to prevent your arousing suspicions that might cause this fascinating invention to be returned." He laughed into his wife's face as he turned his back gratefully to its warmth.

"Uncle Roy and I are agreed that we won't send the stove back, but we could send you back if you don't stop complaining, couldn't we, Uncle Roy?" The warm voice was vibrant with laughter. Her aunt and uncle looked up startled to find Elizabeth, her good humour completely restored, standing in the doorway. The wrinkled folds of the rich garnet velvet gown fell softly without hoops, carressing the lovely, tall figure. Her proud throat was encircled with the gleaming pearls, and her glorious hair was piled high and loose. Elizabeth's dark eyes were warm and luminous with the elusive eagerness of youth. Time had only deepened her lush beauty, enhancing it with strength and assurance. The only visible mark of the years on the glowing face was the deep line between the heavy brows.

"Oh-hh!" gasped Aunt Vadie. "How beautiful you are!"

Uncle Roy bowed with a flourish and Elizabeth, laughing, swept him a deep curtsy.

From that moment preparations went forward for a holiday celebration. The community, too long engrossed in its fight for life, had neglected the gay parties that bring light and laughter, and ease the heavy burdens of care. All eagerly entered into plans for a gala few days of song, games, and dance. The air was redolent with the fragrant odors of Christmas kücken, plumb pudding, and sweet meats stuffed with rare spices that Eleazar brought from Charles Town along with messages from Governor Glen to the Catabaws to meet him for a good talk at Saxe Gotha in the Spring, the Cherokees to gather for the same talk at Ninety Six.

Eleazar was full of himself and eager to be on his way. He promised to be back by Christmas Eve, the date set for the dance in Thomas Brown's store to open the festivities. Games and contests were scheduled for Christmas Day with an open air feast for all on the Common if the day were fine. If not, each family would dine at home and meet again at the store for songs in the afternoon. Excitement was everywhere. Elizabeth's garnet gown hung in the steaming kitchen until it's wrinkles disappeared. Aunt

Vadie, her bad temper completely forgotton, mended gold lace for Roy and searched in her boxes for forgotten finery. Eleazar had asked that he be allowed Nat and Nellie's old cabin for that week so that he might bring a couple of friends, traders he said vaguely, to join in the unheard of goings on. Why, some traders never knew it was Christmas from one year to another, he declared. This was fine business! They couldn't afford to miss it.

Children were sent to the woods for spicy pine boughs and berry laden holly. Their eyes sparkled with youth that had rarely had the opportunity to express itself in the ever present rigors of frontier life. Great battles with acorn ammunition developed, making the forests ring with their glad warlike shouts.

Succulent smoked turkeys and dark red hams were taken down from their hooks and subjected to the various culinary secrets of the nationalities represented in the Carolina backwoods.

The final day arrived and Elizabeth and Aunt Vadie were supervising the last minute decorations in the improvised ballroom. Bungs had been loosened in the kegs of good stout German beer, the spirit of comradery prevailed everywhere.

"Merry Christmas, Miss Betsy!" Elizabeth gave Eleazar a glad hug and shook hands joyfully with O'Gilvie whom he had brought with him.

"How's Nellie, O'Gilvie?"

"Just splendid, Miss Elizabeth."

"And the baby?"

"He's nearly a man! I've never seen an infant thrive so. He should with two women to spoil him."

"Pakahle?"

O'Gilvie shook a puzzled head. "I don't understand it, Miss Elizabeth. Such a complete about face. She's helpful, efficient, and devoted to Nellie – apparently completely contented. You know there's a deep seated feeling of trust you can have about a person. We all feel that about her. Can you explain it?"

"She says there is nothing now for us to be enemies about, so she intends that we be friends. It's a very simple philosophy. Perhaps the world would be a happier, less complicated place if we could all subscribe to it." Elizabeth laughed doubtfully. "I wish Nellie and Nat could be here. Can you believe how the spirits of the people have risen? We must never neglect fun again. It's a wonderful tonic."

"I felt I shouldn't leave them now, but neither Nat nor Nellie would hear to my staying after Mr. Wigan's account of the activities here. The hands are busy with fences and Nellie promises them a good, sound celebration too. We have some new neighbors. They don't have warrants for land as yet, but they are taking it up and seem to plan to settle."

Elizabeth looked worried. "You'd better advise them to go to Charles Town for warrants. You know what trouble Thomas Wallexelleson, the blacksmith, is having trying to protect his land against Mr. Gibson who now has a registered warrant for the same land and is cutting off the timber."

"Let's not worry about it now, Miss Elizabeth. I'll advise our neighbors properly on my return. I plan to stay only a few days and will leave after I discuss the news of our cows with you."

"No news, O'Gilvie. That's another worry."

"Day after tomorrow will be soon enough to worry. Let it not mar your holiday. It's good for us all. We could do with a bit of laughter."

As the day wore on Eleazar grew morose and by lunch time was fairly glum. Elizabeth full of her own chatter didn't notice for a time how silent he was and how often he glanced out the window.

"It's Christmas Eve, Eleazar, what's the matter? No one is allowed to be glum today in my presence. I haven't felt so light hearted in years! Will you dance with me tonight? Did you know that we found two fiddlers with violins with strings all intact. Mr. Mueller says his might hold out if he doesn't saw too hard. Eleazar, please put violin strings on your next list. I shall have to sell more land to pay my debts to you!" Elizabeth laughed gaily, her face flushed with high spirits. "Your friends will surely come, don't worry. But they'd hardly come from that direction," she added seeing his eyes turned toward the Charles Town road. She hurried off to talk with Blossom about her own little dinner party before the ball, not noticing that his eyes remained glued to the Charles Town road.

"Eleazar," she called a few moments later from the direction of the kitchen, "will you teach us that Virginia reel? I'm afraid the minuet is too stiff and stately for our gay mood."

When she received no answer, she thrust her flushed, hot face into the holly draped living room. It was empty. She shrugged and went back to her work with Blossom, humming a little tune.

Chapter Five

Only the fire burned more brightly than the light in Elizabeth's eyes that evening as she gaily touched up the elegant table and pirouetted gracefully for Uncle Roy to admire her. Aunt Vadie watched in wonder and cried within that such beauty and gaiety should be wasted. She knew that the beauty born of great inward strength would last on through the lonely years, but the sudden gaiety would die and become perhaps peace, maybe even content, but never the joy and happiness that should be her destiny. She sighed heavily.

"Now, Aunt Vadie, your face is longer than Mr. Wigan's. By the way," she said suddenly remembering, "did his friends arrive? I have laid places for them. I do hope one is Mr. Grant. I like him. He's so learned. Why do you suppose a man of his education is content to spend his life among the Indians, Uncle Roy?" Elizabeth asked chattily.

"Funny isn't it?" answered Roy. "Take Wigan himself. He's a paradox. He has the heart and mind of an educated man, the body and appearance of a peasant. But come, my dear," he turned to his wife. "Elizabeth is not the only one to be admired on this momentous occasion. I prefer blondes," he bowed gallantly, "smiling blondes," he added, cupping her sweet face in one hand while he stroked the gleaming gold of her hair with the other. Two remarkable women, he thought. From what inward spring did they draw their youth and courage? Vadie's hair was fading and she no longer bustled, but the gentle face changed little with the years. Yes, he had enjoyed some of the rewards of life, and, by Heaven, he hoped to enjoy more. He wasn't dead himself yet!

A heavy hand pounded the thick door. Elizabeth ran to throw it open in glad welcome to Eleazar and his guests. Wigan bowed elegantly. Elizabeth sank in a low curtsy. Her startled eyes looked up and a glad cry broke from her raspberry red lips. She sprang to her feet.

"Why, Andrew Rutledge! What a wonderful surprise!" She held out both her hands to him joyfully. He clasped them warmly and bent to kiss her flushed cheek. "Stand back and let me look at you! Why, Andrew, you haven't — " She stopped short. The color drained from her vivid face. A blond head bent to come in the still open door.

"Am I to be denied the same welcome?" Gavin McBride felt her shoulders tremble beneath his hands as he bent to kiss her now cold cheek. Something she had thought long dead stirred deep within Elizabeth. She withdrew unsteadily from his touch.

"Gavin," her voice was almost a whisper. His blue eyes met her dark ones and held. For a moment the world receded, leaving the two of them alone. "Welcome," Elizabeth's voice when she found it again was husky. "Please excuse me while I see to our dinner." She hastened from the room on shaky legs trying to get hold of herself and control the sudden chill that caused her body to tremble violently. Everybody began to talk at once to cover their emotions.

Gavin's eyes were waiting for her when she returned, her composure restored. The gaiety of the early evening was gone, but the light that burned in her eyes was deeper and surer. She tried to avoid Gavin's eyes which never left her as she served her guests wine to match the color of her gown. She smiled shakily as she raised her glass.

"To us all," she cried, her eyes sparkling.

"To us all," echoed around the candle lit table covered with fine damask and heavy silver that Aunt Vadie had rescued thankfully from its exile in her trunk.

"It's been a long time," said Andrew as they seated themselves.

"Yes, it has," Elizabeth spoke softly, avoiding Gavin's eyes.

"Too long since I last ate," Eleazar declared boldly after clearing his throat loudly.

"Why, Mr. Wigan," scolded Elizabeth, glad to have his matter of fact voice break the tension, "are you disregarding the excellent luncheon I served you?"

"I was too worried about these fellows to eat. I thought they'd spoil my surprise."

Elizabeth laughed. "You and your deceiving ways! I'll never trust you again."

The crisp skin of the smoked wild turkey crackled and split under Uncle Roy's practiced knife. Gay conversation turned back the clock and the long weary disappointing years between dissolved in the happy holiday atmosphere.

Uncle Roy and Aunt Vadie led off the minuet. When Gavin had held out his arm to Elizabeth, she dropped her eyes, her voice was almost inaudible.

"I promised the first to Eleazar."

Gavin and Andrew good naturedly chose two of the much younger women whose husbands were too shy to dance. The festive air added a look of elegance to the simple homespun gowns which had been carefully pressed and ornamented with a sprig of holly if no other touch of finery was available. Some gowns of cherished heavy silk rivaled Elizabeth's own, but none could touch the beauty of her glowing face. The dignified movements of the stately dance did not match the excited mood of the gathering. Eleazar perspired his way through the first dance, and thanking his partner peremptorily he left her and headed for the fiddlers.

"Fellows, that's too slow. Do it like this." He began to pat his foot in a lively tempo. The two musicians' faces broke into a grin and the wailing whine of the dragging minuet changed to a spritely twang of the reel.

"All right, men, grab a girl and let's go!" Eleazar shouted. Catching the idea, the men and women gathered in a great circle and began to clap their hands and pat their feet. Gavin was again at Elizabeth's side. This time she could not refuse him and laid her hand lightly in his own. His fingers closed warmly over it. He looked down at her seriously.

"Couldn't you forget the past just for this evening? Pretend we are two nice people who have met for the first time, there is no past and no future, just tonight. Will you try it?"

"Yes, Gavin, I'll try."

It was not difficult in the tearing tempo and lively rhythm of Eleazar's dance to shut out all but the present. It was all one could do to keep up with his flying feet and shouting voice. The few reluctant bystanders soon began clapping their hands and shuffling their feet to the contagious melody. After the dance, weak with exhaustion and jolly laughter, they rushed for the punch bowl and the beer barrels. So much noise and laughter had never been heard at the Congarees. The woods rang that night with gaiety and the joy of living. Forgotten for the moment were weariness, privation, and fear. The small red figure sliding into the clearing from the narrow northward path cocked his ear in amazement. Onconecaw hesitated a moment at the corner of the store building before gliding on toward the little stone house waiting in the cold moonlight. He was still waiting in the shadow of the house much later when the door of Thomas Brown's store was flung open on tired but happy dancers who called "Merry Christmas" to each other thankfully as they sought their beds.

Laughing and talking gaily the little group turned toward Elizabeth's house. Strangely, she had not found it at all difficult in the excitement of the happy crowd of dancers to treat the evening as a joyful interlude. She had danced the new dances with Gavin, Andrew, Stephen Crell and her uncle. It was wonderful to feel young and free again. The laughter died on her lips.

"Onconecaw!" The little figure that stepped out into the moonlit yard stood before them with the assurance of position and natural poise of his race. The warm feeling left Elizabeth's heart and cold reality returned. How foolishly naive she had been to suppose one could forget the past even for a moment. It closed in on her now as she looked coldly at her old friend. The future? One could not forget it either. It was always ready to spring on the unwary. To meet it meant eternal vigilance for a new battle.

"What do you want?" Elizabeth asked stiffly after she recovered from her first shock.

Onconecaw's face expressed no surprise at the coldness in her voice.

"I came at once, Lady Cuming, after a short visit to my village. But lately did I affect my release from the northern Indians. I bring news."

Elizabeth shuddered and drew her furs more closely around her shoulders.

"Please, could we not discuss it another time. It is late and – and I'm very tired," she ended lamely. Suddenly she was very tired. All her exuberance vanished.

"Tomorrow?" persisted Onconecaw. "I must leave for trip through the Nation. Many chiefs have many talks. They discuss English."

Eleazar pricked up his ears.

"Talks, eh? Maybe you and I had better talk tonight. Tomorrow we'll all meet together after the celebration." Bidding them goodnight, Eleazar led Onconecaw off in the direction of Nat's cabin.

Heavily, Elizabeth led the way into the warm living room dimly lit by fragrant bay candles. After a bowl of hot punch, they all rose to leave save Gavin who lingered.

Elizabeth stood facing the fire, her back to the tall big man whose heart was in his face.

"You see," she said bitterly, not turning. "One cannot discard the past like an old shoe. It's no use!"

"What's no use?"

"Why did you come?" Elizabeth whirled on Gavin angrily. "Why didn't you leave me alone. You have your life and I have mine!"

"The last time we were alone, we quarrelled," he looked steadily into her stormily miserable eyes. "Both of us said angry, hasty words we did not mean. Look what it cost us. Shall be begin again by quarrelling?"

"Begin again? It's too late to begin again!"

"Why?" he asked calmly. "You say you have your life and I have mine. But what kind of lives are they? Empty and wasted. Betsy, my darling, you know as well as I that we belong together." He started toward her. She quickly put the table between them.

"No!" She cried.

"No?" His arms fell to his sides. His eyes held dismay and a certain anger.

"Can't you see, Gavin, that from the pieces of the wreck I've made of my life I can salvage something here to cling to, some purpose to guide me. They need me here. I love this wild, free country. I can't return to Charles Town. There's nothing for me there!"

Before she could prevent it he had rounded the table and grasped her shoulders in hands that hurt. He shook her and forced her eyes to look straight into his own.

"For God's sake, hush that foolish chatter. Why do you think I made the long gruelling trip from Charles Town in the middle of winter? A pleasure trip, mayhap! The trip was certainly not a pleasure but the anticipation of what I'd find at the end of it was." He drew her resisting body into his arms. The good, clean man odor of him assailed Elizabeth's nostrils like a drug. The hurt of his strong arms sent little flames darting through her. "Oh, my darling, I love you so. All down the lonely years you have rarely been out of my thoughts and heart. Now that I've found you again

223

I don't intend to lose you."

"Please, Gavin," Elizabeth whispered, "let me go! It's folly to think we can turn back the clock. I can't go with you."

"I didn't ask you to go with me."

Elizabeth raised her head from his chest. Her eyes were puzzled, "Well, why — ?"

"When Andrew ordered your cows I had him double the order."

Elizabeth waited.

"I thought perhaps we could consolidate."

"Here?"

"Wherever you say. I have a warrant for two hundred acres of land next to your survey at Ninety Six. Did you not point out to the Governor the great need for doctors on the frontier?"

"No, no!" she cried "I can't let you give up all you've worked for for me!"

"My dearest," he said teasingly not attempting to touch her. "I am not giving it up for you." He took her cold hand and caressed it as he spoke seriously into her upturned, unbelieving face. "Now that the heat of youth has passed and I know what I've missed, I would gladly give up anything for you. But the city with it's vapors and its narrowness of mind has no need of a doctor. All it needs is a bedside manner. I can't practice medicine in the face of such dogmatic prejudice. I want to be where I am really needed, where I can do good and relieve suffering."

"Oh, Gavin, do you really mean it?"

"Yes, Betsy, I do." She smiled softly as she realized he was using Margaret's and Blossom's pet name for her.

"But," she said slowly, frowning as she withdrew her hand and rose, "It's been too long, I'm afraid. We've both changed. How can we know — ," she looked at him for help.

"Of course, we've changed. We've grown wiser and more mature. That can only make our love the deeper."

"How can we know that love still exists after so long? How can two people who have seen each other but once in thirteen years — ?"

He sprang up and put his hands on her shoulders, "How can we know? What did you feel when I walked in tonight? What are you feeling now that I touch you?"

Elizabeth's eyes fell. She began to tremble again.

"Afraid?" He tilted her chin and forced her to look into his eyes. "Are you afraid of me, my Betsy?"

"No," she whispered. "I'm afraid of myself. The years have not been kind. Gavin, please give me a little time."

He kissed her fragrant hair gently.

"All the time you need, my dearest – just so it isn't long." He smiled reassuringly. "Good-night. It isn't long until tomorrow."

Christmas Day dawned fair and crisp. In spite of the late hour they had retired after the dancing, the members of the little colony were up bright and early preparing for the big feast. Pit fires were going before dawn and the aroma of barbecuing wild meat floated in the pine scented air. The woodsy odor of burning hickory added tang to the atmosphere. Trestle tables were laid with fine linen sheets from the Old Country. Smiling faces were rosy in the crisp thin air. Here and there spots of Christmas carols broke out.

Chris Beudeker shouted and puffed as he rolled out his kegs of ale, sampling periodically from each barrel. In this activity he had many willing assistants and by noon faces, red with the cold, were redder still with an inner glow. Good fellowship flowed with the ale and new friendships were made and sealed to eternity.

By ten o'clock the games began. Back woods knights astride unshod, wild range ponies whooped and hallooed as they dashed by a suspended greased goose, vainly trying to capture its slippery neck as they flew by. Many tumbles added hilarity and bets ran high. Tilting without lances, Indian fashion, revealed powerful muscles as contestants tugged back and forth endeavoring to unhorse each other. As one was thrown, cheers arose from the victor's group of supporters. The high light was the turkey shoot. The usual show-off distance for markmanship with the dead-heavy English smooth bore musket was sixty yards, and, had an elephant lumbered through the jungles of colonial South Carolina on Christmas day of 1745, a marksman with such a gun might have found his mark – provided the air was not too damp to put out his flash in the pan or the wind not blowing in the gunner's direction causing the burning powder to singe his eyelashes. The betting ran high as the target, a nail head in a foot square block, was set on a fallen log and the line of fire drawn on the cold ground sixty yards away. Herman Geiger, when sober, was a master sharpshooter. He now strutted pompously about already acting possessive toward the plump pair of fine turkeys that had been fattening for weeks as the event's prize. Giggling children climbed trees to keep better tab of the score. Geiger, after laboriously loading his awkward piece of artillery, pulled it up and fired in the general direction of the target. The musket, having no sight, was not placed to the shoulder merely raised and discharged.

A high right corner of the target splintered slightly. A roar arose from the crowd. A truly fine shot! Amazing for the first round. To allow every man time for reloading his cumbersome arm, each contestant took one shot around, two out of three shots determining the winner. The second shot was wide of the mark. The ball thudded dully into a far away tree. One after another took his place at the firing line, rarely did a ball find the target. This was all proper and expected and if a man managed to sink his ball in any visible spot in the vicinity of the block he was a hero.

Eleazar swaggered up trying to look nonchalant and succeeding about as well as a mother hen with a new brood. Tilting a long slender gun, a few inches longer than he was tall, he opened his pouch took out a small round patch greased it lightly and placed it over the muzzle. With his thumb he thrust a ball atop this patch down the bore and shoved both home quickly with a light wooden ramrod in about one fourth the time it took the others to load. Necks craned, eyes sparkled with interest at this lightning operation.

Eleazar looked around his audience disdainfully like a trooper, cleared his throat importantly, raised his gun to his shoulder, sighted down its six-foot barrel, and fired. Astonished silence gripped the spectators.

"Bull's eye!" screamed a child nearest the target falling from his perch in his excitement. Everyone rushed to see. About an inch to the right of the nail head was a tiny, neat hole. A gasp arose. Geiger's face was mottled with rage.

"Vat haf you here?" spoke Thomas Waxelleson in a reverent whisper reaching out to touch this magic fire stick.

"Isn't she a beauty?" Wigan stroked the black walnut stock lovingly. "I've named her Betsy." His eyes met Elizabeth's smiling ones over the heads of the astonished crowd. "You're two of a kind, Miss Betsy," he said making his way toward her.

"Why, Eleazar, it's a wonder! What is it?"

"It's a rifle, Miss Betsy, made in Pennsylvania." He relinquished it to Waxelleson who had followed close on Wigan's heels. The blacksmith tried its long slenderness for balance and raised unbelieving eyes to its owner.

"Vy it veys no more dan a fedder!" Waxelleson cried.

The turkey shoot came to a slow halt while each man examined the wonder rifle. German rifles had been known for over a hundred years but they were few and far between, cumbersome, difficult to load, and almost as inaccurate as the English musket. Something in the colonial atmosphere of America stirred ingenuity and this instrument was the product of a Pennsylvania gunsmith who was tired of being potted at by red savages who could shoot a quiver full of arrows while he pounded one ball down his barrel with an iron ramrod and heavy mallet.

Admiring eyes examined a thing of beauty as well as a lethal looking gadget. The walnut stock was darkened with soot and oil, the butt was protected with a metal plate where it touched the ground in loading. A metal star marked the spot where cheek rested against stock.

"The bullet is smaller than the bore," explained Eleazar in answer to eager questions, "and can be loaded more quickly. The greased patch serves two purposes, to wedge the ball securely to make it follow the rifling and to clean the barrel as it travels."

"Do it again!" shouted the children. "Do it again!"

The shoot turned into an exhibition. The sturdy picture of Eleazar Wigan in his buckskins and furred hat loading his slender rifle, the first product of American manufacture, might well have become the emblem of Independence instead of the eagle.

Wigan was the undisputed champion. He walked away proudly with a fat fowl under each arm while Thomas Waxelleson examined the new gun, measuring and muttering to himself.

Flushed with exertion and excitement, the crowd congregated around laden tables groaning under piles of roast turkey, roast goose, blood red hams, pheasants, quail, and pigeon — their brown skins bursting with juicy goodness. Irresistible spicy fragrance arose from a huge iron pot stirred lovingly by the one lone French inhabitant at the Congarees, Pierre LeBlanc. Bouillabaisse, an inimitable fish stew, added a touch of Latin romance to English and German realism. Pierre often wondered how the tides of fortune had swept him from his sunny, civilized Provence to the wild American continent. Now he shrugged and sipped his good yellow wine made from luscious wild Carolina scuppernongs while he smiled a bit disdainfully at his beefy compatriots swilling great draughts of heady beer.

Elizabeth had greeted Gavin quietly but gladly. In the riotous holiday confusion they had little time to talk. Though their eyes met often, he had a feeling she was deliberately avoiding any tete-a-tete with him. A solid happiness enveloped them all, however, and it was impossible not to enjoy the day.

When no one could eat another morsel, they gathered around Christian Theus to lead them in a great sing. The woods rang with their glad voices and the power of the mounting strains must have risen even to the watchful Cherokee in his mountain fortress, perhaps even helping to dissipate momentarily the gathering dark clouds of Indian hostility. Could such powerful voices be easily stilled? The red man watched and wondered — and waited.

An old German carol rose first. Heads were bared devoutly in the warm December sun.

"Fairest Lord Jesus, Ruler of all nature,
O Thou of God and man the Son,
Thee will I cherish, Thee will I honor.
Thee, my soul's Glory, Joy and Crown."

One gay carol — both English and German — followed another. Shadows were long on the leaf strewn earth when Reverend Theus brought his little flock back to the real meaning of the day. George Whitefield, on his departure from Savannah, had written Elizabeth a farewell, heartening note enclosing another beautiful Wesley hymn that he himself had altered. Christian Theus now lined it out to his enthusiastic choir who echoed his melodious baritone with fervour,

"Hark the herald angels sing,
'Glory to the newborn King;
Peace on earth, and mercy mild;
God and Sinners reconciled,'
Joyful, all ye Nations rise,
Join the triumph of the skies;
With angelic hosts proclaim,
'Christ is born in Bethlehem!'
Hark! the herald angels sing,
'Glory to the newborn King!'"

Strains of the lovely hymn floated back on the evening air as the inhabitants of Saxe Gotha, full of sweet joy and renewed hope, sought their rude but tight cabin homes.

"Born to raise the Sons of earth,
Born to give them second Birth."

Hope found a second birth in the hearts of men that day.

Chapter Six

"Why are you avoiding me?"

"I am not avoiding you."

"You are. You promised me an answer today."

"No, Gavin, I did not."

"Very well then. You led me to believe you would answer me today. I have been very patient with you, Elizabeth. Now, I want my answer."

"My father taught me that if I must say yes or no, to say no."

"I am in no mood for joking or coquetry."

"Oh, Gavin, I am neither joking nor coquetting. It's just as I told you; I'm afraid."

"What have you to be afraid of, my darling?" Gavin tried to draw her to him, but Elizabeth stopped him with a gesture.

"Please sit down, Gavin, and let me try to explain."

She was silent a moment gazing into the flames. She sighed deeply and turned to him, speaking earnestly. "There are many associations here that I cannot forget. Will they creep in, if we should marry, to destroy our peace, our happiness? Haven't I hurt you enough already? I don't want to accept that responsibility again." Her eyes pled with him to understand a feeling, a fear, that she herself but vaguely understood. Disaster had so long dogged her every step that she had begun to distrust her own judgment.

"No one can forget or erase the past; only the very strong can rebuild on disaster, Elizabeth. I believed that you have that strength. If I did not, I would not have come."

"But don't you see, I must believe that too," she cried desperately. "I had already begun laboriously to rebuild my life along the only lines that I thought possible, when you came along and opened up a whole new vista. Will you give me a little time, for your sake as well as mine, to try to straighten out the confusion in my mind?" She looked at his unresponsive face.

"You don't understand!" she cried out. "How can I make you see something I can't understand myself? How can I explain this feeling that everything I touch I will eventually destroy? How?" Her dark eyes were large with sorrow and filled with tears.

"I have only one question to ask you. Do you love me?"

Elizabeth faced him squarely, "I do, Gavin. I have no words to tell you how deeply!"

"To me, nothing else matters. However, some confusion in your mind might arise after such a sudden move on my part. I will concede I have been planning it for months." His voice became matter of fact.

"I intend to journey now to Ninety-Six with O'Gilvie. He advises me that he will go back tomorrow. After I see my new land, I am to return to Charles Town to wind up my affairs. I have promised to accompany Governor Glen's party in the early spring to consult with the Catawbas here, with the Cherokees at Ninety-Six. In May I shall be here again."

Elizabeth waited. Gavin rose to his great height and looked down into her beautiful troubled face.

"I am a man, Elizabeth, not a boy. I shall expect an answer then, and until then I shall not press you."

May! That was four months away! Not to see his beloved face again until then? Her heart quailed. Well, she reminded herself sharply, it's your own doing. What is the matter with you anyway? She sighed wearily.

"Yes, Gavin," was all she could think of to say.

Chapter Seven

Andrew Rutledge left the council chamber carrying in his hand the Governor's message to the Commons. In the corridor Gavin was waiting.

"Come on, Gavin. Let's see what kind of humour these parsimonious boys are in today."

Gavin raised his eyebrows questioningly while he smiled into his friend's shrewd, dark face.

"Governor Glen expects a battle. He's not stupid, however. He's invited members of the Council and Commons to accompany him, and has whispered in their ears that the Board of Trade might question the fact that, as deputies of the King, they have never visited the peoples that they govern. He's cleverly, with my help I must admit, made it seem like a lark, a grand parade of British might. Since they are to spend the money on themselves, and not just on the Governor, perhaps they'll relax the purse strings just a trifle." Andrew laughed sardonically.

"You are a realist, Andrew."

"Politics doesn't welcome dreamers, my friend. Would I be where I am now if I were not a realist?"

Gavin joined in his laugh. True enough, he thought. A raw and unknown neophyte in this dog-eat-dog country would have to see everything as it really was to have reached the dizzy heights of

Andrew Rutledge's assured position – member of the Council, eminent lawyer and husband of an enormously wealthy woman. Gavin wondered fleetingly if Andrew had found satisfaction in his phenomenal rise to fame and fortune. He thought he had. Andrew was an intellectual but not a deep thinker. Was such a paradox possible? He shrugged as they approached the Commons House assembly hall.

"Andrew, what ever became of that man, who was he – Hamilton, I believe, who wanted to settle that area above the Congarees, the land around Nine-Six?"

"John Hamilton. He's one of those dreamers, Gavin. Here we are. Find your seat in the balcony and watch the show. I'll see you later." Andrew hurried off as Gavin sought his place in the spectators' gallery.

He looked down with interest at the crowd of gentlemen below, trying at the last minute to draw in votes for this or that favorite bill. He answered William Bull's salute of welcome. William, as different from Andrew as day and night, had done well too. After his return from the University of Leyden in 1734, he had become a power in the political life of the province also. But he was the member of a fine and established family of solid statesmen and patriots. His rise to speaker of the Commons was not as remarkable as Andrew's rise from complete obscurity. However, Gavin supposed, that fact was what had made this country develop so rapidly. A country which could recognize ability in both unknown and established, and give both an equal right, was bound to become great.

William Bull's gavel interrupted his reveries. A hush fell. Governor Glen's proclamation was read:

> *"Whereas the General Assembly of this Province stands adjourned to the eleventh day of May next, and whereas the urgent affairs of this Province, which greatly concerns the security and welfare thereof, render it highly necessary to call the General Assembly sooner than their said day of adjournment, I have therefore thought fit by and with the advice of his Majesty's Council to issue this my proclamation to summon the several members of the General Assembly to meet at the usual place in Charles Town on Monday next the fourteenth instant and they are hereby required to meet at said time and place accordingly.*
> *Given under my hand and the great seal*

232

of the Province this eleventh day of
April in the nineteenth year of his
Majesty's reign

James Glen

A murmur and rustle broke out after the formal reading. The gavel fell again. William Bull introduced Andrew Rutledge to the members of the Commons House of the Assembly now in session in Charles Town, Province of South Carolina.

Andrew rose, cool and assured. His dark eyes travelled slowly and dramatically over the assembled gentlemen. He adjusted his cravat and a paper on the table.

"Thank you, Mr. Speaker. Gentlemen," he paused for effect as the secretary's pen began to scratch across the foolscap.

"Good theatre," Gavin thought. "What a showman he is!"

Andrew's suave voice — was it just a mite nasal - no, must be a slight cold — continued.

"I am come before you as the Governor's messenger. He has requested that I read to you certain letters he has received from traders Doughtery and Grant in the Cherokee nation. But first the Governor's own message." Andrew paused and set an elaborate pair of spectacles astride his sharp nose. Gavin could scarcely suppress a grin. Andrew's eyes were much keener than his own. More stage business, he'd wager. But Andrew was reading:

Mr. Speaker and Gentlemen:

Since your last adjournment I have received several letters from the Cherokees, Creeks, and Catawbas which inform me of the design the French have and are practicing to debauch those Indians from the British interests. If their efforts are effective they will be most detrimental to the peace and safety of the Province.

I have dispatched an express to the Cherokees to summon the head men of that nation to meet me at Ninety-Six in order to give them a talk and deliver them the presents agreed on at your last meeting. I have appointed the first day of next month for my interview with those Indians at Ninety-Six. As I advised you in your last meeting, the King of the Catawbas and one hundred of his beloved men will gather at the Congarees on the twenty-seventh instant. Mr. Thomas Brown advised me that the settlement at Saxe Gotha is in

233

readiness to receive the envoys of that nation as well as ourselves.

If it meets with your approval, I urgently request that you vote the necessary funds to equip and maintain a retinue of fifty gentlemen and their servants as well as two hundred horsemen. Today is the fourteenth, and to arrive at the Congarees on the appointed day, our contingent should leave Charles Town not later than Monday, April twenty-first, one week from today. In addition to the necessities, I recommend that you also include a sum for the employment of a qualified physician to guard the health of our members in the wilderness and to return them to Charles Town in good order.

I cannot stress to you too emphatically the importance of this mission on which the future good relations with our red neighbors may depend.

James Glen, Governor

For a moment no one stirred. Gavin wondered if it were the contents of the document or the spellbinding voice that had held them enthralled. He would place his heaviest bet on the voice!

Finally the storm broke. The Commons, who voted *no* without thought on all affairs involving money, protested as a matter of course. The debate started and rose to furious proportions. The line of division was apparent. Those who were invited to be a member of the diplomatic mission were in favor of spending the money, naturally not as much as the Governor recommended. Heaven forbid! Did the man think the Bank of England had offices in the Province extending unlimited credit? Those who had not been invited, or whose wives would not let them go, shouted in vociferous protest. The Governor was completely mad — delusions of grandeur, absurd. Not one penny, etc.

When all the arguments pro and con had been spoken, if not heard in the din, a vote was taken and the *ayes* had it. Shocked silence fell in the House. This was heresy! Voting *aye* on a money bill originated and recommended by the Governor! The ayes looked sheepishly around. Not one of them thought he would have enough company to pass the bill. The look of dismay was comical. Belatedly gathering their dignity, and their sole right to originate money bills unto themselves, they coldly advised Andrew Rutledge to inform His Excellency the Governor that if he were suffering from dyspepsia, he could employ his own private physician.

"The health of the Governor is no responsibility of this Government." They had the last word. That should warn the Governor to keep his meddling nose out of their business. They arose and went home sheepishly to pack their boxes in preparation for the trip. To think that they had allowed themselves to be so tricked!

Andrew winked at Gavin. His look plainly said, "There, do you see? What did I tell you?"

Gavin bowed in mock salute.

Two days later, the Commons, apparently completely demoralized by their laxity in allowing the Governor to talk them out of so much money, were again cleverly duped into voting five hundred pounds for a fort at Saxe Gotha and less ostentatious sums for similar fortifications at William's Burg and Orangeburg, allowing four swivel guns for each installation. Again regrasping the reins at the last minute, the money was directed to be taken from the Township Fund.

Now excitement took hold of the society at Charles Town, always glad to welcome any change from the monotony of their days. There were many farewell parties before the grand cortege set out from town under threatening skies.

The long months had passed slowly for Elizabeth, though she threw herself into a fever of work. She became moody, cross, and irritable to the point where Aunt Vadie chided her one day,

"Now, who is acting like a querulous old maid, my dear? You are almost too cross to live with."

"I'm sorry, Aunt Vadie."

"What is the matter with you, child?"

"I wish I knew, Aunt Vadie. I feel terrible!"

"Why must you try to complicate the simple issues of life, Elizabeth? In some matters it is best to follow the heart, not the head."

"But, Aunt Vadie, this is too important!" She looked around the charming room, the home that she had made in the wilderness for another man, the home that had held no happiness, only misery. "The associations are so strong. Could we possibly build a private life for ourselves here where old memories might creep in and destroy us?"

"You would have to control that, my dear."

"I'm tired of controlling things!" Elizabeth sprang to her feet and faced her aunt despairingly, "I'm tired of fighting against overwhelming odds. Why can't I just live like other people? Don't I deserve any happiness?"

"Calm down, my dear, and listen a minute if you can." Aunt Vadie sought for the right words, "When we cease to have odds to fight against, we cease to have life. We're dead! Life is a challenge from the cradle to the grave; when the struggle is over, so is life." She paused, looking at the bright bowed head. She took a deep breath and plunged on.

"You are so used to ordering and directing things that you are singularly blind when it comes to managing your own life. You think clearly when others are involved, but you seem incapable of being rational about yourself. You say you are tired of controlling things. That perhaps answers your other question, why can't you live like other people. No one can control life as he would wish. There are some things you must just let happen — naturally."

"But — ," Elizabeth raised tear-filled eyes and tried to interrupt.

"Wait, Elizabeth, now that I've gotten the courage to start, let me finish." She spoke beseechingly to her niece. "In this world, we have to trade. Nothing is free. For what we want, we have to offer the price required. Just as in the peddler's pack there are many bright things we would like to have. We have to examine our resources and determine, of that we can afford, what we desire the most. For one thing, we must sacrifice another."

"How does that apply to me?" Elizabeth demanded.

"If you think the price of happiness with Gavin is a carefree past, then you cannot afford him! You don't have that to offer. You'd better make another selection. If you think that love and courage are enough — ," she left her sentence unfinished as she looked lovingly at the troubled face and wide grey eyes before her.

"It isn't so simple as that, Aunt Vadie. Oh, what's the matter with me? I'm so confused and mixed up, I don't know where to turn!"

"The whole trouble with you is that you are travelling emotionally the road you should have travelled when you were twenty. But let me warn you, Elizabeth. You are very fortunate that you have another chance after the deliberate havoc you wrought with your lives before. I am amazed that a man as attractive as Gavin McBride should have remained a bachelor so long, even for someone as lovely as you. He's no longer a boy to be played with, however, and I advise you to make up your mind and stop mooning about like a young girl."

"I'm not mooning about! I'm trying — "

"You have a decision to make, and it seems this simple to me.

236

You either want a future of loneliness with only hard work to absorb your many talents, or you want a future built around the sharing of those odds you spoke of with a man who loves you deeply and whom you obviously love. Those same odds will be there in either case. You can not escape them!"

"Aunt Vadie," Elizabeth cried, deep hurt reflected in her eyes. "Are you for me or against me?"

"For you, Elizabeth, with all my heart and hopes. I don't want to see life pass you by again. I have a feeling this will be your last chance."

In the weeks that followed, Elizabeth was thoughtful. She looked at her aunt with eyes sometimes reproachful, sometimes questioning. Aunt Vadie, however, refused to be drawn into any more discussions or harangues. When Elizabeth tried to use her as a sounding board for her thoughts, Aunt Vadie declined to reply. She stated firmly that she had expressed herself definitely and irrevocably. The rest was up to Elizabeth. As she watched the struggle going on in her niece's mind, Aunt Vadie felt better about her. She understood in spite of all she had said, the tumult in Elizabeth's heart. As the days passed and the tension in Elizabeth seemed to relax, Aunt Vadie smiled at the growing look of decision in her eyes. The long, busy days without Gavin, after she had seen him once more, were having their effect.

Preparations went forward for Governor Glen's visit. Excitement ran high. Now the Governor himself would see their crucial needs. He would understand when he saw their untutored children their need for school and church. When he himself made the long trip to their settlement, he would see how difficult it was for Saxe Gothans to journey to Charles Town to transact legal business. News of the Governor's success in Indian matters was travelling and the inhabitants hoped that his visit would restore the equilibrium of friendship between white man and red, and stop the constant raiding, burning, and killing that went on periodically.

Late in April the Catawba chiefs and their followers began to drift in to the settlement and to make their camps on its fringe. Elizabeth invited them to her house and fed and treated them with such tact and consideration that distrust and truculence disappeared from their faces. The Indians put on games that drew interested white observers. The two races hunted and fished together in new-found camaraderie. Hope ran high.

Then it began to rain. Torrents such as they had not

experienced before descended on the greening fields and swelled the sparkling streams. For days the thrifty Germans and Swiss rubbed their hands in glee as they watched the wide fields of grain drinking in the water thirstily. Then they began to shake their heads, recalling the swirling Congaree that had swept over its banks and destroyed their crops once before.

Elizabeth began to worry, in spite of anticipation, about the soaked ground where the gentlemen of the Governor's retinue would have to pitch their tents. The woods were dripping, the open ground, soft and spongy. Relentless grey clouds hovered over even when the rain stopped. Nat came down from Ninety-Six to supervise the construction of a proper shelter for the dignitaries at the great meeting. No building would hold the crowd of red men and white, and all must see and hear the Governor's important talk. Axes bounced on sodden trunks of trees that finally dropped with a slush to make staunch posts for the shelter. Poles across the top were covered with dripping green oak branches. On a sort of dais beneath, couches were fashioned and draped with soft dry deerskins when the great day dawned bright and clear. Saxe Gothans greeted the long absent sun joyfully and early filled the barbecue pits with the driest wood they could find. Their most decent garments were again shaken out and sprigs of yellow jessamine replaced the gay holly of the last celebration. The same jolly feeling prevailed. Another gay dance and great feast had been planned in honor of Governor Glen and his retinue. The two races, awaiting the white chief and his Beloved Men from Charles Town, mingled in unheard of good fellowship. Children ran far down the road and formed a line to relay the first news of arrival to the village. Elizabeth paced about impatiently inspecting everything over and over again. Her hands were cold with nervousness. Finally a shout went up and rippled down the line of volunteer sentries. Everyone was immediately electrified. The Governor's bugler, spotting the first excited child, sent the brassy tones of his instrument ahead of the colorful retinue.

Riding a magnificent white charger, the Governor was smiling and bowing graciously to the lines of people waving and shouting a glad welcome. Just behind him rode Gavin McBride and Eleazar Wigan, both simply clad in soft buckskins. Gavin's choice had annoyed James Glen, who loved pageantry and thought the Governor's physician should be more fittingly attired. But in the confusion of departure, he neglected to chide his doctor who, he had to admit privately, was an impressive figure in any outfit.

Brave in scarlet coats and tall shakos, rode the stiff British regulars with the Union Jack flying proudly in a light breeze. The splendor of the fifty gentlemen of the Province almost rivaled the bravery of the soldiers' scarlet tunics. The awed inhabitants were struck dumb by the gorgeousness of fine laces and satins and velvets. The overall effect of the parade was so astonishing that the peaked, pinched faces above the satins and velvets went unnoticed.

Elizabeth was waiting on the little porch with Thomas Brown and Stephen Crell, who immediately stepped down to bow a greeting to the Governor. Clem grasped his mount's bridle and grinned toothily, glad to see such quality again. There was just time for Gavin's questioning eyes to find his answer in Elizabeth's glad face before the Governor spoke.

"So, this is my famous kinswoman!"

Elizabeth flushed and swept him a formal curtsy. "Welcome, your Excellency!"

"Your Excellency! I expected a more cousinly greeting." He laughed as he dismounted stiffly. "Come, Miss Elizabeth. Let me salute you properly."

Elizabeth joined in his friendly laughter as she allowed her cheek to be soundly bussed. The Governor turned with a flourish and introduced his followers in a body. Thomas Brown and Stephen Crell took charge of the billeting while Governor Glen, Gavin, and Eleazar Wigan followed Elizabeth into the stone house where Aunt Vadie was waiting.

"Why, Jamie Glen! Who would ever think a naughty boy like you would live to become a great governor? I would have thought your poor brothers or cousins that you drilled mercilessly in your private army would have dispatched you in revenge before you reached maturity!"

Governor Glen joined in the delighted laughter at his own expense.

"Now, Miss Vadie. Is that fair to show me up before my people? A governor should be remote and mysterious and grand, not made of mortal clay."

"We'll not tell on you, Sir." Eleazar grinned.

The Governor's face was suddenly serious.

"Where are our friends, the Catawbas? We are travelling exactly on schedule, to the deep annoyance of some of our guests, eh, Dr. McBride?"

Thomas Brown entered at that point, a look of concern on his face. He shook hands all around and the little group sat down while Aunt Vadie fetched refreshments.

"The Catawbas, Your Excellency," said Brown in answer to the

Governor's question, "are encamped at a short distance from here on the banks of the Congaree. They have been most friendly and seem in a good mood, thanks in part to Mrs. Fenwick here." He smiled at Elizabeth who returned his admiring look gratefully. "Why they aren't here today to greet you, I don't understand."

"They probably don't want to seem too easy, Sir," said Eleazar shrewdly. "They need to be courted a bit. It's up to us to make the first move. Besides the day of meeting is Monday; today is Sunday."

"But your arrival was scheduled for Sunday," puzzled Brown, ruffling his flaming hair with a beefy hand. "However, Wigan knows the Indians better than anyone. I suppose he is right."

"The hunters in our party killed several fine buck yesterday and we had them dressed and prepared to help meet our needs here. Our supplies are very low. Mr. Wigan, have the venison sent to King Haigler. Go yourself and ask the king and his headmen to do me the honor of meeting with me tomorrow morning for our talk. Tell them that after that they are all invited to a great feast." He turned questioningly to Elizabeth. "I supposed that can be managed?"

"Indeed so, Governor Glen. The inhabitants of Saxe Gotha have been preparing just such a feast for weeks."

Gavin and Elizabeth had been trying vainly to manage a private word and now the Governor turned his energetic attention on his physician.

"Well, Dr. McBride, I hope that ample chest of yours holds enough potions to keep our weak-stomached brethren on their feet until the conference is over. We can't afford to show either internal or external weakness in this country."

"The bad weather and inadequate tents are responsible, Governor. These men are not used to camping out in torrential spring rains."

"Serves their parsimonious souls right!" growled James Glen. "They were too close to vote the Province's funds for adequate supplies, and then refused to spend their own money to keep their stingy hides dry! To pull money out of their pockets for public benefit is like pouring molasses in January!" He snorted in disgust. "Go on, McBride; stop their fluxes and fevers for me until I can drag them home again. Then I'll turn them over to Dale. That will be sweet revenge, won't it, Doctor?" He grinned and realized Elizabeth's presence suddenly.

"Pardon me, Miss Elizabeth." His tone was embarrassed. "I forgot you were here."

"I'm used to it, Governor Glen," Elizabeth smiled. "I don't shock easily." Her eyes followed Gavin as he left the room, bowing his gold head to go out the door.

The sickness infecting the Low Country gentlemen kept Gavin busy until midnight. He finally turned in, groaning wearily, on one of Nat's improvised beds. Elizabeth had sent him some supper by Eleazar after she had waited in disappointment for his return. Governor Glen talked and questioned incessantly. His energy and enterprise reminded Elizabeth of her own father. No detail was so inconsequential that it escaped his notice. Elizabeth heard with delight of the money voted for the reconditioning or rebuilding of the old fort. Now perhaps they could sleep in some manner of peace.

"A fort without a garrison will be ineffective," she suggested hesitantly.

"Give me time, give me time." James Glen smiled. "Mary would like you. I wish you could be friends." He thought fondly of his wife. "She would like this country too. She feels closed in in Charles Town after Scotland."

"Wait until you see Ninety-Six!" Elizabeth's eyes sparkled as she told James Glen of the beautiful rising country above the fall line where one could get tantalizing glimpses of the blue Cherokee mountains, so like their own Scottish crags. The Governor watched the lively play of emotions across the vibrant face and ceased to wonder that McBride wanted to desert lowland safety for the uncertainties of the frontier. He reflected that with such an inducement, he'd better keep his physician occupied until he had at least talked with the Cherokees, lest he lose a needed doctor's services too soon.

This he accomplished so cleverly that Elizabeth did not see Gavin again until the next day when all gathered around the improvised throne room to hear the Governor's talk. Under Nat's green canopy Governor Glen sat in impressive dignity. The Union Jack flapped gaily above. Two lines of scarlet clad soldiers stood at ramrod attention. King Haigler, his face hideously painted, attired in a magnificent dyed feather cape that touched the ground at his heels strode calmly down the lines of foot soldiers. Drums, which had begun to roll softly as his approach was announced, increased in speed and volume until the Indian king stood before the British Governor, who arose courteously, raised his arm in salute, and descended to the sodden ground to lead his guest to a place of honor at his right hand. The two seated themselves. Small cannon boomed out in the sudden silence, as the drums ceased their rolling. The two brilliant corteges, red and white, drew in to flank their respective representatives.

"Whose guest is whom?" wondered Gavin ironically. He wished Andrew could be here to watch the show. Only he could appreciate such good theatre. The feeling of tense expectancy in the crowd gripped him also. He had looked around for Elizabeth, but could not find her. She stood with Aunt Vadie and Uncle Roy discreetly in the background. She could see the back of his bright head and hoped that its constant turning meant he was searching for her.

The Governor beckoned to Eleazar who stepped forward to interpret the momentous talk. The Governor stood, bent his body slightly to King Haigler, and addressed them all. He may have needed an interpreter but he had no need of an amplifier for his booming voice. He was obviously enjoying himself hugely, though he took his responsibility with deep respect.

"We hear, far away in Charles Town, that the French are trying to seduce the Catawba to their interests." Eleazar hastily and competently translated. The Governor opened his mouth to continue but Haigler raised his hand to interrupt. Governor Glen waited.

"All know the Catawba have refused to desert their English friends. Has the Great Governor brought the gifts of powder and ammunition the Catawba requested?"

The Governor was rocked back on his heels. A little of his starch wilted.

"Wow!" thought Eleazar, trying to keep from shaking with inward laughter. "That's putting it on the line! Poor Governor. All those wasted hours writing that pretty speech."

The Governor hastily picked up the pieces of his shattered dignity. He summoned two guards peremptorily to bring forth the promised cases of powder and ammunition, and tried to go on with his speech. Haigler interrupted him again while he calmly and personally opened the cases and checked their contents. He grunted finally with satisfaction, sat back, and signified with an arrogant gesture that the Governor had his undivided attention.

Nettled, the Governor tried again.

"I must remind you that your English brothers have endeavored always to keep peace among the different tribes. You must cease your constant quarrelling among yourselves — "

King Haigler's silencing hand flew up again.

"The Catawbas will stand by the people of Carolina. However, the Cherokee have not done well by us. It is impossible that we continue in friendship with the Cherokee. They harbor Northern Indians who are our enemies; they fit out our enemies the Choctaws, and also desire peace with the French."

Grasping firmly at control of the situation that seemed to be slipping out of his capable hands, James Glen tried to impress Haigler and his Beloved Men with the necessity for good feeling among themselves as well as toward their white brothers. Glen felt that, contrary to the wide spread policy of divide and conquer, friendship and peace would benefit white colonization. Should they continue to bicker jealously among themselves, one nation might vent on the British his rage against his tribal enemy. He managed to get in a suitable harangue uninterrupted. Gavin wondered if King Haigler, whose blank face showed neither feeling nor interest, listened to a word of Eleazar's translation. His suspicions that he had not were confirmed, as the Governor's voice died away. Haigler was pointing, a first gleam of interest in his eyes, at a nearby drum.

"The Catawba king desires a drum and flag to impress the French and Virginians when they travel north," Eleazar, conscious of Glen's exasperation, kept his face straight with difficulty. The deep seated import of Indian imperviousness to reason was not laughable, he knew, but, for the moment, it was comical.

The rest of the conclave was uphill work in the face of such bland indifference. Though Glen felt that he had the Catawbas safely in his hand for the moment he would have liked some more tangible expression of loyalty. He felt tired and defeated and a bit ridiculous in front of his council members. Though they dared not express disapproval openly, he found their faces a bit strained when the time came for feasting. Healths were drunk to every Catawba chief, both living and dead; guns were fired after each toast. A fine glow possessed the entire company by the time they started on the Beloved Men. Yes, indeed. The Governor was a fine fellow and a great statesman. The Province could not be in better hands. Hurrah for Governor James Glen!

The Governor, himself an abstemious man, retired late, his face a study, his tongue in cheek, but not before he had sent his personal physician to attend some ailing gentlemen of His Majesty's Council.

Chapter Eight

Elizabeth looked at Eleazar with annoyance when he stuck his tousled head through the door to say good night. He grinned.

"Too much belly ache?"

Elizabeth stamped her foot. "Is he deliberately planning this? He won't give us a minute alone."

"Maybe he hates to lose such a good physician. He's afraid you'll get your hooks into him before he finishes his blessed parade. He's bound to keep his gentlemen alive till he shows them off to all these red devils. After that, if my guess is correct, he'd just as soon throw them in the bay!" Eleazar looked over his shoulder into the starlit night. "Where is he?"

"Gone out on some pretended inspection. I tried to out sit him last night, but I went to sleep in my chair." Elizabeth was ready to cry with rage.

"Seriously, King Haigler was more impressed than he made out. You yourself complained to the Governor that these savages could only be kept under with fear. That Governor's right. He'll make Christians out of these pagans yet. We leave tomorrow for Ninety-Six," he added abruptly.

"No!" cried Elizabeth. "You can't!"

"Yas'm. I'm afraid we can. Why don't you go to?"

"Me? I couldn't!"

"Why not? The Cherokee will have their squaws there. Why can't you and Miss Vadie represent the British? She wants to see Nellie and you said that you were going back in the spring. O'Gilvie is going, too. He'll look after you."

"Will Governor Glen let us?"

Eleazar grinned. "The rest of us know better than to stop you when you get your head set. The Governor will learn too, I guess."

"What would I do without you?" She hugged Eleazar and went to find her Aunt.

Eleazar, letting himself out, heard Aunt Vadie's indignant voice, "No, I certainly won't."

"Yes, Sweetheart, you will," said Elizabeth; "won't she, Uncle Roy?"

"She usually does," Uncle Roy's muffled voice answered.

Governor James Glen never understood how he was maneuvered into it, but on Tuesday, April twenty-ninth, 1746, his diplomatic mission to the Cherokee Nation was increased by two ladies, whose company he reluctantly found very diverting, one well-informed overseer, one silent half breed whose shadowy presence at Elizabeth's side gave him the creeps.

The journey was accomplished with some rain, but no mishap. The only diversion was the tussle between the Governor and his charming cousin over a giant, young blond doctor who was hugely enjoying himself while he pretended not to notice. Elizabeth's charm was scintillating. Gavin watched her with wonder. Had he not loved her during all the past hopeless years, he knew he would have fallen in love with her again.

By the time the long journey was over, Elizabeth and Aunt Vadie were thoroughly tired. The great unwieldly retinue extended the trip beyond its necessary limits. Elizabeth decided her two day desperate dash to help Nellie was less fatiguing than the creeping pace of a great crowd. She wondered what would happen to these unbending British regulars if a hostile tribe should suddenly descend on them. Eleazar, and even Gavin, could melt into the forest. Remembering her escape up the tree from the wolves, a comic vision of these picture book soldiers caught in such a dilemma made her smile to herself. The Charles Town gentlemen had all complimented her lush beauty and contagious smile with unfeigned admiration. Even the startling riding costume, after the first shocked gasp, had come in for its share of approval. Mentally each tried it on his own mate, some with doubtful shakes of the head.

The reception at Ninety-Six was more heartening. Nat had raced ahead unencumbered to prepare a suitable shelter for the distinguished notables and to advise Nellie of her own visitors. Down the path they were met by Onconecaw and a great crowd of Cherokees on horseback. Delighted to be greeted in his own tongue, Governor Glen, after giving the prescribed Indian greeting, pumped Onconecaw's welcoming hand, placing his left hand on the little Indian's shoulder in genuine friendliness. Onconecaw's eyes fell on Elizabeth in pleased surprise. He drew his horse up before her own and quickly dismounted. Placing his right hand across his gorgeously painted chest, he inclined his head slightly.

"Onconecaw and his brothers salute the Lady Cuming."

Elizabeth hesitated while a gasp of amazement rippled over the crowd. Such an honor was unheard of! She moved impulsively to dismount. Gavin, seeing her movement, sprang to the ground and held up his arms to her. Smiling into his eyes she dismounted, and turned to Onconecaw, her left hand still on Gavin's arm.

"Onconecaw, you do me undeserved honor." She extended her hand to him simply. He took it briefly in his own after the colonists' fashion. Looking from her vivid face to her companion, he spoke softly for her ears alone.

" 'Tis good."

She flushed but returned his gaze steadily.

Next day the Governor was seated under the canopy with the Cherokee Emperor, who was a mere lad, and his great chiefs at his right hand. The Emperor's extreme youth was a stroke in his, Glen's, favor, thought the Governor, who had no intention of letting this meeting get out of hand as had the last. However, looking at the powerful faces of the young Emperor's guardians, Skyagunsta, the Owl and Kollonah, the Raven, he plunged headlong into his prepared speech, intending no interruption.

"I speak to the Emperor, Beloved Men, and warriors of the Cherokees, and I desire you to carry my talk to your nation.

"As I and my Beloved Men," he indicated his gaudy gentlemen with a sweeping gesture, "have come to see you at so great a distance from Charles Town and to shake hands with you, I hope that you will esteem it as a mark of the regard I have for your nation and that you will look upon us and consider us as your friends and brothers."

He decided quickly after a glance at their greedy faces that he had better skip quickly to a paragraph he had intended for the climax. Eleazar inwardly approved as he translated deftly. This

247

Governor was all right. Quick learner!

"I have brought with me presents of such things as you desired to defend your lives against your and our enemy."

Grunts of approval greeted this statement and his listeners became more attentive.

"– and they shall be delivered to you tomorrow upon reward of your answer."

"Bless his bones," thought Eleazar. "He is a sly one!"

The grunts of approval ceased. Cherokee looked at Cherokee and finally seemed to agree tacitly to let it pass. Since the goods were on the spot they'd have them one way or another. Waiting a moment for their decision to jell, James Glen's booming voice again commanded their attention.

"I have been informed and have good reason to believe that the French, with whom we are now at war, have been endeavoring to win our Indians to their interest and to make peace with them, and to withdraw their hearts and affections from the English by telling lies and deceiving them."

Elizabeth's attention wandered. She looked with wonder at Onconecaw whose friendship she had tried to reject when he visited the settlement at Saxe Gotha after his release from captivity.

"We can no longer be friends," she had told him coldly. "Your people and my people are enemies. Your people have done me cruel wrong. We have no longer a common meeting ground!"

"Lady Cuming," Onconecaw had spoken with wisdom far beyond his years and training. "Our nations are perhaps enemies, yes. But you and I see beyond the enmity born of greed. Can we not be, are we not already, ambassadors to effect a better integration that we both know must and will come? It was in endeavoring to save your man from the Nottawega that I angered them and was led far North into long captivity. There I had much time for thought. I learned that the Indian may have little chance with the English; with the French he would have none at all. I go to do what I can to hold the Cherokee to the English."

Her thoughts came back to the Governor's impressive voice.

"When many of your people went over the wide water and saw the great King George who is like a father to you all, he spoke good words to you, gave you large presents and, I hope, is still remembered in your nation. Give no credit to the lies and falsehoods spread among you by the French, our enemies, nor listen to their fine speeches and promises."

The sky was overcast and its glowering mood cast a feeling of gloom over white men and red alike. The white men were sick and worn out from the unaccustomed hardships of the journey. The glow of adventure had faded; they were only tired men who wanted more than anything a good, clean bed. The red men were still suspicious and inclined to want to wipe out the white and put an end to all their problems. But, Onconecaw had warned them, you are not free, wild, and independent men such as your forefathers were. You are softened by English-made luxuries which you yourselves have not learned to make, but must have at any cost. If you destroy the English, you destroy yourselves. He did not add that he often thought they were bound for destruction in any case.

The Governor besought his listeners to remain friendly with the Catawba and cease to harbor the dreadful Nottawega. On this note the meeting broke up to be resumed again in the morning to hear the Cherokee reply. There was no feast until the next day and all retired early with no feeling of elation.

The next day was grey and unseasonably cool for May. Elizabeth was up early to see her beloved mountains, but they were elusive. Only a leaden sky met her searching gaze. Her spirits sank. The Governor still stood solidly between her and Gavin. For one bright moment they had exchanged glances yesterday after the talk. Her arm tingled as she remembered the pressure of his hand. "Tomorrow, darling," he had whispered, "we'll escape the old dragon! From here he must go on without me."

Speaking for the Emperor before the colorful crowd, his guardians, the Owl and the Raven, accepted from the English Governor of South Carolina undying friendship.

When it came to Raven's turn, he spoke softly, "We have harkened attentively to Your Excellency's talk and we remember the promise of presents which you have made for French scalps, and we will perform what we promised. We hope Your Excellency will do the same."

Hastily Governor Glen corrected him, "Not for scalps, but for live enemies we promise reward."

The Raven regarded the white leader with mounting unbelief and disgust.

"No scalps?" he asked.

"No scalps," was the reply.

Disappointment and chagrin were written all over the Indian's face as he replied, "When we are in the woods hunting, we take a great deal of pains. We walk much and come home weary. But of so great value to us is a scalp, that if we should happily in our way

249

meet with one, it is sufficient recompense to us for all our labor. However," he gave the Indian equivalent of a shrug, "what Your Excellency told us in your talk last night we will carefully observe and what you have said shall not be spoilt."

Onconecaw stepped forward leading a child by the hand. He raised his own arm and a respectful silence fell. He turned his slight frame and looked at each man gathered in this momentous meeting at the budding settlement of Ninety-Six.

"You spoke last evening of some of us who had crossed the great water to visit your King, our common father. I, alone, remain of those who made this long journey and saw the glory and splendor of King George and his court. At that time a bright chain of friendship was fastened from the breast of your King to the breast of our Emperor, the great Moytoy. The Lady Cuming was there also. Of all the fine people who were present at the linking of our races, only the two of us remain. Many moons, many years have passed. Tarnish has been allowed to dull the bright chain. Today we remove the stain from that chain that it may shine again brightly."

He pushed the child forward. Suddenly the sun broke through the dismal clouds and bathed the little boy in unearthly light. The audience was obviously impressed.

"To this child I have told of that long ago visit. Today he witnesses the strengthening of the bonds of friendship between our two great nations. To his sons and his sons' sons he will tell his story that it may govern the hearts of man and keep peace in this beautiful land!"

The land that his wide-flung arms indicated was indeed beautiful as it came to vibrant life under the rays of a warm May sun. Away in the distance Elizabeth saw a faint glimmer of the beckoning blue hills. Her heart beat thankfully that she was here in this wonderful new country. But the Governor was speaking again. She brought her attention back to him with difficulty.

"Onconecaw, for the great work that you have done for our two nations, I give you the name Attakulla-kulla, Little Carpenter. You, I understand, are skilled in this trade. Not for this ability, but for your efforts as a builder of peace in the hearts of man, I give you this name."

"Thank you, Excellency," said the little Indian, deeply touched.

Something tugged at Elizabeth's sleeve. She looked around to find Billy beckoning her. She followed his urgent gestures without question. He led her to her horse that was saddled and indicated that she was to mount. Puzzled but not alarmed, she did as he directed. He pointed up the northward path and slapped the horse's rump sharply. The horse sprang forward and broke into a run. Before Elizabeth could stop him, he had flashed around a bend in the path, out of sight of the tiny settlement. Elizabeth reined him in sharply and turned, annoyed at Billy's act, to lead him back. Gavin stepped out of the woods. The two looked at each other a moment without speaking. Silently Gavin held out his arms. Elizabeth slid into them and he held her close a moment. He released her and drew her to a seat on a fallen tree.

"What is your answer, Elizabeth? I can wait no longer."

Elizabeth swallowed hard and wet her lips.

"Are you still afraid?" he asked taking her hand gently.

"Only of the ghosts of the past, Gavin."

"They cannot reach us here. I intend to settle at Ninety-Six. Will you stay with me?"

"Oh Gavin," she cried joyfully. "Do you really mean it?"

"I do, dearest. Listen. Already the Governor has in mind trying to purchase these lands for settlers who want to come in from Virginia and Pennsylvania. He is daily bombarded with requests from people who would have come already but are afraid of the Indians. If he can buy the land from the Cherokees — they have no towns here — we can build our future safely. Will you stay, Elizabeth?" he pled. "I want you so!"

"Oh Gavin, am I too old?"

"Are you, my dear?" He drew her gently into his arms. His lips rested softly on her own. Then a fire like the exploding of a thousand rockets burst into a flame that enveloped them both. After a while she drew back shakily, her eyes reflecting the stars.

"Gavin, Gavin!" she cried in wonder. "I'm young and alive and oh, Gavin, hurry. We have lost so much time already."

There was no gentleness when he swept her back into his hungry arms.

EPILOGUE

Andrew Rutledge again left the Council Chamber and walked, this time alone, down the corridor to the room where the Commons House of Assembly of the Province of South Carolina was in session. The corridor was drafty in the chill March wind. Andrew slapped his arms with his hands, in one of which were important looking papers, messages to the Commons from His Excellency James Glen. He thought of another cold March day when he, a young unknown lawyer, had entered another drafty council chamber far away in London. Then he had listened to another group of men who, like the provincial gentlemen he would address today in the Governor's name, held the destiny of Carolina in their hands. What the gentlemen in London had proposed, the gentlemen in South Carolina had accomplished. Sixteen years ago! Was it possible? He didn't feel that much older. He did feel a bit lonely. Well, one can't have everything, he told himself as he entered the chamber.

Speaker William Bull's gavel fell and order took the place of pleasant chaos. Andrew Rutledge arose as he was introduced and bowed elegantly to the speaker and assembled gentlemen. His eyes unconsciously sought the balcony. Gavin McBride was not there to smile to him, but in his place sat a youngster with eager adoring eyes. He winked companionably at his seven year old nephew,

John Rutledge, and began to read in his compelling voice:

Let it be known and remembered by all Men on whom the Sun doth shine That we Conotochiskio and Testoe of Toogoloo . . .

Andrew's suave voice did not falter as he rolled the unpronounceable, heathen names off his tongue. He had spent some hours in his office schooling himself in order that he might achieve just such seeming unstudied nonchalance. He could not resist a grin at his nephew who alone had been present at the private readings of the treaty, and understood his uncle's seemingly easy perfection that in truth took countless hours of discipline and practice. John flashed a return look of praise as the smooth, slightly nasal voice went on.

. . . and other Chiefs of our several Towns by and with the good liking and consent and agreement of our several Towns and for the better keeping the Chain of Friendship between our good friends and brothers the Sons and Subjects of the Great King George of Great Britain . . . in consideration of four hundred weight of Gun Powder Eight hundred pounds weight of Bullets twenty pounds of Vermillion, and two hundred pounds weight of Beads with their bags, together with a fowling piece, At our Town, Kewohee Given and delivered to us for ourselves and our Towns by His EXCELLENCY JAMES GLEN ESQ.
   . . . Have given Granted and Sold . . . unto the Great King George and his Successors for the use and benefit of his people of the said Province, All that Tract or Parcel of land lying and being South and Easterly of a certain branch of stream of water commonly called Long Canes within about sixty miles more or less of our Towns from the Path on 96 . . . TO HAVE HOLD USE AND ENJOY THE said Tract and Parcel of Lands with all the Goods and benefits therefrom arising . . . as long as the moon doth shine by night or the Sun by day continues to give warmth and Heat, on the 12th day of February in the year 1747 and in the 20th year of His Majesty's Reign.

Also read in the Assembly that windy March day of 1747 was a petition by one Nathaniel Hayne of Ninety-Six praying to have the sole privilege of making and licensing a machine of his own invention for the ginning or cleaning of the rough seed cotton

. . . such as has been sown and propagated in this Province and

254

is a commodity very easily and plentifully produced here being well adapted to this soil and climate. That the said machine with the labor and attendance of a Negro man and two boys will, in the space of twelve hours, gin (clean from the seed) eighty pounds weight of cotton . . .

Thus the tiny flame of friendship lighted by that dazzlingly attractive felon, Sir Alexander Cuming, grew through the years. Nutured by his fearless daughter and her friend Attakullakulla, the Little Carpenter of British-Cherokee relations, cemented by the wisdom of such men as Robert Johnson, South Carolina's own William Bull, and Jamie Glen, the wizard of Indian diplomacy, peace lay for a time on the troubled land. The dark bloody hours of 1760, brought on by the typical British bigotry of Governor Littleton were as yet far in the mysterious future.

And so, for a time, the dream lived on . . .